A LONG TIME DEAD

A Joe Turner Mystery

T.L. BEQUETTE

Black Rose Writing | Texas

The author grants the final approval for this literary material.

First printing

This is a work of fiction. Names, characters, businesses, places, events, and incidents are either the products of the author's imagination or used in a fictitious manner. Any resemblance to actual persons, living or dead, or actual events is purely coincidental.

ISBN: 978-1-68513-256-9
PUBLISHED BY BLACK ROSE WRITING
www.blackrosewriting.com

Printed in the United States of America
Suggested Retail Price (SRP) $22.95

A LONG TIME DEAD is printed in Baskerville

*As a planet-friendly publisher, Black Rose Writing does its best to eliminate unnecessary waste to reduce paper usage and energy costs, while never compromising the reading experience. As a result, the final word count vs. page count may not meet common expectations.

Praise for
The Joe Turner Mystery Series

"T. L. Bequette masterfully builds his series, creating growth in his characters through each novel. Combining supreme character building and a fast-paced mystery… readers won't be able to set the book down until the final page. In short, Joe Turner is well on the way to becoming a fixture in contemporary mystery fiction."

–Chanticleer Book Reviews

"After his rousing debut, *Good Lookin'* (2021), Bequette returns with a tale that solidifies Turner as a charmingly reliable champion of the innocent."

–Kirkus Reviews

"5/5 Stars. A fantastic read for fans of courtroom drama, light detective work, and endings with a twist… that will keep you interested from cover to cover."

–San Francisco Book Reviews

"Fascinating… entices the reader on the opening page to dive into a stunningly readable and exciting effort. I am waiting impatiently for the next book in what I hope is a long series."

–Mark Hewitt, award-winning author of the *Duncan Hunter Thriller* series

A LONG TIME DEAD

PROLOGUE

Rotterdam, The Netherlands

Owen dove out of the slow-moving taxi onto the street, protecting his head as the pavement gouged his shoulders and knees. Charged with adrenaline, he rolled to his feet and sprinted with the traffic before dodging to the sidewalk. Glancing behind him, he saw another cab, seventy yards back, its back door swinging open. "Think," Owen said aloud, weaving his way up the crowded sidewalk. Against a trained officer, running wasn't the answer. He was already winded. What had that bald prick said about being chased? Crowd…Disguise…Damn! What was the third thing?

Three and a half blocks up a hill, flags marked a swanky hotel. Although he'd taken up running, his daily routine involved more of a leisurely jog. Certainly, he hadn't sprinted since high school, and now his thirty-four-year-old body was rebelling. Afraid to look behind him, he expected to be tackled any second. After twenty seconds, the hotel seemed no closer. His sprint had slowed to a gasping plod up the ever-steepening hill, each stride was now a hot iron to his calves. Cursing his worthless daily jogs, he panted out a mantra through burning lungs: "Oh shit. Oh shit. Oh shit." Finally reaching the hotel, he pulled himself up a short flight of steps, gasping for air as he clung to the wrought-iron railing for support. Doubled over at the waist, Owen looked back at his pursuer at the hotel's entrance. He was young and stocky, wearing a dress shirt and blazer, looking composed and fresh. He'd closed the gap to forty yards when Owen ducked into the crowded hotel lobby, desperate to control his breathing. Crowd…Disguise…What was the fucking third thing!

CHAPTER 1

"I've got a new slogan for my law practice, Andy," Joe called to his partner, the personal injury lawyer in the next office.

"Let me guess. 'Joe Turner, only slightly worse than the public defender.'"

"Hilarious. It's 'Criminal Defense. Only for the Innocent,'" Joe said proudly.

Andy appeared in Joe's doorway. "Don't all your clients tell you they're innocent, anyway?"

"Of course," Joe answered. "That's the genius of the marketing."

"Glad to see you're embracing the sliminess of your profession, Turner."

"Oh, this from Mr. 1-800-INJURED? You stocked up on neck braces?" Joe jeered as his partner walked away.

"Beats heavy lifting," Andy called, closing the door to his office.

Joe checked his watch. His client, an alleged drug dealer, was late or had more pressing business than his pending felony charges. Joe's client show-up rate was running at about fifty percent, so he walked to the fridge in the corner of his office, maneuvering past the stacks of boxes. He and Andy had moved into their new digs in downtown Oakland three months ago, but half his files and office supplies remained unpacked.

Joe cracked a beer and took a long drink. Looking down at a box labeled "Red Sox," he idly opened the lid and pulled up a chair. Joe had grown up in California, but his father, a Bostonian, had passed on to Joe the love of his team. His dad had been murdered before their World Series championship in 2004, so for Joe, the team was sacred.

After law school, before returning to the west coast, Joe had lived in Boston for four years, first taking a job with the Suffolk County D.A., then starting his criminal defense practice.

Inside the box was Red Sox memorabilia Joe used for office decor. There were team pennants, photos with players, and autographed baseballs. His eyes fell to a plain white envelope resting near the box's bottom. He picked it up, smiling as he read the message scrawled across its broken seal. "Do not open until after Game Five."

Joe peaked inside the envelope. There were two ticket stubs for Game Six of the 2013 World Series, a crinkled credit card receipt, and a photo with Joe and his mom at the game. Memories flooded back—his time in Boston, the game, and the tickets, gifted from a friend that he hadn't seen since.

CHAPTER 2

On a damp, gray February morning in Tetbury, Owen Prescott typed at his desk, a mug of tea at arm's reach, his cat snuggled to his socks in the front room of his cozy stone cottage. He heard Mrs. Pembroke's sensible heels on the cobblestone path to his front door. "Something suspicious afoot if you ask me," she said as she entered, in mid-conversation with herself.

Owen had purchased the one-bedroom guest cottage from Mrs. Pembroke upon his arrival in the English village ten years ago, but the stout and talkative middle-aged occupant of the main house still had the run of the place. Owen didn't mind, especially on Saturday mornings when she brought warm croissants from Balfry's, the village bakery.

"Skulking around the village, snooping about. And Mr. Firth from the city office said she'd come in asking for the Residents' Directory," she said, dismay in her high-pitched voice. She set down the box of croissants on the kitchen table. "Imagine the cheek of her."

"Good morning, Mrs. Pembroke. And who's this? The woman with the long black hair again?" he said, bemused.

"Yes, long black hair. Black as night. Having a gander all over the village. Seems very fishy to me, wouldn't you say?"

When he'd moved in, Owen had explained that as a famous American novelist, he hoped his new home would provide a quiet sanctuary where he could live in peace under his pen name, Ancil Bradford. When he asked Mrs. Pembroke to keep his identity a secret, she had embraced her role as protector and confidant with enthusiasm.

"You certainly are aware of things," Owen said, delicately, moving toward the table. "Thank you for the croissants, by the way. And I certainly appreciate your vigilance."

"In other words, I'm off me trolley, then."

"No, I didn't…"

"No, Mr. Bradford, I understand," she said, in mock condescension, taking a croissant and heading toward the door. "It's just poor, daft Mrs. Pembroke imagining things again."

"Mrs. Pembroke," Owen said calmly, suppressing a smile. "You are anything but daft, and I very much appreciate you looking after me."

"Well, thank you. And mark my words, Mr. Bradford, something's up with this one. Up to something sinister, if you ask me. And now I'm off to…" The door shut, muffling her running commentary as she continued down the path.

Owen sampled a warm croissant and reflected on his decade-long adventure into anonymity. There had been some close calls in the first few years. Once, he had recognized one of his high school teachers before they saw him. Another time, he'd seen a woman stare at him as he passed by her table at an outdoor café, then point and whisper to her partner. He had tried not to quicken his pace as he walked past and had spent the next few weeks waiting for a knock on the door.

Back when his family attorney asked him to choose a spot outside the U.S., he hadn't hesitated. Ever since he'd taken a year abroad in college at Oxford, he'd dreamed of a writer's life in the Cotswolds region of England, with its quaint villages of honey-colored stone.

All things considered, his time in the village of Tetbury had not disappointed. The charming hamlet had good old-fashioned pubs and plenty of places for people-watching with a cup of tea—the wellspring for many of his stories. Since he'd arrived, he'd published three novels under his pen name and while they hadn't enjoyed the wild success of his first, they'd been well received.

Lately though, after nearly a decade of isolation, Owen craved human interaction. Always an introvert, communication with friends or family had never been essential to his happiness. Although talking with his mother had been difficult, he'd managed it every two months on a tight schedule. But the isolation of his life was taking its toll.

He had strictly adhered to the rules—refuse to engage in casual conversation, avoid eye contact and retreat at the first sound of an American accent. Over the years, however instinctive his stifled persona had become, its maintenance was far from pleasant. He missed seeing new faces, hearing interesting voices, and sharing a laugh, to say nothing of cavorting with the opposite sex. He desperately missed the thrill of someone new, the scent and feel of another, and the ache of lustful passion.

But in the end, Owen knew it was how it had to be. He smiled as he sat down at his desk, brushing crumbs from his sweater. So, thank goodness for Mrs. Pembroke. It was true that his landlady's eyes and ears had proven a comfort, especially in the early days, before his beard had grown out and he'd gotten into shape. He was genuinely grateful that she seemed aware of everything that happened in Tetbury. At times like this, though, he felt guilty for his deception.

CHAPTER 3

Boston, 2013

Owen slid his phone from his nightstand and sighed when he saw the screen. He closed his eyes, collapsing back onto his pillows. "Hello, Joe. It's early."

"Only you would think it's early."

"I'm sort of busy. What's up?"

"In other words, you're with a woman. You're unbelievable, you know that? I just called to remind you about the book signing this afternoon."

Owen groaned. "Really, Turner? This is the third one this week. Do these things really sell books?"

"Look, Mr. Superstar," Joe groused. "As I told you about a million times before you talked me into this gig, I'm not a literary agent. I can barely spell it. But that's what the agent manual says. So, until you do us both a favor and fire my ass, then yes, I need you there."

"Hey wait, we got the 'Sox game tonight! What the fuck, Joe!"

"Believe me, I know. The signing was scheduled weeks ago. We can catch the last few innings of the game after. Besides, your stalker will expect you there."

"Stalker is a bit harsh. She's just overly enamored with me. And who could blame her?"

"I still think you should consider a restraining order."

"You have to admit, as stalkers go, she's been very little trouble. And if things go south, you've got a potential criminal client."

"I think you actually like having a stalker."

"It has a certain cachet." Owen noticed the water running in the shower. "Anyway, if she boils my pet rabbit, I'll call you."

"Hey, did you ever know a Professor Anendale?" Joe asked, trying to sound casual. "Taught an advanced course in creative writing, I believe."

Owen thought for a moment. "Oh God, yes. Is he still spreading those rumors about me stealing my book from him?"

"Well, don't panic, but it seems he's suing you. Claims that the two of you collaborated to write *Orchards* together."

"What?" Owen sat up in bed. "He can't be serious. That washed up hack? I barely know him. How in the..."

"Take it easy. I've read up on this. It happens all the time with best-sellers. These leeches file frivolous suits, hoping we'll pay them a small settlement just to go away."

"But Joe, I..."

"Seriously, Owen, it's nothing to worry about. I'll see you this afternoon. And hey, if the 'Sox make the series this year, we have to go. Any chance you can scare up tickets? You know, being a star and all."

"Don't jinx our team. They have to get there first. See ya."

Owen heard the shower shut off. That would be...shit, what's her name? Was it Audrey or Paula. He felt like it was an "au" name. Okay, Mr. Smooth, what's her name, idiot!

The bathroom door swung open and a statuesque brunette in a satin robe strode to the edge of the bed. Owen hung up on Joe, tossing his phone aside. "Hello, Lauren," he said, with an unintended emphasis on her name as it popped into his head.

She laughed and sat down next to him. "Hello, Owen," she said, accentuating his name. He guided her in for a kiss. "How about we re-enact that famous sex scene?"

"Oh, that again?" he answered, feigning boredom.

"Ha!" She playfully shoved him back to the bed. "I'll tell you what, Mr. big-time author, maybe we can try an original that will make it into your next book." She swung a long leg over his body and straddled him. "Or better yet," she whispered, leaning down, her damp hair draped on his chest, "it might be too hot for words."

CHAPTER 4

Owen was a successful writer using the pen name Ancil Bradford. That much was true. He had settled in Tetbury to live in anonymity. Also, very definitely true. His lie—really more of an important omission—was the reason he had chosen this secret life.

Pressing his cheek against the cool window of the train as the lush hills of the Cotswolds rolled past, Owen stared vacantly, evaluating his simple life. In many ways, it was full. Besides his prolific writing, he'd found time for pleasure reading, daily workouts, and long walks in the English countryside. He'd grown vegetables in his garden, learned to make beer and was teaching himself to play guitar. He wondered what had occupied so much of his time in the states—a combination of cell phone screen time, commuting, and chasing women, he supposed. All had been eliminated from his life.

Still, with each passing day, the monotony had worn on him and more so the lack of human contact. With apologies to Mrs. Pembroke, while she was entertaining, his friendship with the woman nearly twice his age was a small shrub in the barren plains of his social life.

Owen had come to realize that conversation and socializing provided stimuli that allowed his brain to relax by merely reacting to the thoughts of others. Without this, all his thoughts came from within. More than once, he'd wondered about the long-term sanity of a brain turned in on itself.

He also missed traveling. He sipped his tea and smiled at the irony as the train conductor announced the next stop. But this wasn't really traveling. He left the village only to communicate with his mother. The exact timing of the calls was calculated on an impossibly complicated mathematical formula set out by his family's shady "advisor." That's the generic name his dad called him. Roughly every two months, Owen would take a half-day trip, buy a burner phone, make the call, ditch the phone and travel back to England.

Airports were to be strictly avoided, so he would either take the train north to Scotland, west to Wales, or travel to Europe by ferry across the North Sea, or through the Chunnel. There was no sightseeing, no wandering the streets to sample the culture, and no communicating with anyone. Today, it had been Frankfurt, but might as well have been Muncie, Indiana.

For a while, he had gotten a thrill from the secret excursions, but that had long since worn off. He decided that living the life of a fugitive would be much more exciting if he could stop when it got boring. In a nutshell, that's what he'd failed to fully appreciate about his decision to leave Boston: the complete and utter finality of it all.

Reclining in his seat on the train, he recalled sitting in his father's study in their summer home in Connecticut on that fateful night. The advisor was there, a short and stocky man with a shaved head who wore too much cologne. So were two attorneys, a young one that seemed bright but kept his opinion to himself, and an older gray-haired man who wore a three-piece suit and spoke as if paid by the word. His father had sat with perfect posture behind his desk, peering down over his spectacles with his military bearing, looking like he had every other time Owen had disappointed him over the years—disapproving, with a hint of apathy.

Leaving had seemed premature to Owen, but what did he know? The consensus was formed that the trip was the only reasonable decision, so he'd been forced to agree. Not because he had a burning desire to spend the rest of his life living as a fugitive, but because it seemed a reasonable alternative to a lifetime in prison.

CHAPTER 5

Alyssa Wagner, the newly minted FBI special agent, stared at the list of cold case files on her computer screen in the Bureau's Boston Field Office. Fresh out of a Computer Science PhD Program and the FBI's Training Academy at Quantico, the coding wizard had been recruited by the NSA and every heavyweight in Silicon Valley. But having already made a small fortune with two startups while still in grad school, she'd opted for adventure.

The Fugitive Unit was a typical assignment for young special agents, and Wagner was determined to bring her unique skill set to bear and make a name for herself. As she scrolled the list of files, one name caught her eye.

A native of Boston, Alyssa recalled the Owen Prescott disappearance as a teenager and was immediately intrigued by the idea of bringing the fugitive to justice. That would grab some attention in the Bureau.

Alyssa perused the file on her computer, buzzing through the material nearly as quickly as she could scroll. During the decade since his disappearance, there had been nearly three-dozen suspected sightings world-wide, all reported by vacationers from the Boston area. Interviews had been conducted and BOLOS, or "Be on the look outs," had been issued to local police in the areas of the sightings. Months of wiretaps of the family's estate and a girlfriend had produced nothing.

Artificial intelligence had rendered Prescott's face at his current age of thirty-four, along with images showing different hairstyles and facial hair, all based on facial hair growth patterns of his ancestors.

There had been no hits on FR, or Facial Recognition, now utilized at most airports in the world. Alyssa had written her thesis on the mathematics of the technology. In her mind, the search for Owen Prescott thus far may as well have been undertaken by a gumshoe from the fifties with a pencil and notepad.

"Sam, what if Cyclops had FR?" she asked, calling to special agent Sam Fields in the next cubicle.

"Well, that would be one powerful thing." He rose and peered over at Alyssa. "But it doesn't."

Cyclops was the world's largest network of video footage. In cooperation with the FBI and other law enforcement organizations around the world, the International Criminal Police Organization, commonly known as Interpol, had linked millions of video surveillance feeds around the globe. Law enforcement agencies, municipalities and small business had been incentivized to join in. The result was a network that blanketed an astounding percentage of the world's population centers.

"It just sucks," Alyssa said. "This guy is no doubt on video somewhere, but so long as he avoids airports, FR can't help us."

"That's about the size of it." Sam replied, retaking his seat out of sight.

Alyssa logged on to Cyclops and stared at the screen, her nimble mind processing the problem. "If Cyclops had facial recognition, it would be a different story."

"And if your aunt had balls, she'd be your uncle, Wagner." While facial recognition software could be applied to a single video system, it was out of the question for Cyclops, which used thousands of different video formats.

Sam heard the rattle of her keyboard over the short wall. He'd witnessed Alyssa's single-minded focus before. "Writing FR software for Cyclops, Alyssa? I think the idea is to catch the fugitives before they die."

But Alyssa didn't hear him. She was already writing code.

CHAPTER 6

Hanover, New Hampshire, 2013

Owen's shirt stuck to his back as he sat in the bookstore on a muggy late-summer afternoon in New England. "Good evening." He took the middle-aged woman's copy of *Orchards of Grace* and scribbled his well-practiced signature on the inside cover.

"My Annie is an English major here," she said, nudging her embarrassed daughter toward the table stacked with books.

The young woman rolled her eyes and waved awkwardly. "Hello," she mumbled.

"Well done, Annie. I'll expect you to be sitting here in a few years." He handed her the book and sneaked a peek past her where the line now extended down three aisles in Palsgraf's, the independent bookstore a block from Dartmouth, his undergraduate alma mater in Hanover, New Hampshire.

Owen cracked a wry smile and cursed Joe under his breath. He had to hand it to him, though. For as reluctant as his childhood friend had been to take on the role of his agent, he'd grown to embrace the position. From day one, Joe had hounded his publisher for ads, blanketed social media, and scheduled speaking engagements and book signings.

"Hi, thanks for coming," he said, grinning through a sigh as the next patron stepped up. He had been out late last night, and this looked like a slog.

At least the buxom, young auburn-haired event coordinator walked by occasionally in her tight jeans. Sent by his publisher, Owen thought she may have flirted with him earlier. "I like your shirt," she had said. "Not many men can pull off paisley."

Owen was still adapting to the sudden spike in his attractiveness at age twenty-four. He had always held his own with the opposite sex, relying on his personality, wit and boyish good looks to compensate for his somewhat rounded frame. But as soon as *Orchards* had hit the best-seller list, his every joke had become hilarious, every comment more insightful. His recent success begat confidence and even the occasional workout. Now, although he didn't exactly see himself as a swaggering sex object, he was trending in that direction.

He even had his own real live stalker, as Joe had referenced. Her stalking had been limited to leaving notes for him here and there—on his car or at his place setting at a banquet. They were loving messages with the occasional reference that indicated she was following his life very closely—"Have fun golfing today" or "Don't forget to pick up your shirts. It's been a week." Once she'd left flowers for him at Joe's office, with a note that read simply, "I can't wait until we're together," which seemed odd, since they'd never spoken. The notes were always signed, "Your Spirit Mate, Desiree R."

A local gumshoe Joe hired had found Desiree Richins listed in a Breastwing alumni directory. She'd been two years ahead of him in the prestigious creative writing graduate school. Owen had seen only a glimpse of her once, scampering away from his car. She was a smallish woman with an unkempt blonde mane who seemed harmless enough.

After another hour of signing, Owen stood and stretched, massaging his left hand, then wiping his sweaty brow with a shirt sleeve. Thankfully, the store had closed and there were only a dozen or so left in the queue. He felt hands on both his shoulders and warm breath on his neck. "Can I get you something, Owen? Water, whiskey, heroin?"

He laughed. Even he could recognize that as flirting. "Thank you, April, a water would be great. For now, anyway," he added, staring hard into her blue-gray eyes. She waited for him outside the store and soon they were drinking at O'Hara's, one of his old favorite spots as a college student.

"So, I suppose you'd love to talk about your book," she said sarcastically.

"Absolutely. What shall it be? I can tell you what a damn fine writer I am, or go on about my inspiration, or my creative process? Although I should warn you, I have no idea what creative process means."

"Then definitely, your process." They laughed and drank well into the night. She was a grad student in design and possessed a sharp wit. Owen loved her wide smile and freckles that disappeared into her cleavage.

"I was convinced you'd have one eye glued to the Red Sox game tonight. Not a fan?" April asked, touching his arm.

"I root for them, of course. It's not like I'm some lunatic Yankees fan," Owen joked. "But I'm not like my family or my agent. For them, I feel like if the Red Sox lose..."

"Shh! Are you trying to get us killed?" she asked, looking around fearfully in mock outrage.

After three gin and tonics, each were sending unmistakable signals with subtle touches and coy smiles.

"April is an awesome name," Owen remarked. "Great nickname possibilities."

"Is that right? Is that important?" she asked, as they stood to leave.

"Extremely. I'm a huge nickname guy. You could go with Api or A-train?"

"A-train? What am I, a professional football player? What's your nickname?"

"Don't have one. I've given myself many cool ones, but they never stuck. O'Dawg or Owenator."

"Owenator. I can't imagine why they never stuck," she said, snickering. "How about Wennie?"

"Wennie? You're not getting it. It's supposed to be cool."

"Are you at the Dryden Inn?" she asked as they walked out of the bar, arm in arm.

"Yes, it's a short walk. Would you…"

"Yes," she cut in. "I would love a dip in the hotel pool."

"You are full of surprises, April Monsen." They strolled to the hotel, leaning into each other, only partially for balance. At the hotel, she veered to the pool, pulling him with her.

"What, you thought I was kidding?" she asked.

"It's after hours. I think it's closed," he said, following her through the gate. But she was already pulling off her clothes. Owen began undressing as well, wobbling on the pool deck as he shed his shoes and pants, wondering if she would stop at her underwear. A stolen glance and he had his answer, as porcelain skin shone in the moonlight. They eased their naked bodies into the heated pool, pressing themselves against each other and tasting kisses with hints of chlorine.

Suddenly, a motion-activated light turned their dark and peaceful world fluorescent blue, exposing them to the hotel that towered above them. Laughing, they swam frantically for the deck, scrambling to pull on robes that were stacked by the pool.

April gathered her clothes and headed for the lobby, turning back to him. "C'mon, what are you doing?" she said, still laughing.

"I can't find my shirt. It was right here," he said, exasperated, chuckling at his plight.

"Oh, forget it. You look better out of the shirt, anyway."

"But you liked that shirt. You said I was one of the few people who" —he stopped, mid-sentence, overcome with drunken laughter— "who could pull off paisley."

"I was just hitting on you," she said, now also laughing deliriously.

"Fine," he said, giving up the search, and the two stumbled off to his room.

CHAPTER 7

At times like this, Owen often thought back to his first night in his cottage. He'd sat there in his front room, feeling sorry for himself, staring at a painting depicting a fox hunt played out in the English countryside. A month later, he fed the painting to his fireplace and had never looked back, soldiering through his life in hiding.

Now, Owen felt more alive than he had in years, guiding his Leyland Rover through the country lanes of the Cotswold meadows. The pale green bucket of bolts had come with the house, he supposed, because Mrs. Pembroke couldn't sell the oddly shaped vehicle. It was a two-seater with the engine in the rear and very little leg room. Its boxy front end and tapered rear made it appear to be traveling backwards.

Owen had rolled it out of the detached garage the day before, dubious after six weeks of dormancy. But after a few turns of the ignition, it had coughed and sputtered itself to life. Now, still far from comfortable driving on the left, his heart pumped with anticipation of what lay ahead.

He had read about it in the *Gloucestershire Echo* a month ago, the weekly newspaper that served Tetbury. Sir Alex Wixom, the famous British novelist who had most influenced Owen's writing, would be speaking at Oxford. He'd purchased a ticket online and had counted the days. He was nervous about his appearance in public—at a literary gathering, no less—but as he weaved east through the meadows and pastures of the Upper Thames, his excitement for the event far surpassed his anxiety.

He would be cautious, to be sure. As usual, he would avoid all eye contact and be on the alert for American accents. He'd sit at the back at the lecture with his face buried in the program. Surely, that would be enough. His altered appearance alone should safeguard his identity. Having long since said goodbye to his love handles, his 6'2" frame was lean. His brown hair had grown to his shoulders, and a mustache and beard now covered his angular face.

Owen arrived two hours early, chiding himself for his eagerness as he rolled the gurgling Rover to a stop on a quiet, leafy street near the edge of campus. What he would give to stroll the grounds of his old college, Balliol, with its medieval halls and peaceful gardens. It had been there during his year abroad where he'd discovered his love of writing. But rather than walk the cobbled streets of Oxford, or have a pint at the *Bird and Baby*, he would remain disciplined and wait in his car until it was time to make his way to the theatre. This was not the time to be greedy.

CHAPTER 8

Hanover, New Hampshire, 2013

The shrill ring of the hotel room phone, an ice pick to Owen's ear, had him scrambling in the dark to make it stop. Disoriented, he'd assumed it was a wake-up call, and nearly hung up before hearing his roommate, Will's, voice.

"Hey, sorry to bug you so early but your phone was off and I thought this was important." Owen grunted a reply, holding his throbbing head in one hand. A phone call from his roommate was rare under any circumstances. An actuarial scientist and mathematician who consulted with wealth management firms, William Nelander kept socializing to a minimum, preferring instead to be alone with his equations.

"Our place was broken into last night. I was staying at Melanie's and got a call from our neighbors this morning. I'm on my way there now."

The words seeped through the thick fog that enveloped Owen's mind. "Someone broke in? Who?" he asked stupidly. Then, as more words from Will thudded the perimeter of his consciousness, a single coherent thought floated to the surface and bubbled free. Professor What's-His-Name's lawsuit.

On the hard drives of two laptops—one in Owen's office, one in his bedroom—resided every draft of *Orchards of Grace.* Every plot outline, synopsis and character note was there, not to mention outlines and drafts of other novels in progress. Joe had seemed so confident, but what if someone succeeded in taking credit for his best seller? Even if it cast doubt, his reputation would be ruined.

"Okay, I'm on my way," Owen said, and tossed the phone aside. He walked into the bathroom and drank out of the faucet, then doused his face. He pulled on jeans and a tee-shirt and searched for his shoes.

To his left, a lump in the bed moved. Shit! Owen had completely forgotten about her. He searched his brain. April. He scanned the room, trying to piece together the evening—the drinks without dinner, the pool. His eyes fell on the robes at the foot of the bed, then to an empty wine bottle on the desk. He swallowed, tasting its tannins, and went back to the bathroom to gargle mouthwash.

He sat down next to the lump. "Hey," Owen said tentatively, nudging the pile of bedding. It shifted slightly. Another nudge brought a feint murmur but no movement. He decided on a note. He was a writer, after all.

"You're leaving?" came a voice from the lump after he stood. The tone was harsh.

"Hey, there you are," he said, sitting on the bed again. "Yeah, so, um, I'm sort of in a panic and need to leave right away."

"What happened?" The tone was softer.

"My apartment got broken into last night."

The lump was silent. Then, "Your apartment in Boston was broken into. That's your emergency?" Harsh again.

"Yeah, it's just that…"

"So, you need to rush home and what? Catch the burglar?"

"No, but I—"

"Whatever. Fine. Go."

"April, I feel badly leaving…"

"Leaving me here with no ride after we…Fuck it. Just go."

Owen gathered his things and stopped at the door on the way out. "So, I had a nice time. I left my number on the desk. Please call and I'll send you an Uber." A fist slowly emerged from the lump. A middle finger emerged from the fist.

CHAPTER 9

Margo Stark loved the colors and scents of England in early spring. She had lived in the Midlands for three years as a child and her memories were painted with meadows of daffodils and brilliant sprays of wild orchids that peeked from the giant stones of her patio.

Today she had lost track of time in the Oxford University Botanical Garden, strolling in Bluebell Wood, where stately oaks rise from a knee-high pool of lapis. Now she was hustling up the sidewalk on Broad Street toward the iconic Sheldon Theater. A freelance writer, she had detoured north from a writer's conference in London and didn't want to be late for the lecture.

She jogged up the steps, through the grand doors and into the ornate foyer, where the last few patrons were slowly making their way inside the theater.

She scanned the line, her eyes stopping on a fit-looking man in his mid-thirties with longish hair and a beard. Slowly, recognition washed over her. She could scarcely believe her eyes.

CHAPTER 10

Boston 2013

On the two-hour drive back to Boston, sipping a coffee snagged from the hotel lobby, Owen's head was clearing. As usual, he had overreacted, at least in leaving April stranded. She was right, of course. What did he expect to accomplish at his apartment that couldn't be done a few hours later?

There was no question, though, that the break-in could prove disastrous. Of course, all his literary works in progress were saved to the cloud, as was the final galley proof of *Orchards of Grace,* published earlier in the year. But he had begun writing the best-seller over three years ago when he was still in graduate school. So all his notes from the early days—the plot outlines, early drafts, character notes—existed exclusively on the laptops.

Another thing about the break-in bothered Owen. The burglary occurred on one of the very few nights that both he and Will were away. Parking for their two-story Beacon Hill townhouse was underground, so there was no way to tell if it was occupied from the street. Either the burglars kept track of their comings and goings, or he and Will had been very lucky to have avoided a home invasion.

Owen's thoughts had drifted back to April when his phone buzzed.

"Hi, Will. What are the odds that the one night we're both gone is the night we're burglarized?" Before his sentence was complete, Owen knew what was coming.

"Nine, probability quotient for x, .438," he mumbled into the phone before announcing clearly, "I'd say somewhere just south of .0004 percent."

"Thanks, Will. Do we have an inventory of our losses?"

"It seems they took your laptops. I think that's it." The words, crystal clear through the car speakers, echoed in Owen's ears. It was the worst news he could have received. Surely, the burglary was related to the lawsuit. "Owen?... Hello?"

"Yeah, sorry. I'm about thirty minutes out. See you soon."

"Hey, there's something else." Will paused, as if searching for the words.

"Yeah?"

"It's difficult to explain. You'll see when you get here." Numbers were his first language, so his response wasn't surprising.

After leaving a panicked message for Joe, Owen put on his classic rock playlist and forced himself to relax. He reflected on his rather erratic behavior of late. He'd been drinking too much, not writing enough, and blowing off his marketing obligations. Owen pictured his father, sitting in his study, peering down over his reading glasses, smug sneer in place, reveling in yet another of his son's disappointments. No matter how successful he was as a writer, he would never understand why Owen had declined a fascinating career moving around his family's giant pile of money.

Owen had to admit that he had a storied history of snatching failure from the jaws of success, mostly through his own doing. Self-sabotage, his dad called it. These recent accomplishments, though, were like nothing before. To screw this up, he mused, one of his normal irresponsible stumbles wouldn't do. To undermine his current success would take a truly reckless blunder on a grand scale. Maybe this was the start. These and other self-destructive thoughts tumbled through his mind all the way into his garage in Boston.

Will greeted him in the elevator. "Greetings, Owen." It was his roommate's standard formal greeting.

To say that Will was socially awkward was only half true. While his lack of empathy and social graces certainly made other people uncomfortable, it didn't bother Will in the least. On the elevator ride up, he brought Owen up to speed as only he could.

"It seems entry was made by crudely bashing a window," he began. "Of course, a more savvy burglar would have pried open a door or broken the glass on our back door. As I mentioned, only your laptops were taken, which is curious, given that they left behind many other more expensive items—my neutron calculators, for example.

"Nor was there a search for cash or jewelry. After a quick online survey, considering the current rate of inflation, given that our estimated insurance recovery time is likely sixty-eight days, I reported to the police that our loss, including the window replacement, totaled approximately $2,713.00. Of course, this is only an estimate. The officer told me the prospects for recovering your computers is less than ten percent, but I think that's way off."

"You think ten percent is way off?"

"Yes, given the current crime rate, the closure rate of burglary cases by the Boston PD for this year and last, not to mention the recent layoffs suffered by that department, I'd say the number is much closer to 7.6 percent." When Owen had first met Will, he often thought such comments were a joke. Over the years, he'd learned that Will seldom joked, and never when it came to numbers.

Owen entered the apartment to find that it looked remarkably normal. A backpack where he kept one laptop had been thoughtfully returned to its place, slung over the back of a kitchen stool. The other, in his bedroom, had been carefully removed without upsetting the ordered clutter on his desk.

Owen had forgotten Will's inability to describe another aspect of the burglary, so what greeted him in the dining room was all the more jarring.

In the least used room in their apartment, two place settings were arranged across from each other on the dining room table. Between them sat a white birthday cake, its icing intricately decorated with books and balloons. Red script on its top read, "Happy Half-Birthday, Owen! Love, Your Spirit Mate."

Owen shivered and approached the table cautiously from behind one of the place settings, as if afraid it was booby-trapped. "So, Will," he called behind him, afraid to take his eyes off the table, "I assume this was here when you arrived?" Owen heard the quake in his own voice and already knew the answer.

On each place mat rested a glass of Pinot Noir. The one nearest him was two-thirds full, the one across the table, nearly empty. Owen steadied himself, both hands on top of the chair in front of him. His fingers touched paper on the chair. Slowly, he walked around the table, almost afraid to look. There, taped to the chair's headrest, facing the table, was a life-size photograph of his own face.

A rush of nauseous warmth enveloped him and his legs turned to jelly. In slow motion, he collapsed to the table on his forearms and wiped the sweat from his face with both hands. He looked up again, taking in the macabre tableau. He pictured the woman enjoying the wine and an imaginary romantic evening with his face, frozen in a smile.

The good news was the burglary now seemed unlikely to be related to the lawsuit. But so much for his friendly, harmless stalker. He needed to call Joe about that restraining order. He'd never acknowledged his half-birthday, and he didn't care to again.

CHAPTER 11

If Margo hadn't seen him walk, she may not have recognized him. He had certainly lost weight, and the beard softened his pronounced jawline. She would have to take a closer look to be certain, but that swaying walk was unmistakable. She couldn't make out his eyes, but they would be telling. As seen in the photos, they were green, and she recalled wondering if he wore colored contacts.

The story had dominated the press back in 2013, when she was starting her career as a freelance journalist. Owen Prescott, the darling of the class of Breastwing graduates, was reveling in the success of his novel, *Orchards of Grace*, an acclaimed work of literary fiction about a boy's adventure of self-discovery through the minefield of his foster upbringing in rural Georgia. It had won a Cupcarthe Pyramid and a string of other prizes for fiction. Margo had found the book captivating and had attended more than one lecture by Prescott after its publication.

Then came a lawsuit by a former professor, Norvel Anendale, claiming that Owen had stolen the book idea and plagiarized much of the book. The suit was covered on the back pages, but most assumed the lawsuit was baseless—a fraudulent money grab fueled by jealousy and greed.

Margo would never forget where she was when she heard Owen was the prime suspect in Anendale's murder. She'd been watching a movie while house-sitting for her aunt in Weston when the local news cut into regular programming. Camera footage showed Owen from a week earlier, walking into the police station as reporters and camera crews shouted questions in his direction. It was then that she noticed Owen's peculiar gait—a saunter that had his torso rotating more than usual. She even recalled a radio personality poking fun at it. That walk, replayed countless times on television, had been singed into Margo's memory.

For weeks, Owen's arrest had dominated the news in the provincial city. Prescott's fame was heightened by his family's presence in Boston as wealthy philanthropists who'd made their money in steel and now presided over an aerospace engineering empire. Margo recalled the press conference, where an exhausted-looking Owen stood in silence as his New York attorney predicted a swift acquittal.

Then out of nowhere, on the eve of the day he would be formally charged with murder, he had vanished. The family sent out a press release. Regrettably, they had lost contact with their son and would do everything in their power to find him. Both Owen and the family were looking forward to seeing justice served.

Of course, few believed a word of it. Clearly, he had fled to avoid a trial, and most were certain the family was financing his life as a fugitive. Over the next few years, there had been a few reported sightings of Owen, but none had panned out. Occasionally, a newspaper would revive the story on the anniversary of Anendale's murder, but mostly, Owen Prescott's disappearance itself vanished from the minds of Bostonians.

Margo sat through the lecture, her mind preoccupied by her discovery. Owen had taken a seat near the back of the theater, and she didn't dare turn to look at him. She couldn't claim to know the famous writer. Of course, she'd been aware of him at Breastwing, and they traveled in the same literary circles. But she was certain he wouldn't remember her, especially given the change in her own appearance in the last decade. She needed one more look to confirm, but she had to be cautious.

Margo's career as a fiction writer had not panned out. She'd published a few short stories in literary journals, then had turned to journalism. After stints with two newspapers, she'd found her niche as a freelance investigative reporter. Her career was mainly financed by her husband, but she enjoyed her job immensely, traveling around, uncovering scandals and writing features for newspapers and magazines.

Margo stood quickly as the lecture ended and was at the back of the theater before the applause had died down. The tall figure in the back row was still clapping as she headed out into the cool night at dusk. She crossed the street and stood in the shadows on the sidewalk with a clear view of the well-lit entrance to the theatre. She pulled back her brown hair, draped her shawl over her head and put on sunglasses, checking her appearance in a storefront window.

Owing to construction in the area, upon exiting the theatre, all patrons would cross the street. She would wait to see him exit the theatre, then walk past him, crossing the street in the opposite direction.

Owen was one of the first to exit, quickly descending the steps and heading for the crosswalk. Margo began her stroll across the street, lining herself up to pass close by him. Not wanting to stare, she planned to avert her face until he was near, then steal a quick glance as he passed. Two paces from him, as she was lifting her head, her heel caught something in the street, propelling her forward, face-first toward the pavement.

She landed on the street on her hands and knees, all pain obscured for the moment by her utter embarrassment. As she scrambled to her feet, she felt a hand on her shoulder and looked up into striking green eyes.

CHAPTER 12

The code had taken Alyssa three weeks to write, working all hours of the day and night. For a fellow coder like Sam, it was the height of elegance.

First, she had reverse-engineered the facial recognition software. Rather than taking facial measurements of millions of faces, her software imprinted the algorithmic representation of Owen's face on the vast network of videos. He was the only fugitive she sought, after all. The math behind her program also made her facial recognition much more precise than those used at airports. The genius of Alyssa's idea was based on the reality that no two human faces shared more than a few identical measurements.

For each face that appeared on the video, the software would begin comparing it to Owen's face, one miniscule measurement at a time. For nearly every face, one measurement would mean elimination. The quick dismissal of every face that wasn't Owen Prescott's meant sidestepping the enormous bandwidth necessary for most FR programs, which captured all the biometrics of millions of faces. This simplicity meant that the code easily applied to the thousands of different platforms running on Cyclops.

Sam, ever the company man, had suggested that Alyssa run the idea up the chain of command. But it had occurred to her that a fugitive from 2013 wouldn't be the FBI's first priority. Also, offering up her program to the bureau at large would mean months of delay. Besides, her charge was to use the resources available to catch a fugitive, and that was precisely what she was doing.

In less than a week, she had her software—she'd taken to calling it Pres-catch—up and running on her Cyclops feed. Besides working in real time, the software began searching the previous two years of archived footage.

Alyssa was thrilled when the first hit appeared on her screen. Two years ago, Prescott was caught on video in front of a store in Stuttgart, Germany. Then about two months later, he was near a train station in London and later the same day, in Paris.

The sightings continued at those approximate intervals until the first one in real time, in Amsterdam. Alyssa had been monitoring the video in her office when the hit came and had alerted their field office there, but too late. She realized the challenge would be getting boots on the ground before he was gone. Unfortunately, his constant movement made that nearly impossible. Alyssa figured that her best bet was to catch him stranded somewhere, perhaps waiting for a train.

Over the next several months, there'd been a smattering of other video sightings in Dover, Vienna, Edinburgh and Brussels, but all met with the same result. The sightings kept occurring every few months, sometimes in different cities on the same day. Alyssa suspected that Prescott lived in a remote location safe from cameras and traveled occasionally, probably to communicate with his family. She didn't see any pattern to the timing of the trips, so they were either random, or more likely randomized by a formula to prevent a pattern from emerging organically.

Alyssa patiently updated Owen's wanted photo based on the new footage. Prescott certainly didn't look like a killer, at least based on her FBI profiling classes. But what did she know about that? It wasn't real science, after all. What Alyssa Wagner knew for sure was that every day, the web of Cyclops spread wider, slowly creeping over the world, shrinking Owen Prescott's islands of safety. This guy was smart, but she liked her chances.

CHAPTER 13

Boston 2013

Professor Norvel Lambeth Anendale sat in his dimly lit study, his spindly frame cradled by the worn leather of his oversized chesterfield. A stack of essays rose to knee level from the floor in front of him. To his left, a highball glass of single malt scotch sweated on the agate top of a side table.

His summer term creative writing classes were the most tiresome, filled as they were with slackers playing catch-up on credits. The authors of the essays before him had proven no exception. But then, the entire Department of Fiction at Breastwing was different now. In his day, in order to write, you had to read the classics — Dickens, Shaw, Austen. He'd paid his dues, studying the syntax, elegance and flow of the greats.

He sipped his drink, savoring the singe at the back of his throat, then the wave of warmth as his senses dulled. Now, the department emphasized…he smirked. He hadn't a clue, really. Perhaps holding hands in a circle and sharing their feelings about writing.

It was no wonder the graduates of the renowned Breastwing College of Writing were producing such drivel—narrative stream of consciousness memoirs, poetry without meter, and novels that read like comic books. Not like in his day, when the graduates—himself, among them—had elevated the written word.

But that was then. It had been twenty-five, no, Jesus, twenty-seven years since his *Cake Batter Blues* had won a Cupcarthe Pyramid for best debut novel. A prideful smile played at the corner of his lips. His novel had been a sweeping epic, not like one of these trite novellas that pass for literature today. Another sip. His tired eyes traveled to a bookshelf behind his desk, where the foot-high granite pyramid sat collecting dust amidst old textbooks.

The professor let his mind drift back to those heady days as a young author. He would toil as a professor's assistant by day, his mind filling with thoughts of his new bride, Lydia, and his manuscript—plot twists, metaphors, and dialogue. Then he would race home to Lydia to make love, then let the pent-up words spill out, filling the pages of his masterpiece.

After publication, he had been the talk of American literati, he and his beautiful companion. But then came the accident and everything changed.

For months after her death, he would sit in front of his computer for hours, trying desperately to write himself free, tethered fast by the memories of that awful night. It wasn't so much writer's block as a complete lack of concentration. After a few months on the best-seller's list, sales for *Cake Batter* dwindled. Book signings and speaking engagements began to dry up and soon, he was yesterday's news.

Even after he'd pulled himself out of his malaise, the ideas and words that once flowed from a faucet now had to be wrung from a damp rag. The questions didn't help. When would he publish again? Would it be a sequel or a different genre altogether?

Anendale rattled the ice in his glass and finished his drink. He knew his drinking hadn't helped with his writing but he had it under control, despite the murmurs from his sanctimonious colleagues in the Fiction Department. He'd lost his position as department chair last year and had seen the raised eyebrows at the college mixers.

Now, in the summer term, without the daily class routine, the days ran together. They began with coffee at home, in the kitchen where Lydia used to make her famous omelets. Then his morning constitutional to clear the cobwebs, across the street and around the brick and ivy of the campus. On Tuesdays and Thursdays, he'd teach an afternoon class. If not, he would read on his patio, snacking on cheese until dining alone, across from the photo of beautiful Lydia, the one of her in the garden on their wedding day.

Really, his day had devolved into waiting to pour his first drink. He started with a proper Manhattan, carefully shaving zest from an orange, adding bitters and vermouth, patiently measuring as the anticipation built. Next, the clink of an ice cube sounded the end of another day's torment. Then the first whiffs of smoke and peat were at his nose and the caramel liquid was washing over the ice cube, filling his empty soul. After the first cocktail, he didn't bother with anything but the bourbon.

The professor stared at the stack of essays, no doubt filled as they were with the immature prattle of the privileged. He resented the young authors of this generation who wrote without a thimble-full of discipline. He'd tried to read their latest offering, a best-seller by the Prescott kid. What was it, "Orchards of something?" Couldn't get through it. It meandered around like a stray dog in a park. "No clarity, no precision," he said aloud, hearing the bitterness in his stuffy New England accent.

But Owen Prescott was the anointed darling of Breastwing. Over the years, the graduate school had been a training ground for the nation's best authors. Even now, months after publication and you couldn't turn a corner on campus without seeing his smug face—in the bookstore, on fliers, and at university events. Anendale recalled Prescott's efforts in his Advanced Creative Writing class as utterly unremarkable. He could turn a phrase, he supposed, but was raw and untrained. Anendale fished the twist of orange peel from his glass, sucking the sweet liquor from it.

Orchards had begun as a short story in that class three years ago. He'd seen the potential in the tale but knew his student wouldn't do it justice. In a moment of weakness, he had offered Prescott an opportunity to collaborate. He chuckled bitterly at the memory. Imagine, he, a department head with a Cupcarthe Pyramid to his name, offering to write with a student.

He recalled Prescott's flippant response like it was yesterday. "Thanks, but I think I work better alone," he'd said without a hint of humility.

The professor rose with his glass in hand, steadying himself against the table, then wobbled to the kitchen for another drink. On the way, a leg nudged the stack of essays. They slid, in slow motion, to a heap on the hardwood floor.

CHAPTER 14

As a crowd gathered around them in the middle of the street, Owen turned up the collar of his peacoat, retracting his head like a tortoise, and scurried out of the intersection and down the street. Head down, sticking to the shadows, he jogged back to his car. "Fuck, fuck, fuck," he whispered to himself with each stride. So much for not calling attention to yourself or interacting with strangers. And an American, at that! He wasn't sure how he knew, but she at least gave the impression of an American.

He reached his car and scanned the neighborhood before climbing in. There was something about the encounter that was unsettling, apart from attracting unwanted attention. Years of living as a fugitive had sharpened his awareness of his surroundings.

As he had descended the stairs outside the theater, he had noticed the woman from across the street, standing in the shadows against the building. She had moved from her position only when he had entered the intersection. And was it his imagination or had she seemed to veer to her left in the street until directly in line with him? And sunglasses had been an odd choice at this hour, he thought. It's probably why she'd tripped.

A few nervous turns of the ignition and gentle taps of the gas coaxed his jalopy to life and soon he was sputtering his way out of Oxford, the bustling city giving way to the rolling hills and sheep pastures of Oxfordshire. As usual, the isolation of the road eased his mind. The encounter had lasted for, at most, a few seconds, and he was probably just being paranoid about the movements of the woman in the street. Come to think of it, what possible motivation would anyone have to throw themselves face first on the pavement? And it wasn't like he could have just stepped over her. Societal code dictated he at least check on her well-being.

Owen replayed his interaction with the woman in his mind. He had to admit; it had been thrilling. His hand on her small shoulder, feeling the hair beneath the soft fabric, their faces inches apart when she rose, seeing his reflection in the sunglasses. He thought he'd detected an air of panic in her movements as she scrambled to her feet.

Briefly, he wondered if he had imagined something when their eyes met. Had there been a moment between them? He let his mind wander to another time, when he may have insisted that he be allowed to at least escort her off the street. He would make a crack about women throwing themselves at him, then ask her for a cup of tea. Two Americans, their chance meeting in England straight out of a romcom. Perhaps it would end with her telling him she'd been falling for him from the moment she saw him or something equally trite.

He chuckled at himself. So starved for romance he must be, finding it in the briefest of encounters. He wondered if she'd seen his desperation for a connection in his face? He may have actually freaked her out.

Deep in his romantic ruminations, Owen hadn't noticed the car following him out of Oxford. A mix of anxiety and excitement surged through Margo as she followed from a safe distance, her hands in a death grip on the wheel. Driving on the left, the narrow country lanes, the ever-darkening skies—all of it had her unblinking eyes glued to the road.

But it was her covert mission that had her body clenched taut. "What the fuck are you doing, Margo?" she asked herself aloud. But she knew exactly what she was doing. In her world, Owen Prescott had been one of the most well-known missing persons ever, and she'd found him. She couldn't let the opportunity pass.

Suddenly, she realized she may need gas. She hadn't refueled since leaving London this morning. She stole glances at the strange dash display, finally locating the fuel gauge. Thank goodness all was well.

But when her eyes were back on the road, the taillights of her target had disappeared. Shit! Had he turned off without her knowing it? Within minutes, she sped past a turnoff where a sign read "Tetbury." Past the sign, the road crested a hill where she could make out a long and straight road ahead. There was not a car to be seen. Margo sighed with satisfaction, loosening her grip on the wheel. "Tetbury," she said to herself. "I'm going to find you, Owen Prescott."

In fact, Owen had finally noticed the headlights in his rear-view mirror about thirty minutes into his drive. The country roads of the Cotswolds were truly a labyrinth, so when the car was still behind him on the outskirts of Tetbury, he'd rounded a sharp turn and quickly darted off the road, cutting his lights. The car had sped past and continued on the main road, bypassing the Tetbury turnoff, and Owen breathed a sigh of relief.

In a few minutes, he was sputtering through the familiar streets of his village, feeling its soothing familiarity. Past the town hall, the sweet shop on the corner and Wigan's barbershop. A left down the cobbled main street, with its pastel store fronts and honey-hued cottages. Another left just past St. Marks, a medieval church with the cemetery out front, over the ancient stone bridge that spans the trickling River Avon. A right on Old Mill Lane and Mrs. Pembroke's stately stone manor was just past a meadow on the left, his cottage tucked in behind.

Soon after tucking his rover into its shed and enduring a scolding from Guildy, his cat, for his late arrival, Owen enjoyed the peace and solitude of his back patio with a beer and a peanut butter sandwich. After years of solitude, the crowd at the lecture had nearly short-circuited his senses. He thought of the woman on the crosswalk and his needless evasive actions on the drive home. He chastised himself again for his paranoia, but knew it was a part of his life.

CHAPTER 15

Boston 2013

"Welcome to the Sheffield Club, Mr. Prescott." The diminutive man clasped his hands in front of himself and bowed slightly, as if accepting imaginary applause for his own introduction. He wore a tweed jacket with velvet elbow patches over a green turtleneck and sported a self-satisfied smile. "Follow me, please."

Owen could stomach the book signings. He could tune out and default to repeating the same generic greetings and expressions of gratitude. Even the university-sponsored mixers were okay, provided there was enough alcohol to mute the social awkwardness.

But the events where he had to speak about his writing were altogether awful, combining Owen's two least favorite activities: public speaking and talking about himself. Not to mention the Sheffield Club was a collection of the most self-important self-proclaimed intellectuals in Boston. Owen's father was a member, so he hated it.

He followed elbow patches across the marble floor of the lobby, where the walls were lined with huge paintings of jowly white men looking pensively into the distance. Presumably, they were past presidents or grand pooh-bahs or whatever they called their leaders.

The club was the frequent host of lectures and discussions aired on public radio, and the members fashioned themselves a public forum for highly elevated discourse. As a teenager, Owen's dad had dragged him to a half dozen lectures, none of which he cared to remember.

Elbow patches paused before opening a thick leather-padded door. "If you'll just follow me into the parlor." The room was stunning, with massive windows on one wall that overlooked Boston Harbor. Gothic gargoyle candleholders jutted from stone walls, lighting ornately carved bookshelves of mahogany. Four massive black granite arches soared to the fifty-foot-high ceiling, meeting at the center of a brilliant dome of golden stained glass. Furnished with overstuffed leather chairs and marble topped side tables, Owen could well imagine the guys in the paintings lounging around, checking the market while smoking cigars and sipping expensive liquor.

Thankfully, Owen caught sight of Joe, looking awkward himself. "Welcome to the parlor, Joseph," he snickered. "What is this, Downton Abbey?"

"Owen, please behave yourself," Joe whispered. "There are powerful people here, not to mention critics. Nice of you to dress up," he said sarcastically.

"What's wrong with this?" Owen said defensively, looking at his wrinkled khakis and blue button-down shirt. He took a glass of red wine off a tray from a passing server. "Besides, true intellectuals don't care about appearances."

"After your burglary, I guess I should be glad you're not in hiding. I've got a buddy's firm working on the restraining order, by the way. Tonight, just try not to piss anyone off," Joe said under his breath.

Owen scanned the room, his eyes falling on a familiar angular figure dressed in black. "Turner, what the fuck is he doing here?"

"Oh, Scieri. Yeah, maybe I didn't mention it. You two are sharing the stage tonight," Joe mumbled, turning away.

"What did you say, Joe?" Owen was suddenly seething.

"Oh, c'mon, Owen..." Owen grabbed his friend's elbow and spun him behind a granite statue.

"What the fuck, Joe! Are you kidding me?" he whispered through clenched teeth. "You're ambushing me with my mortal enemy?" Owen gulped down his wine and walked away, partly to keep from throttling his friend.

Dominic Scieri had been a year ahead of Owen at Breastwing. He'd published a critically acclaimed and controversial book of poetry two years ago that called attention to American ghettos. The book had been the biggest deal in town before *Orchards of Grace* made it yesterday's news.

The poet represented everything Owen hated about the world of literature. While Scieri cultivated the persona of an eccentric intellectual who had no interest in the trappings of fame, he'd lapped up every drop of attention.

The poet had hired a New York publicist to "build his brand," on the heels of Scieri's latest publication, an anthology of inscrutable modern poetry entitled, *Words on a Page*. As near as Owen could tell, his brand consisted of the new black getup and pronouncing his name with an absurd rolling "r" as if he was first generation Italian.

Owen found another glass of red and rubbed his suddenly tense neck. Although he thought Scieri's poetry was trash—at least the latest book was—he knew the real reason for his vitriol had been Scieri's comment about his novel at the University Club last month. The moderator had asked him to comment on his former classmate's book. "Well," he'd said with an air of authority, "*Orchards* is an amazing book, and I'm so happy for Owen. I mean, I think we can all agree he's not exactly a wordsmith, but he can really spin a yarn."

Owen had tried not to let the backhanded compliment bother him. It had gotten no press and *Orchards'* sales spoke for themselves. The book had received a few lukewarm reviews, but it was Scieri's comment that still echoed in his head. Owen hated to admit it, but that there was some truth in the comment made its sting more lasting.

Joe approached Owen gingerly as the crowd was taking their seats in rows of chairs in front of a dais. "Hey, sorry about the booking. I should have told you."

Owen finished his second glass and traded the empty for another. "No worries. I overreacted. I've been in a foul mood ever since screwing up my date with April."

"April, the Hanover girl, right?"

Owen nodded. He'd sensed leaving her behind was a colossal mistake, and suddenly had no desire to date anyone else. Just yesterday, he'd passed on being set up with an underwear model.

"So, do you have anything prepared?" Joe asked, eyeing Owen's wine.

"No, I thought I'd start with some ethnic jokes. You know, loosen these guys up a bit. Then maybe a dirty limerick."

"Hilarious, Owen. Hey, I hope it's okay, but Dominic wanted you to speak first."

"Of course he did, Joe." Owen sighed, determined to take the high road. "Sure," he said, shrugging.

"Thanks. Break a leg."

Owen felt the wine rounding the hard edges of his mind and took his place at the head table behind the lectern to the right of a large man who proudly introduced himself as Carothers Eshmont, the club president. "Hello, Owen," came a smarmy greeting to his left.

Owen looked down the table where Scieri sat on the other side of their host. "Hello, Dominic, nice turtleneck." After some opening remarks by the president, Owen stood and walked to the lectern. "When my agent booked this event for me," he began, "I was nervous. The Sheffield Club, such an august group of deep thinkers. What can I possibly have to say that would be of interest? But my agent assured me I could just talk about writing *Orchards of Grace.*

"To me, though, talking about writing the novel didn't seem at all interesting. 'Let's see,' I thought. 'I had some ideas and I wrote them down.' It hardly seemed worthy of a lecture at the Sheffield Club.

"But my agent, Joe Turner, who is here tonight, assured me it would be perfectly fine. And so I thought maybe he was right. Perhaps having some ideas and writing them down is interesting enough, after all.

"Then," Owen said, pausing for comedic affect, "just a moment ago, I noticed at the bottom of tonight's agenda, the title of next week's lecture. If you haven't seen it, it reads, 'The Linear Syncope of Existential Thought in Post-modern Society.'" The laughter from the crowd calmed Owen's nerves and the rest of the talk went smoothly.

Last week while cleaning out his garage, in an old notebook from an English class, Owen had found the very beginnings of his best-selling novel. After covering some of the book's literary themes, he retrieved the notebook from his satchel and shared with the crowd his original thoughts about the book. Apart from vague notes about the storyline and protagonist, Owen told the group that he was struck by how little was done by way of organization. "So, I suppose it was very much as simple as I told you it was in my opening remarks," Owen said, replacing the notebook in his satchel. "It seems I had some ideas and wrote them down."

After hearty applause, he returned to his seat. For all Owen's disdain for the Sheffield Club, he was satisfied and glad he'd gone first after all.

He drank more wine as he half-listened to Scieri, then joined him on the dais for a question-and-answer session. "Mr. Scieri," a man in the front row asked, "Can you tell us your opinion of Mr. Prescott's novel?"

"Ah, I think *Orchards* is a lovely little novel. Really, brilliant in its simplicity." Owen seethed, as an uncomfortable silence filled the room. Lovely little novel? Who did this jackass think he was?

The next question came from a tall, erudite looking woman in the back. "Dominic," she began, as if she knew the poet personally, "Your first poem, "Prisms in Repose," is so incredibly emotionally evocative…"

"Evocative of what?" Owen heard himself asking into his microphone. "Sorry for interrupting, ma'am, but I was just curious what emotion was being so incredibly evoked by Mr. Scieri's poem?"

The questioner froze. "Well," she said after a pause, "I suppose I don't know for sure."

"And if I may," Scieri said, smiling condescendingly, "That's the thing, isn't it? The questioner is spot on. I've crafted the verse so as to capture an ambiguity that's present in everyone."

"Mr. Prescott," came the inevitable next question, "Do you have an opinion of Mr. Scieri's latest anthology?"

Owen had been formulating his answer before the question was complete. "Well, I think *Words on a Page* is a very descriptive title," he said with a glance at Scieri, savoring the moment, "but I may have substituted the first word of the title for another."

The president thanked the men amid enthusiastic applause, the two shook hands, both staring daggers through fake smiles.

Later, after the requisite glad-handing, Owen was about to leave when he felt a light tap on his shoulder. "Hey, April," he said, his goofy smile betraying his delight. "I didn't expect to see you here. I've really thought of you, uh, a lot. I mean," he said, feeling himself babble, "you've been on my mind."

"Well, you know, I never did get that explanation of your process."

"We were going to head over to the Plume for drinks. I don't suppose…"

"Actually, no," she smiled with a gleam in her eye. "I'm leaving with Dominic."

CHAPTER 16

Margo could no longer summon the energy to hate Kenneth, her domineering husband. God knows their decade-long marriage had been volatile. Without the buffer of children, the previous separations had been marked by drunken threats of violence, snooping investigators and email hacks. She'd left him twice before, but this time felt different.

Both times she'd moved out, Ken, twenty years her senior, had vowed to leave her penniless. He was a business magnate, and she knew his army of lawyers could well make it happen. Margo was pretty sure he had cheated on her—a far cry from at the beginning of their courtship, when it seemed he would do anything for her. But twice she'd come crawling back to her very comfortable life. For the most part, Ken had financed her job as an investigative journalist, flying around the country, learning fascinating things and writing about them. She'd sold a few articles, but mostly, it was an expensive hobby that was good for her ego.

But when she had moved to a modest apartment in Beacon Hill last month, Ken had hardly protested. He'd sat calmly, discussing her living arrangements and her monetary expectations. He'd made it clear that she would never enjoy his wealth but agreed to be reasonable and civil.

Upon her return to Boston, she hadn't bothered to tell him about her latest adventure across the pond. He would just furrow his untrimmed brow, close his eyes and shake his head, not bothering to waste the energy of speech. Besides, he'd find out when he got the credit card bill.

Now, as her train from London rolled into the village of Kemble, the stop nearest her destination, Margo wondered what was different this time. Their age gap had become more pronounced after he retired. Even with more time on his hands, he exercised less, expediting the softening of his pasty body. He was no longer the sexy captain of industry, and his constant moping presence in the house had become almost unbearable.

They had reduced the rarity of sex to an afterthought, more of a maintenance to see if everything still worked. Still, part of her loved him, she supposed, and she suspected the same of him. As a couple, she thought, sadly, as the train eased to a halt, they'd just run out of steam.

After her red-eye flight from Boston, a coffee at the train station and the cool air of the English countryside gave Margo a second wind, and soon her scheduled ride was pulling up at her new digs. She'd found the studio apartment online, and its location in the middle of the village seemed perfectly suited for her unique endeavor, so ideal that she'd look past its location above a pub.

The Piper's Arms looked well maintained from the outside, smartly painted, its wrought iron pub sign depicting a hand-painted bagpiper above the year 1743. Margo entered and was surprised to find it a quarter filled in the middle of the afternoon. A portly man bounced from behind the bar to take her bags. "You must be our Yank," he said in a heavy Scottish brogue. "Brodie Dundas, at your service."

"Hello, I'm Margo. Pleasure to meet you."

"Aye, the pleasure is mine, and follow me, Ms. Margo." She followed the owner of the pub back to a door opposite the sign for "Toilets," then up steep stairs to her flat. "Not the most glamorous of entrances, but you'll be happy to know there is private access from the alley outside."

After pointing out some nuances to the place—tricks to opening the window and directions for the heater—Dundas made her promise to come down for supper later and left her alone to get settled. She looked around her flat. It was a bit musty, but she was relieved to recognize it from the online photos. The kitchen was tiny, which suited her fine. Two feet of formica counter space separated a one-burner electric stove and a squat, rounded refrigerator from a different era. The bed appeared to fold into the wall, but she wouldn't bother with that. The only extravagance was an oak rolltop desk, no doubt long since judged too heavy to move.

Flopping down on the bed, Margo was happily surprised by silence, the solid construction of the old place muting the din of the bar below. Growing up with four siblings, she had always relished quiet. Her therapist had encouraged meditation in darker times, and quiet introspection had often pulled her from the depths of despair. But those days were over now. She had broken free from her marriage and was living a thrilling adventure.

She rose from the bed and walked to the window that overlooked Sibley Lane, the main street of Tetbury. She parted the heavy drapes, raised the shutters and lifted a window to let in the light afternoon breeze. Having forgotten that the pub was half underground, Margo was surprised to find herself only twelve feet above the cobblestone street.

Looking down past a flower box of pink and violet impatiens, she saw the town post office directly across the street, Balfry's Bakery to its right and Anne's Boutique to its left. Further left, there appeared to be a coffee shop and another pub. The discreet observation post seemed ideal for her purposes. Unless Owen Prescott was a true hermit, it seemed only a matter of time before their paths crossed again.

After a cat nap and a shower, she was soon seated downstairs over a plate of fish and chips and a regrettable glass of warm white wine. Margo looked around the pub and reflected on the last week, half wondering what she was doing living in a tiny village in the middle of nowhere. But why the hell not? Would she rather be home in Ken's giant house, comfortable and bored to tears? It was Tuesday afternoon there. She'd have just finished a therapy session that she didn't need. He'd be back soon from his weekly golf game, snoring in his recliner while she thought about dinner.

Margo smiled, reveling in her newfound freedom and purpose. Soon her eyelids became heavy and she was thankful her bed was only steps away.

She had just closed the door to her apartment behind her when, downstairs, Dundas, greeted his next patron. "Awrite Ancil! Been a while. Something thick and dark fer ye? And I think your favorite seat in the corner is open."

CHAPTER 17

Boston 2013

Owen hooked his satchel on a purse hook and took a seat at the bar in the Plume and Feather, a popular pub a short walk from the Sheffield Club. He'd developed many of his characters here, holed up in a corner table wearing a hoodie, nursing a beer and people watching with a notepad. But tonight, especially after April's poisonous dagger, there was serious drinking to be done.

He was halfway through his first gin and tonic by the time Joe pulled up a stool beside him. "That went well, I thought, even if it was clear you guys hate each other."

Owen gulped the rest of his drink and motioned the bartender for two more, then shared his tale of woe.

Joe sighed. "Owen, as someone who hasn't had a date in months, you'll excuse me if I don't shed a tear for you."

"April was different, Joe."

Joe rolled his eyes. "This was the book signing in New Hampshire, right? It was one night, for God's sake. And as I recall, it didn't exactly end well."

"It went spectacularly well right until the end."

Just then, Owen caught sight of April being seated at a booth. "Shit."

"What?"

"It's April. Seven o'clock. Don't look."

"Where?" Joe turned his stool to the left, looking behind him.

"What are you doing, Turner?"

"I don't see her," Joe answered, confused.

"I said seven o'clock, you idiot. That's behind me. Over my right shoulder," Owen said, exasperated.

"What are you talking about? Twelve o'clock is here, so…"

"No, Joe," Owen said, lowering his voice. "You're facing the bar, not me. So twelve is the bar, so…what are you laughing at?" he asked, but he knew when he felt the tap on his shoulder.

Owen spun his stool to face her.

"Hello," Owen said, turning red. "Joe, this is April Monsen. I like to call her Alley. April, Joe."

"Nice try, Owen. I think Alley is short for Alice. Hi Joe. It's a pleasure. So, Owen, having your friend see if I'm looking at you? Very mature. What's next, a note with a 'do you like me' box?"

"Actually, I asked him to see if your date was pointing a gun at me."

"My date?"

"Yeah, you know, my mortal enemy. Is this your revenge for Hanover?" Owen stole a glance toward her booth but didn't see Dominic.

April slid onto an open stool next to him. "Mortal enemy? What are you, a superhero?"

"Oh, I have superpowers. Maybe someday you'll experience them."

"Careful there, cowboy," she said, laughing. "Don't forget I may have already had that opportunity."

He blushed. "I was hoping you would remember as much of that night as I do."

"Oh, I remember," she joked, "right down to the role play."

"Role play. Really?"

"Yeah, you were dead set on selling me life insurance. Super hot."

He laughed out loud. "You may be the funniest woman I know. And I didn't get a chance to apologize for, you know..."

"Deflowering me and leaving me stranded?" she asked, with a chiding smirk.

"Deflowering? Oh my. Well, that would explain the passion behind your last gesture that morning."

"Yes, well, that may have been a little harsh."

"So, are you seriously dating Dominic?"

"And why would that be so horrible?"

"I don't know. Just never pictured you as the giant reptile type."

She smiled wide, like she could no longer keep a secret. "He's my brother," she said, relishing Owen's mortified reaction.

"Oh, God. April. I'm so sorry." He covered his face with both hands.

"Now," she said proudly, "I have my revenge. The look on your face makes us even."

Owen peaked from behind his hands and groaned. "Really? Your brother?"

"Yeah, he took our mom's maiden name as a pen name. Thought it sounded more literary, I guess."

"I'm really so sorry. He's obviously super talented. I'm just too dense to appreciate poetry. He's really, um..."

"No worries," she said, throwing the stammering Owen a lifeline. "Dom can be a real jerk when he wants to. He's said some pretty mean things about you, too."

"Oh, I'm sure. Let me guess. 'No-talent hack?'"

"Honestly, I'm afraid he would see that as an insult to no-talent hacks. Seriously, if you guys knew each other, you'd find you're a lot alike. I wish I could knock your heads together like the three stooges."

"Well, for your sake, I'm calling a truce."

"I'll let him know. He'll be here soon."

"Hey, at the risk of repeating another Hanover fiasco, do you feel like hanging out tonight?"

"No chance, Prescott," she said, without hesitating.

"Well, that was fairly assertive."

"I'd better get back to my friends," she said, hopping down off her stool. "Call me for coffee tomorrow?" she asked, eyebrows raised.

"I will. Have fun."

Owen turned to face his drink in a considerably better mood.

"She's something else," Joe said.

"Yeah. I tried to tell you."

Joe nodded. "I have to admit, it seems like you guys have known each other for a long time. Don't screw it up, though. Her dad's on the police commission."

"I have no such intention."

The two talked shop for the next hour—next week's schedule, publisher news, and the timeline for his next book. Owen told his agent that he missed writing and couldn't wait to get some free time. It was past eleven when Joe left Owen at the bar. The music was louder and the place had filled up, college kids and young professionals now three-deep behind Owen's barstool.

He sipped his third gin and tonic, letting the warmth massage his mind and fog his senses. Highlights of his successful night at the lectern bumped through his mind against the backdrop of April's smile. He felt a nudge from behind as someone reached for a drink on the bar. He shifted on his stool, his movements slow now, as if weighted down by an invisible coat. Another nudge. It was probably time to go.

Before Owen got to his feet, a small hand reached under the bar and inside his satchel.

CHAPTER 18

Brodie Dundas was one of Owen's favorite people in Tetbury. He didn't know him except to say hello, but he was relentlessly cheerful and seemed to have a Scottish proverb for every occasion. Owen got the gist of most of them and loved the sounds of his inscrutable Gaelic expressions. The mathematical formula had scheduled a phone call trip across the North Sea for the following day, so it was time for some people watching, writing, and beer, followed by a good night's sleep. Presently, Dundas set a dark foamy pint glass on his corner table.

"Thanks Brodie. This will taste good."

"Come in to do a wee bit of scribblin', did ye?" the bar owner asked.

"Yes, I hope so."

"Heid doon arse up, then!" Owen smiled and tipped his glass, assuming Dundas had told him to get on with it or good luck or something similar.

Owen sipped his beer and took in the scene. Blue-collar men played darts, serious drinkers hunched at the bar and families enjoyed dinner as Dundas bounded about, making cheerful Scottish sounds. Owen wondered why the English pub feel couldn't be duplicated in the states.

His Oxford excursion had been eye-opening in a way he never would have predicted. He had looked forward to the day for weeks, anticipating the energy of the crowd and the intellectual stimulation. The lecture had been fine, but he'd found the crowded theater claustrophobic, setting him on edge. Although Oxford was barely a city by American standards, compared to Tetbury, he'd found the pace frenetic and unsettling. He was sure it was to blame for his paranoia on the ride home.

He took out his notebook and watched the dart throwers, chiding each other with jaunty shoves and animated celebrations. They were mechanics by the look of them, a "J. Burns Auto" patch on the chest pockets of their faded, grease-streaked coveralls. To his left, a middle-aged, well-dressed couple spoke quietly over large meat and vegetable-filled pasties. Between them, their teenage son slumped in his seat, his face half-shrouded by an angle of brown hair.

Soon, Owen's ideas flowed, and his fingers danced on his laptop. Two hours and two pints later, he stretched in his chair. Dundas approached from behind the bar.

"You know, Owen, if you're lookin' for bonnie lasses for inspiration, you're better off on a weekend."

"So, you're saying there are beautiful women?" Owen asked in mock disbelief. "Here, in Tetbury?"

"Aye. On the weekend, you can't swing a dead cat."

"Well, thanks again, Brodie. I've gotten a lot done." Owen tipped his glass and downed the last swallow.

"Aye, beer won't solve your problems," the proprietor said, "but then again, neither will milk." The Scot and his pub never disappointed.

Back at his cottage, Mrs. Pembroke was just dropping off carrots and broad beans from her winter garden. Along with his daily runs, she knew her fresh vegetables had helped Owen transform his diet and shed the weight. Mainly, though, she was eager to report the latest on the mysterious woman with the long black hair. Mrs. Pembroke had been away for two weeks visiting her sister in Durham and hadn't had the chance before she left. She let herself in and set about washing the vegetables, hoping that Owen would be back by the time she finished.

Owen's intrepid protector had heard from her hairdresser, Mrs. Copley, that yesterday, the woman was seen strutting down Sibley Lane, as nice as you please, peering through every storefront she passed. Also, the Vicar Elsinore, who, upon her description, knew immediately the woman in question, had seen her lurking at a church social, scanning the crowd. When he politely inquired, she told him, in a decidedly American accent, that she was doing some research for a sociology study. "Load of rubbish, if you ask me." That's what the Vicar had thought of it.

Finished washing with no sign of Ancil, Mrs. Pembroke set the vegetables on the counter and set off on the short walk home, thinking about her tenant. She certainly enjoyed Ancil's company. They didn't have lengthy chats, but just his presence made her less lonely. And even if he was anything but handy, it was good having a man around to do the occasional heavy lifting. For these reasons, she overlooked her not buying the American's story. Not for one second.

From the moment he told the tale of his retreat to Tetbury to escape the trappings of fame, she'd been dubious. For one, she'd barely heard of a writer being recognizable to the public. She liked her murder mysteries but wouldn't know one of her favorite authors from a grocery clerk. And to be sure, authors liked solitude, but at least from what she'd heard, the U.S. was a big country. Why did he have to travel to a different continent for some peace and quiet?

And the pen name business. How daft did she look, after all? Of course, writers used pen names, but they didn't go around living by their pen names. In fact, presumably it was their pen names that were famous. So, if it was solitude they were after, it seemed like assuming their pen name in every-day life would be one of the few ways they could be recognized.

But whatever he was up to, she was happy to go along with it. She quite enjoyed their shared secret and whatever their purpose, found her covert activities exhilarating. For now, anyway, she was happy to go on being gullible old Mrs. Pembroke.

CHAPTER 19

Owen had always known his father was ashamed of his son's fear of confrontation. Once, at summer scout camp, which he hated, his dad entered nine-year old Owen in a wooden car race. Each boy was given axels, four wheels, and a small block of wood from which to carve a car that was raced down a ramp.

Of course, pursuing his lifelong quest to crush all competitors in every walk of life, his father had taken the kit from Owen and emerged from his wood shop with a sleek car that had made the other boys' efforts look pathetic. "I calibrated the aerodynamics. It's a few milligrams over the weight limit, but their scale won't detect it. I had it sprayed at our plant with the new coating we use on our missiles to reduce airflow resistance. The specs are perfect," he'd told Owen. In other words, don't screw it up.

The cars ran two at a time, propelled by gravity down side-by-side tracks. The boys would place their cars at the top of the track then wait for them at the bottom of the ramp while the starter released the gate. In the championship race, Owen's car raced against his friend, Isaac Hanlon's. Isaac had managed to file down the corners of his block of wood. It didn't resemble a car but it had performed well.

Before the race, Owen's dad called him over. "I've been watching," he said, spraying graphite on the car's wheels. "The track on the right is slightly faster. Make sure you get that side."

But when Owen approached the start line, Isaac's car was already resting on the preferred track.

The starter, a ridiculous looking man in full scout uniform and red, knee-high socks addressed the boys in a tone as serious as his father's. "Gentlemen, this is the championship match. The winner of two out of three races will be our champion. Owen, since you are undefeated, it's your choice of track."

"Oh, sorry," said Isaac, reaching to remove his car, then pausing to look at Owen with innocent eyes. "Do you want me to move it?"

"No, it's fine," said Owen. "I'll take the other track." Looking back, Owen wondered if he had secretly wanted his dad to lose. He certainly hadn't cared in the least who won the stupid race. He'd had nothing to do with the car. Really, though, it was just that he hated confrontations.

That his dad's perfectly engineered car had cruised to victory in two consecutive races hadn't spared him a belittling rant about standing up for yourself and two hours locked in the closet. "No son of mine will allow anyone to walk all over him," he said, slamming the door, entirely missing the irony.

These stints in the cramped broom closet with the padlock were designed "to test his mind." They'd begun at age six, when he was still afraid of the dark. Once, when his mom was away, his father had forgotten about him. Panicking late at night, Owen had bloodied both fists pounding on the door. As an adult, Owen knew that the forced confinements were responsible for his chronic claustrophobia.

The wooden car race and countless other episodes still made their way into Owen's consciousness as an adult. None had been more damaging to his psyche than the goose incident. That's the way it had been referred to by most of his therapists.

It had started with his father's terrible idea to take him hunting for ducks and geese when he was eleven in the marshes of northeastern Massachusetts. By then, Owen had begun to speak his mind. He wouldn't exactly stand up to his father but mainly voiced his displeasure with pre-teen sarcasm. "So, let me get this straight, Dad," he'd said, trudging out to the duck blind at an ungodly hour. "It's just you and me, mano a mano with the unarmed ducks?"

In truth, he hadn't objected to the excursion—first, because it wouldn't have mattered, and second, because he had no intention of killing another life form. He had no idea if he could hit a target but he was certain he could miss when called upon.

Nearing the end of the stint in the blind, the birds had kept their distance, and everything had gone reasonably well—that is, except for the bone-chilling cold and his father's lecture in the car criticizing his inability to survive in nature. Inevitably, though, in late morning, an unsuspecting flock of geese appeared overhead, flying in a perfect V formation, their white breasts highlighted against a cobalt sky, dark wings beating muffled flutters through the morning calm.

Shotgun blasts shattered the peaceful scene. His dad stood, firing and reloading in a rapid, terrifying cadence. Owen fumbled with the safety on his gun, then emptied his gun into the air, aiming at blue sky. But then a bird fell, and Owen's nightmare began.

His father had shot it, of course. But it wasn't dead yet and he thought Owen should kill it—some bullshit about respecting the animal. *Hey dad, here's a thought. How about you respect the goose by not shooting it out of the fucking sky.*

"Owen, we aren't leaving until you carry that goose back to the truck. We eat what we harvest and the humane thing is to kill it now." *Harvest. Is that what murder is called when the victim is an animal?* But Owen knew better than to call his bluff. Once, when he was seven, he'd refused to clean a fish and had gone without dinner and spent a freezing night outside the family tent.

Owen approached the goose, which appeared much bigger on land. Thankfully, though, during his walk to the bird across the soggy field, it appeared to have expired. But a nudge with Owen's sneaker proved him wrong. Suddenly, the bird rose, its long neck craning in the air, his beak releasing a grotesque, gurgling cackle as its wings beat frantically, splattering Owen with blood from its wounds. Startled off his feet, Owen scrambled up and looked at the goose, now slumped again in a heap, its head resting atop its quivering body. He saw fear and sadness in the goose's black eyes and cursed his father.

Owen knew he had to kill the animal, as it was suffering. He grabbed his shotgun, ejected the remaining shells, and opened the chamber. He grabbed the barrel-end and drove the wooden stock down on the bird's head. A glancing blow produced a terrifying hissing sound and more flapping, but Owen numbed himself to the trauma. Now straddling the bird on his knees, his eyes blurred with tears, he began maniacally reining more blows down until the goose's head was a red and black pulp and the noises stopped. Collapsing to the bird's side, he convulsed in dry heaves.

After a time, he stood, determined to complete the task. Now sobbing loudly, he grabbed the goose by its neck and slung its body over his back for the walk back to the truck. His hands felt the sinews within the animal's fragile neck. Its down feathers were soft against his cheek as its lifeless body rested heavily on his shoulders. A few times on the walk, the bird's wings spasmed, beating his back with forceful slaps.

Owen struggled under the weight of the animal as a collage of images flooded his mind: the peaceful morning, the chaotic explosions of gunfire, the goose's terrified eyes pleading for mercy, then the feel of warm blood splattering his face. Just minutes ago, the majestic animal had effortlessly soared overhead and now it flopped lifeless against his back. Reaching the truck where his dad sat relaxing on its tailgate, Owen had just one thought.

He wished he had one more shell in his gun.

CHAPTER 20

Rotterdam, The Netherlands

Owen enjoyed his chats with his mother on the phone. She was relentlessly upbeat and could always make him laugh. A great observer of the human condition and a marvelous storyteller, no one could tease humor out of everyday life like Margo Elizabeth Prescott.

Lately, though, the aging rasp that had crept into her voice made Owen sad. She had always been his person—trusting confidant, friend and champion. He knew she'd suffered under the thumb of his dad and his household of spartan discipline. But she'd stood up to him when Owen chose writing as a career and had believed in him through his low points. Owen also knew she believed in his innocence—maybe the only one in his family.

Owen could never bring himself to ask after his father. She would have known he was just being polite, anyway. It wasn't because of his dad's insistence on his flight for the sake of the family, nor his thinly veiled disdain for his career choice. Owen conceded that his father loved him, on some unhealthy level. But well before he'd turned down the appointment to West Point, Captain Edgar Rockwell Prescott, United States Army, retired, had clarified that he didn't like his son, and the feeling was mutual.

Owen had watched him bully his mother, berating her in private for some imperceptible failure to maintain his vision of the perfect household and ignoring her in public, as if her presence was an imposition. He'd never seen violence but its unspoken threat had always loomed. Owen had responded by retreating from all his father's interests—horseracing, guns and chess. His father loved football, so Owen had become the only teenager he knew who knew more about English professional soccer.

Now and then, usually at the end of his conversation with his mother, she would allow herself to believe she would see him again. Today, she'd said, "Well, Owen Bradley, I enjoy our chats but I sure will love it when you're back in Boston."

"I will too, mom," he'd replied, not wanting to ruin their tender moment. Owen had actually decided that he would risk a trip back to the U.S. to see her before she was gone, but hadn't told her yet. He didn't want to think about her death, let alone reference it in their conversation.

Cool rain on his bare arms stirred Owen from thoughts of his mom as he sat on a park bench in Rotterdam. He glanced at his watch. The ride he'd called for was late and the Dutch bus schedule was incomprehensible. To catch the ferry back to England, he had to hurry. He hurried back to the busy street and within five minutes had hailed a cab. He climbed in, relieved to be off the street. The family advisor with the shaved head had warned him repeatedly against loitering in public. "The ferry, please," he said, confident the driver spoke English.

As they pulled away from the curb, the cab's mounted radio crackled. The driver put on his headset and spoke rapidly, alarm in his voice as he looked up at his rear-view mirror, first at his passenger, then at the traffic behind him. Dutch was a Germanic language, and Owen had found that his four years of high school German allowed him to catch a few words here and there.

"Gevolgd?" The driver ended his sentence loudly, spinning in his seat to look at Owen. The word registered slowly.

"Gefolgt." Owen whispered the German derivation, its meaning easing toward him slowly at first, then pinging off his skull like a wrench on concrete. "Followed."

"Hey, some American prick is…" The driver hadn't finished his sentence before Owen was out of the cab on the pavement, rolling to his feet.

After his exhausting sprint, he scanned the crowded hotel lobby, desperate to control his breathing. He pulled on an olive-green raincoat and matching fedora that hung from a peg in the foyer and breezed past the questioning looks of the bellhops. Not feeling like an elevator wait, he weaved his way through the lobby and ducked into the hotel bar. He walked past its only patron and took the stool next to him, shielded from the bar's entrance. The man looked around the empty bar and scowled, apparently not thrilled with Owen's choice of seats.

Peering past the man, Owen caught sight of the muscles in the sport coat questioning the bellhops, showing them his phone and, no doubt, Owen's face. The bellhops were gesturing to the foyer and pantomiming the coat and hat theft. He watched as his pursuer walked past the bar, scanning the lobby. Then he headed up one side of the grand double staircase that led to a balcony, disappearing from view.

He returned to his seat at the bar next to the scowling Dutchman. It was only a matter of time before his pursuer descended the stairs and checked the bar. Think, Owen, he told himself. Crowd…Disguise…Damn! What was the third thing? He had to make a move.

CHAPTER 21

Boston 2013

Fall had been their favorite time of the year. That was the cruel irony. In the morning, they would walk across campus for coffee, headed west, the sun at their backs showing off the brilliant shades of autumn as the first frosts crunched under their shoes. Now, the shortening days and sweater weather brought with them a profound sadness. Professor Anendale missed his Lydia. This time of year, more than ever.

At least the gut-wrenching flashbacks to that awful fall night were becoming less frequent. But now, as he sat wrapped in a blanket on his chesterfield, rattling his glass of bourbon, he could feel one coming, dancing on the edges of his mind, taunting him. He inhaled, his body clenching for the onslaught. But since setting foot in the Sheffield Club last night, he'd seen it coming, and now his brain desperately groped for a distraction. Finally, he seized on the lawsuit, and exhaled.

He didn't need the money, but it would be nice to treat himself to a piece of art or take a trip. Who knows, maybe a leave of absence and a change of scenery would rekindle his writing. More than the money, though, it would be good to see that little brat sweat.

Prescott's lecture had been predictably uninspired and jejune. "Hey, I'm just the common man who tells stories." Anendale had sat in the back in the very room where he'd lectured about his masterpiece—alone on the dais, not sharing it with some beatnik poet. The professor had forced himself to attend Owen's lecture despite what his own big night had wrought all those years ago. He certainly hadn't gone tonight because he cared in the least what the kid had to say about his frivolous novel. On some level, perhaps, he'd gone hoping to face down his demons.

He also wanted to assure himself that Prescott was the same mediocre writer from his class that had failed to distinguish himself in the least. And somewhere in the middle of his trite little self-deprecating speech, he'd heard the smugness that was seared into his memory. "I think I work better on my own." Anendale said the words aloud again, chasing them with another sip of bourbon.

His memories of the details of his collaboration with Prescott had faded, but they would come back to him. Of course, nobody at the Sheffield Club had mustered the courage to ask about his lawsuit. Soon enough, though, he would be forced to address the matter. Yes, the professor thought to himself, it would be nice to bring that smug kid to his knees. Maybe he needed to experience a little pain?

He sipped his drink and sighed. His diversion had worked. The demons on the edge of his mind had retreated, and better days were on the horizon. The *Post* would publish his feature soon. That would get the bastard's attention.

Then there was next week's mystery visitor. The caller had been cryptic—an unsolicited offer of assistance with the lawsuit. Something about papers that might be useful. He'd never thought to ask for a name. Anyway, they were coming Thursday night.

But while the professor's mind rested, softened by his drink, the forces had silently reassembled on the perimeter of his consciousness. Now, they overran his weakened defenses. As usual, the images were blurred in the beginning. As he grabbed a glass of red from a passing waiter, he could make out Lydia's sleek figure across the room, talking with some professors who'd come to support him. He caught her eye and she beamed, her chestnut hair shining in the glow of the golden dome of the Sheffield Club's parlor.

He hadn't even wanted Lydia to go. She'd seen him give the very lecture at least twice before. But she loved to dress up and be social. Any excuse to put on heels and a dress, she used to say.

The flashbacks centered on the drinks, for some reason. After his lecture, he recalled a whiskey sour with some club members. No more than two, anyway. For some reason, though, the drinks flooded every memory—the gentle burn, the subtle aroma of peat, and the sweetness of the soaked cherries.

The images are more defined as they walked arm and arm to his roadster. He is wobbly on his feet in the memory, feeling for the ground, nearly tripping on the curb. It hadn't been that way at all.

Anendale tried desperately to break from the memory—he always did, at this point—as he saw the car appear in his staggering approach. Panicking, he jerked from side to side to dodge his antagonists, but it was no use. They had made it inside him now, flooding his senses.

Then he was behind the wheel, seeing his beloved Lydia clearly now—her delicate head on his shoulder, her scent of jasmine and vanilla. Her hand was on his knee, as usual, laughing at his jokes with her infectious giggle. And then the car was moving and strangely impossible to drive. His roadster usually handled like a dream. The slightest nudge of the wheel caused a drastic swerve, then overcorrections, then the screeching tires and blinding lights. He let out an audible groan before he heard the sickening crack against the dashboard.

Groggy, he reached for his Lydia's lifeless form and held her to him, rocking her small, limp body. You'll be fine, Lydia. He heard his words slur. Maybe a concussion, but you'll be as good as new, thank God. Then he cradled her head and felt the oozing sticky warmth in the crook of his arm.

He'd stumbled out of the car, laying her across in the driver's seat. He hadn't thought of where he'd set her down. Of course he hadn't, not at a time like that. He only wanted her to be well and safe. But when the officers asked if she was the driver...

That was always the end of the flashback, as it was tonight—a final dagger of cowardice to his neck. The professor was left, as he always was, damp with perspiration and quietly sobbing in his chair.

CHAPTER 22

Rotterdam, The Netherlands

The sport coat scouring the hotel lobby below was filled with the sturdy frame of CIA agent Merrick Appler, a former Green Beret who had tested off the charts on the civil service exam. In Rotterdam as part of an inter-agency task force, he wasn't thrilled about being ordered to chase down a random fugitive on his day off, not to mention with no notice.

Appler figured this guy, Prescott, was still somewhere in the lobby, but he needed the high ground to spot him. He was confident he could make it down the stairs in time if his target tried to make a run for it.

Five minutes passed. The agent, scanning the lobby for the trench coat and fedora, hadn't seen his target right away, moving through the crowd toward the exit. But now, his sharp eyes caught a flash of olive green through the glass door of the foyer and he was swooping down the staircase as his prey slipped out into the night.

"Owen Prescott," Agent Appler called, drawing his service revolver as he slowed his approach, "You are under arrest. Show your hands." The agent had caught up with him a half a block from the hotel, walking quickly on the sidewalk in the lengthening shadows of early evening. Agent Appler had seen this before in pursuits. The fugitive likely knew that running would only call attention to himself, so he was walking quickly, pathetically hoping against hope.

"Prescott, stop!" he yelled. After hesitating, his prey turned toward him, the Dutchman's confused scowl turning to terror when he saw the gun. "Fuck." The agent holstered his pistol and sprinted toward the hotel, but he knew it was too late.

Owen, with new life in his legs, was sprinting again, weaving a crooked path from the hotel through the side streets of the city. Finally, he hailed another cab and was on his way to the ferry, his body still convulsing with adrenaline as the cab arrived at the station. Once on the ship, he scrambled to the upper deck overlooking the loading ramp. Not until the ship pulled away from the dock did Owen exhale in relief. "Diversion," he whispered to himself, smiling. "Crowd...Disguise...Diversion."

He slumped to a bench on the deck, its metal cooling the back of his damp shirt. He shook his head at the dumb luck of his escape. The man he'd sat next to in the bar, it turned out, was scowling because he'd recognized his own trench coat and fedora. Owen happily returned them, and the timing of their owner's exit had been perfect. Owen had followed the agent out of the hotel at a safe distance, then had sprinted in the opposite direction.

He usually dozed on the twelve-hour voyage back to England, but not tonight. Over the past decade, he had allowed his mind to fantasize that his fugitive status had been faded by time, that his new life was his only reality. He'd often pictured a manila police folder with his name on it, buried in a stack of files, under a dead plant in a dark and abandoned storeroom.

Now, as he replayed in his mind the image of the agent showing his phone to the bellhops, he knew his life in Tetbury had done nothing to change his reality. He may have burned the painting, but he was still that hunted fox, and now for the first time, the hounds had picked up his scent.

CHAPTER 23

Boston, 2013

Owen sat on his couch, staring at his phone. Apparently, his newfound confidence with women was not all-encompassing. He had always been terrible on the phone. At age twenty-four, he still worried that his voice would crack, and he could never think of anything clever to say unless he worked it out in advance. Inevitably, though, when he prepared something, he would forget his line or awkwardly try to wedge it into the conversation. Also, he never heard the rhythm of the conversation on the phone and was forever talking over people.

Owen also knew that part of the source of his anxiety was April. Despite their limited time together, she understood him almost better than he understood himself. She was whip smart and funny and each of their brief visits had left him wanting more time with her. He thought about things she'd said long after they'd parted, picturing her wide smile and warm brown eyes.

He stared at the phone, breathed deeply, and pressed her name. Leaving messages was much easier, which was why he was calling in the middle of the afternoon. April had mentioned that...

"Hello...hello?"

Shit. "Oh, hi, April. It's Owen."

"Hi there. Are you okay?"

"Sorry, yeah, I guess I expected to get your voicemail. You had mentioned that your work was strict about personal calls."

"Well, if you'd like I can hang up and you can call back and leave a message," she said, chuckling.

"No, thanks. I mean, obviously not. I mean, of course you were joking," he said, haltingly, hitting his forehead with his fist. "Um, I guess I was wondering if you would, that is, you'd mentioned coffee." Good God, Owen, you've actually lost the power of speech.

"It's true, I did mention coffee," she chided.

"Good," Owen finally said after a pregnant pause.

April laughed. "Good what, Owen?" she asked, teasing him, then ended his agony. "So, if you're free tomorrow, I have a fun idea. Can you pick me up at noon?"

"Okay, great."

"I'll text you my address."

"Okay, that's really great." April waited, sure he'd ask what she had planned, but Owen was hunkered down in phone call survival mode.

"Okay…" She paused again, eyebrows raised. "Well…"

"I look forward…" Owen finally said, talking over her.

April frowned into her phone and shook her head. She felt like she was on the phone with her five-year-old nephew. "Okay, bye Owen."

"Bye."

Owen tossed his phone on the couch beside him and buried his head in his hands.

Sometime after he stopped being mortified by his phone performance, Owen realized that he should have inquired about April's allegedly fun activity. His mind immediately went to his nightmare scenarios of theme parks and roller skating. He had no idea what to wear but eventually settled on jeans, a sweater and dress boots, thinking that his footwear might somehow preclude roller skating.

But as often was the case for Owen, the things he worried about the most turned out to work out just fine. She was waiting outside her downtown apartment, dressed in jeans, a sweater and canvas sneakers.

"Hi Prescott," she said, leaning for a kiss. "I'd been wanting to do that on Thursday but I was afraid my brother would have made me walk home."

"So, what's the mystery fun?" he asked, already feeling better now that he wasn't on the telephone.

"Do you golf," she asked, her smile lighting up his car.

"Golf, as loosely defined, yes," Owen said enthusiastically, feeling relief wash over him.

"Good. I thought we could try a driving range. I'm a lost cause myself, but I do enjoy when I hit it well."

"I know what you mean. That perfect strike feels great. It usually happens for me on my last shot, after a day filled with duffs, chunks and hosel rockets."

"Oh, golf terms, you must be good."

"No, I've had to learn those to describe my awful shots. Anyway, good idea. It's not a fancy club that will require a collared shirt, is it?"

"Fuck no. I hate those places." Owen smiled at her answer, and April smiled back.

As advertised, the driving range, situated near the highway in a blue-collar suburb, was anything but exclusive. They rented clubs, bought a large bucket of balls and two beers from the chain-smoking proprietor and commenced pounding balls into an unkempt fairway that was more dirt than grass.

"So, you really suck on the phone," April said between swings.

"Don't know what you're talking about, Monsen. I felt like I carried the conversation."

"Really?" she asked, laughing.

"Yeah, you were really awkward, which is understandable, given your giant crush on me and all."

"Ha! You writers are so modest."

"Thank you. And I'd appreciate you addressing me as an author," Owen replied in mid-swing, letting fly the best shot of the day.

"I'm sure you would. How about a little contest. Farthest from the one-hundred-yard marker buys dinner?"

"Oh, that would be a grave mistake on your part. I'm just rounding into form," he replied, failing to suppress a smile about their dinner plans.

"I'll risk it. You first." Owen swung mightily, sending his ball dribbling pathetically toward the target.

"Prescott won't be happy with that one," April said in her best announcer voice. "One wonders if the moment was too big for him."

"Hilarious. Your turn, tiger."

April pulled her hair back in a ponytail, abruptly assuming a commanding presence. She took graceful practice swings, her club head precisely clipping the mat. Next, clearly in a well-practiced routine, she positioned herself behind the ball, raising her club to align herself with the target, as Owen stared, incredulous. She addressed the ball and repeated the languid swing, launching the ball in a magnificent arch before a soft landing fifteen feet from the marker.

Owen stared in stunned silence. "What the fuck was that?" he finally asked, as April, curtsied and put down her club. "Don't answer. I've been hustled."

"I probably just got lucky," she said, leaning in for a kiss. "Either that," she said, kissing him again, "or four years of college golf finally paid off."

"Impressive. I assume fast food is okay for dinner?"

After drinks, they settled on pizza, delivered to Owen's apartment.

"Don't mind my roommate's pizza scraps from last night," Owen said, picking up the pizza box from his porch. "We leave leftover pizza for a homeless guy who lives near here. Apparently, he wasn't interested last night."

"That's thoughtful of you," she said. "You seem too good to be true, Prescott. You're not about to abduct me and lock me in your basement, are you?"

"Not tonight. Looks like my roommate is at his girlfriend's," Owen said, as they walked in.

"Well, then I guess I can take his bed," April deadpanned.

"Nice place, Owen," she said, walking into the living room. "What a wonderful tree," she said, gesturing to the giant oak centered in their bay window in a park across the street. Its thick, black limbs, draped with Spanish moss, snaked low from its trunk, some only a few feet from the ground.

"Yeah, the famous Suffolk Oak. Isn't it cool looking? Once I took a notepad and sat on one of its low limbs for inspiration."

"Yeah?"

"Sounded like a good idea, but it was a little uncomfortable."

"Well, your couch looks comfortable," she said, plopping down and snuggling to him. Their conversation came easy, each lapping up details of each other's lives between passionate kisses and caresses. "I've always found," Owen said, pausing, his breath heavy on her neck as she traced a nail over his swelling bulge.

"Yes? You've found?"

"I've found the transition between here and the bedroom to be awkward."

She kissed him deeply, then rose from the couch, looking down into his eyes as she wriggled her jeans to her knees. "You're right," she whispered, guiding his face into her. "Who needs the bedroom."

CHAPTER 24

It was late morning in Boston when Owen made his escape, sprinting from the hotel in Rotterdam. Alyssa never had felt more helpless, watching bits and pieces of real-time footage of the futile pursuit on Cyclops from her desk. The local agent had been off duty so without an earpiece. Without an audio connection, she'd been a spectator, tracking the action from sixteen separate video feeds on her bank of four computer screens.

The chase on the street had been spotty, but once Prescott had entered the hotel, she'd seen everything—his entry into the bar, the exchange of the trench coat, and the agent's ascent to the balcony. "No, he's behind you," she'd yelled at the screens as the agent made his ill-fated dash from the hotel.

Sitting at her desk in the fiasco's aftermath, she had resolved to be more proactive. No more sitting back, congratulating herself on her program, watching Cyclops and hoping. If Alyssa was correct, Prescott lived somewhere rural, away from people and off the ever-expanding video network. The only logical explanation for his travels was for occasional communication with his family. For that he required a city where it was easy to find the untraceable burner phones he used for the calls.

With help from her cubicle neighbor, Sam, whom she suspected of some very tepid flirting, she'd pulled up a map of western Europe and plotted the sightings of Prescott with small emojis of his bearded face. They had to have some fun, after all. The pattern formed a rough perimeter, with sightings in Edinburgh to the north, Dublin and Belfast to the west, Calais and Dunkirk to the south and Amsterdam, Rotterdam, and Brussels to the east.

In the middle of the perimeter was England, and Alyssa had become convinced that Prescott lived there. All of the video sightings were within a day's travel of the country with combinations of cars, trains and ferries. Also, the only video of Prescott in different cities on the same day included a sighting in the English port cities of either Hull or Dover, where he'd been likely either leaving or returning to the country on a ferry across the North Sea or the Strait of Dover.

Where, in the country, Prescott lay his head was a more difficult problem. Surveillance cameras were his enemy, so Alyssa could likely eliminate London and probably the more heavily populated Midlands. She didn't think the South West Peninsula of England was a good bet for the sake of convenience, as there had been far fewer sightings in France to the south than in other countries. Still, that left the rural east, the vast north, and the southwest region as possibilities, or even somewhere in Wales.

At 10:00 p.m., Sam called it a night. "I think I'll probably have a beer at Isely's before I head home," he said, his half-invitation hanging awkwardly in the air.

Alyssa smiled at his pathetic effort. "Have fun, Sam. I think I'll keep at it."

"Hey, speaking of Isely's, maybe our boy is living on the Isle of Mann. Probably not many cameras there."

"That's true," Alyssa said, her eyes glued to her computer screen.

"You know, though, they say no man is an island."

Alyssa shut her eyes, cringing. "Good night, Sam," she said, calling over her cubicle.

Alyssa had turned to Prescott's books and short stories, speed reading in search of any references that might be helpful. Despite being more of a non-fiction fan, she found the books enjoyable but bereft of clues. Next, she scoured the internet, watching webcasts of his lectures and interviews during the height of his success.

It was past midnight when Alyssa pulled up the scratchy audio of an interview with Prescott, taped by a student radio station. He was addressing how his life has changed since the runaway success of his breakthrough novel.

"Believe it or not, I miss writing," he told the interviewer. "Obviously, I'm humbled by my success, but I'd love to get away for a few months and just hole up somewhere and write."

"Do you have a place in mind?"

"Yes," Owen answered, without hesitation. "When I studied at Oxford, we toured the Cotswolds. It was filled with these quaint, sleepy villages. I've always thought that someday I'd love to go there, rent a cottage and just write."

"Would you now?" Alyssa said aloud, quickly pulling up a map of the area.

Alyssa was shrinking the world of her fugitive, but she needed some local expertise. Apart from the shooting range, the special agent had found her access to the international network of intelligence officers the coolest part of her job. At some point in her life, she had assumed that Interpol and MI5 only existed in spy films. It was just past 1:00 a.m. when she picked up the secured line on her desk and dialed.

Thirty-two hundred miles across the Atlantic, in Tetbury, Owen was pulling his Rover into its shed. It was Saturday, so the four-hour drive from the ferry in Hull had been easy. Still, to use an English phrase he'd grown fond of, he was knackered.

One hundred miles due east of Tetbury, an operator picked up the secured line, FBI showing on the phone's screen. "Good morning, Scotland Yard." The clipped British accent made Alyssa smile. Her job was so cool, and her fugitive's days of freedom were numbered.

CHAPTER 25

Owen never knew what would trigger what he called being in the writing zone. Sometimes it was something as simple as a good night's sleep, when ideas would fill his head to be poured out on paper in the morning. This time, it had been his terrifying exploits in Rotterdam that had flipped the switch. For the past two weeks, probably to escape the reality of his life in hiding, he'd been in the zone and had scarcely left his desk.

The zone was rare, but when it happened, it seemed as if his novels wrote themselves. His writing career, in its early stages, had been marked with failure and self-doubt. Before *Orchards*—a story resurrected from his days at Breastwing—his first novel had been panned and his second, unpublished.

But when Owen found himself in this Zen-like state, he felt as if he'd been put on the earth to write. He saw the plot and intertwining subplots with clarity from above, as if diagramed on a grid. Characters formed in his mind as real people he'd known for years, their nuanced traits and personalities meshing perfectly with one another. As quickly as he conjured the story, the precise words filled the pages, painting a vivid tapestry. Currently, he was writing a thriller. Write what you know, he supposed.

Owen had learned that in order to maximize the zone, he had to relax and surrender to the feeling. So, he sat at his computer with a glass of Pinot Noir and gave in to his temporary genius. He also knew that the feeling could be fleeting, so he worked through the night, breaking only to stretch his back, pour his wine, and, of course, to feed Guildy. Owen had always considered himself a dog person, but the playful tabby had come with the house and he had grown fond of her.

Still entranced in his craft after sunrise, he hadn't heard Mrs. Pembroke's first knocks on the front door of his cottage. Finally, the persistent raps slowly registered. "Damn," he whispered to himself, remembering his date.

"Mrs. Pembroke, I hate to be rude, but I'm just now in the middle of…"

"What? More writing?" she asked, a subtle smirk at his wine glass before pushing past him. "I won't hear of it, Ancil Bradford. You work hard enough as it is."

"Honestly, Mrs. Pembroke, it's just that I'm in the midst of a unique…" his voice trailed off, defeated, as Mrs. Pembroke had already turned on the kettle and retrieved cups from the cupboard.

Soon, she was on to her favorite topic, recounting the comings and goings of the mysterious woman with long, jet-black hair. Owen, with one eye cast longingly at his laptop, nodded and managed a look of concern. Mrs. Pembroke seemed more than ever convinced that skullduggery was afoot. Apart from her genuine concern, there seemed something different about his landlady, but he couldn't put his finger on it.

While Owen appreciated her vigilance, he was becoming concerned that perhaps his spirited confidant had loosened her grasp on reality. He didn't think she was, to use her words "off her trolley," but she seemed obsessed with the mystery woman's actions. For starters, Owen found it disconcerting that he had yet to lay eyes on the woman. Even if she existed, her actions as described by Mrs. Pembroke—inquiries in the light of day—seemed fairly innocuous.

But as his friend enthusiastically detailed her latest observations, Owen decided against any cautionary comments.

Mrs. Pembroke was clearly enjoying her investigation. Widowed fifteen years ago, the wealthy woman of sixty-seven had moved to Tetbury from London, where she'd purchased the four-bedroom Victorian manor and guest house on four acres. She'd thrown herself into the community, joining clubs and serving in charitable organizations.

Although firmly ensconced in the village, it was clear to Owen that her role of amateur sleuth provided a welcome zest to her daily life. So, Owen thought to himself, what was the harm if she tilted at a few windmills now and then?

Her investigative update complete, Mrs. Pembroke checked her watch for the third time and rose to leave. "Mrs. Pembroke," Owen asked casually, "Are you wearing lipstick?" Somewhere during their conversation, he had managed to pry his attention away from his manuscript to take stock of his guest. She was speaking more rapidly than usual, checking her watch nervously, and jumping from topic to topic. Apart from the lipstick, she seemed, as she might have put it herself, "in a considerable dither."

"Oh, yes," she replied with a furtive hand to her mouth. "Is it too much?" she asked anxiously.

"Not at all. No, I think it suits you. And where might you be off to on this fine day, if I may ask?"

"Just for a walk in the town garden with a friend. The bluebells are in bloom. It should be quite nice."

"And this wouldn't be with a certain gentleman named Mr. Boles, would it, Mrs. Pembroke?" It would be the third time this week that she would enjoy an excursion with this "friend," who was new in town.

She waved off his chiding tone. "Never you mind, Mr. Bradford. Never you mind about me," she said on her way out the door, but her flushed face betrayed herself.

"Well, have fun, then." And she was off, checking her watch again as her low heels beat a steady cadence down his cobblestone path to the street.

One half mile away, in the heart of Tetbury, Margo opened her window and settled in a comfortable chair above Sibley Street. She had slept until nearly ten, taken a morning run, then stopped in to pick up coffee at Mason's Biscuit and Tea Shop. Later, she'd stock up on groceries and kitchen supplies.

Her plan was simple. When she wasn't scanning the downtown village from her perch above Tetbury's main street, she would sprinkle herself throughout the village, walking the narrow streets and frequenting the quaint shops. Unless Owen Prescott had become a complete recluse, she was confident their paths would cross. For now, excited and confident about her endeavor, she sipped coffee from her catbird's seat.

CHAPTER 26

Boston 2013

Owen shielded his eyes with the newspaper as the morning sun peeked through the blinds. "Wow, Lily," he said quietly, "apparently golf is just one of your many talents."

"Not bad, but too hard to say," she murmured into his chest. "Too many Ls."

"Well, I like it."

April lifted her head from his chest. "I knew there was something wrong with you," she said, collapsing back down. "You're an early riser."

"It's 9:00 a.m. Not exactly the crack of dawn."

"Shouldn't you be off to catch a burglar or something?"

"Very funny. You'll never let me live that down, will you?"

"Not a chance," she said into the sheets.

Owen's phone buzzed on the nightstand. "Mind if I take this? It's my agent."

"Oh, by all means, Mr. Fancy Author," she said before burrowing under the covers.

"What's up, Turner?...Joe says hello, April." A hand emerged from the covers and waved. "She says 'Hi,' too...So, any news on the lawsuit or stalker fronts?... Oh, okay, that's good news, I guess. Although since the burglary, I haven't gotten any creepy notes or anything. Maybe she's given up..."

Owen laughed heartily. "Joe says maybe the stalker sent you to spy, April." Nothing came from the covers. "So, Joe, I'd better go. April is not exactly a morning person. Oh, and Joe, it's not a done deal, but I might have a line on some World Series tickets....Okay, calm down. I'm not certain, but maybe. Bye."

Owen read the paper, relived the previous night and reflected on his relationship with April, which seemed to gather momentum by the day. Normally, at this stage, he would caution himself against getting too serious. Historically, subsequent stages would involve finding fault with his partner, then outright relationship sabotage. Now, all that was the furthest thing from his mind.

Thirty minutes later, April stirred and snuggled to him. "Hey, weird dream," she said.

"Yeah?"

"You, me and Dominic were at a modern art museum."

"That sounds like more of a nightmare."

"You each had exhibits and were criticizing each other's."

"Of course we were."

"Dom's exhibit was an apple with a knife sticking out of it, wrapped in bloody bandages."

"Seems right. I can't imagine why I was critical."

"Yours was just this handwritten sign." April paused to laugh. "It said 'Imagine stupid shit here,'" she said before dissolving into laughter.

"What?" Owen laughed. "Is that what you think of my appreciation for art? You must think I'm a Neanderthal."

"Not at all," she said, once she'd stopped laughing. "Just more of a no bullshit guy. More like my dad."

"Isn't he a bigwig with the police department?"

"He's on the police commission. And no, he can't help you with your parking tickets."

"What makes you think I have parking tickets?"

"Seem like the type. Part scofflaw, part absent-minded."

"As a matter of fact, I have a few, but I was more wondering if he could look up this stalker person and see if she has any prior violent offenses. I'd like to know how worried I should be."

"I'll ask him. Do you have a court date for the restraining order?"

"Joe says it's next week. No update on the lawsuit."

"Who is suing you, again?" she asked, yawning into the sheets?

"Professor Anendale. Did you ever take one of his classes? He taught a prose seminar and creative writing."

"Sounds familiar, but I don't think so."

"Older, sort of shriveled up guy. Smells like a distillery."

"Oh, that guy! Yes, total boozer! Didn't he write some best-seller a hundred years ago?"

"Yes, *Cake Batter Blues*. He won a Cupcarthe Pyramid and never lets his class forget it."

"It's crazy how he can just say he wrote *Orchards* without any proof."

"I know. It's annoying as hell, even though Joe says the lawsuit is going nowhere. Apparently, it happens all the time. It's just a shakedown."

"A shakedown?" she asked, giggling. "Who are you, a detective from the fifties?"

"That's what Joe called it," Owen said, laughing. "Anyway, he's just hoping to get paid off."

"So, I happened to notice that you were fine on the phone with Joe," April said, kissing his chest. "Why do you suppose that is, Mr. Prescott?"

"Without conceding that I was bad on the phone in our call, of course…"

"Of course…" she cut in, rolling her eyes.

"I can only imagine…" he said, holding her face in both hands, "that some calls are more important than others." She climbed on top of him as they kissed, long and slow.

"You've been up already?" she said, before kissing him again.

"Yeah, sorry about my breath. I helped myself to the coffeemaker."

"Listen, Prescott," she said, sitting up to straddle him, her hands on his shoulders.

"This seems serious."

"Quite serious. I am, I think you would agree, a very low-maintenance woman."

"I would agree, Lily."

"And I only have a few hard and fast rules."

"Hard and fast. I like that rule already."

"Sunday mornings," she said, ignoring him, "are meant for…" April paused. "Can you guess, Prescott?"

"Coffee and donuts?"

"No. Well, okay donuts. But you're wrong."

"Are you always this critical in the morning?"

"Sunday mornings are for sleeping a long time." She kissed his lips, then his neck, her soft breasts dragging against him. "Sunday mornings are for nuzzling each other awake for slow, steamy sex." She kissed his chest, then his stomach. "Then more sex. Then more sleep," she whispered as he murmured sounds of pleasure. "So, no Mr. Owenator, not coffee and donuts."

"I stand corrected."

"Happy to straighten you out," she said, and trailed kisses down his stomach, disappearing under the covers.

CHAPTER 27

As Mrs. Pembroke approached the town square, she was admittedly quite atwitter. She hadn't been looking for a gentleman, she thought to herself as she approached the town square where she'd planned to meet Mr. Boles, but his company had stirred something in her long since dormant.

Goodness knows her late husband, Phillip Longfellow Pembroke, had been a fine husband, providing an income from his inheritance and his employment as a banker. But he was so often wrapped up in his work and affairs at his gentleman's club—he was club viceroy eight years running—he couldn't be expected to cater to her needs. Looking back, though, after their two children were off, it would have been nice to have a night out on occasion.

But this George Boles was a different kettle of fish. A bit rough around the edges to be sure, but a gentleman, in his own sincere way. He was prone to pronouncements of Mrs. Pembroke's beauty, which was embarrassing but, she had to admit, not altogether bad. Also, despite his tendency to overindulge in both food and drink, he exuded a certain robust air that she found attractive.

A traveling salesman in prosthetics, of all things, he'd recently taken on the whole of the South Midlands and had moved to Tetbury just two weeks ago. Mrs. Pembroke's heart fluttered as she saw him sitting on a park bench. As was his custom, he wore a three-piece gray herringbone suit and matching flat cap.

"Mrs. Pembroke," he rose and took off his cap, "if you don't mind me sayin', the sight of you is good for sore eyes."

"Oh, Mr. Boles, you flatter me no end. And you look dapper as ever."

"Shall we?" he said, offering his arm. She took it, and off they went on the short walk to the village garden. Mrs. Pembroke, a member of the Garden Club, pointed out her favorites as they strolled the rows of bluebells, primrose, and daffodils.

"We likely won't see the roses this year until June, but I fancy these early bloomers myself. I believe the snowdrops are my favorite. How about you, Mr. Boles?"

"To be honest, Mrs. Pembroke, I wouldn't know a snowdrop from Adam's off ox, but they're all quite lovely."

"Well, I'll bet you can spot the snowdrops, at least?"

"Oh, well yes, I'd say those white droopy ones."

"See there, I'll teach you, Mr. Boles."

The two strolled the grounds, arm in arm, stealing glances at each other's smiles along the way. "Well, I'm feeling a bit peckish. Fancy a cup of tea and a scone, Mr. Boles?" Mrs. Pembroke asked, their tour completed.

"Mrs. Pembroke, I've never been known to turn down a scone. Where shall we go?"

"Balfrey's. It's only around the corner. Do you know it?"

"Sorry, no. I'm still getting my Tetbury bearings."

"Would it help if I told you it was directly across from the Piper's Arms public house?"

"Well then, I daresay I know exactly where it is," he said, and the two set off on their walk.

"I hope you enjoyed the garden," Mrs. Pembroke said as they reached Sibley Street and turned left.

"Well, I know the flower in that garden I fancy," he said, patting her hand on his arm.

"Mr. Boles, you'll give me the big head if you're not careful."

"Oh Mrs. Pembroke, I daresay a woman like you has your pick of suitors. This tenant of yours you've mentioned. Are you two…" He paused.

"Oh, good heavens no, Mr. Boles. He's half my age."

"Well, that's a relief. What's he do for himself, this tenant?"

Mrs. Pembroke had always been discreet about Ancil's secret, whatever it was. Often, she'd wanted to tell someone, as she was proud of her role in his concealment. But she and Mr. Boles were getting on so well, and she preferred they not have secrets.

She stopped and nodded across the street, where an OPEN sign just appeared in the front window of Balfreys. "Perfect timing for us," Mr. Boles said with a wink as they waited for the traffic to clear.

"Mr. Boles, the truth is," Mrs. Pembroke said taking a deep breath, "my tenant, Ancil, is a famous writer, living in seclusion. It's quite exciting, really."

Just eight feet above them, Margo sipped her coffee and smiled.

CHAPTER 28

As Owen had suspected, Mrs. Pembroke's social visit had popped his fragile bubble of creative headspace with a straight pin. In the week since, he'd managed only a few pages before taking a two-day break to clear his head. Today though, determined to recapture his writing mojo, he'd risen early and taken a run. After feeding Guildy, he set off for his favorite coffee shop, laptop in tow.

As he made his way through the narrow streets, the morning light shining soft on the butterscotch stone buildings, the village began to awaken. Shutters rose in the windows of McNaughton's Sweet Shop and the aroma of fresh rolls wafted from Balfrey's.

Across the street, the metal garage door of the Towne Auto Shop clattered open, catching Owen's attention. His eyes followed the noise to find, of all things, a very buxom woman with long black hair striding in the opposite direction.

While relieved to find that the woman existed outside the mind of Mrs. Pembroke, he chuckled to himself that her description omitted any reference to what was obviously her most distinctive physical trait. Owen tried not to stare, a courtesy ignored by the auto shop mechanics, who walked out to the sidewalk to gaze from behind as she strutted down Sibley Street, bursting beneath a tight cashmere sweater.

Arriving at Bunson's Nook, Owen set up his laptop at a corner table out of earshot from the line of patrons. The tall barista in his twenties with a scraggly chin beard and colorful tattoos that crawled up both forearms, called to him. "Black currant tea, Ancil?"

"Coffee for a change. Thanks, Tommy."

Owen settled in, drawing on people he'd observed in Tetbury to form characters for his thriller. There was the thin, fidgety baker Mrs. Balfrey called Nel. Apart from being perpetually covered in flour, the jittery man looked nothing like a baker. Owen could see him more as a disorganized pathologist, overwhelmed with the backlog of autopsies to perform. Next came the chatty butcher with the shifty eyes—perhaps a street urchin angling to trade information about a murder.

Soon, the characters were drawn and a subplot took shape. Owen lost himself in his writing and Tommy refilled his coffee cup without asking. After three hours, Owen looked up from his screen to find the coffee shop nearly empty, the morning rush over. He stretched in his seat, absently rubbing a hand over the stubble of his newly shorn buzz cut and trimmed beard. Somehow, his pursuers must have obtained photos of him with a full beard and long hair. While he knew they could account for haircuts, there was no reason to make it easy for them.

He smiled to himself about his haircut decision. Whether to shave his head and beard had become a game of rock, paper, scissors. If he thought that they thought that he thought he would shave, then he shouldn't, and so on. In the end, he'd compromised. With a short haircut and trimmed beard, he wouldn't be a dead ringer for either extreme.

Later, after a satisfying day of writing, Owen stretched in his seat and gazed out the window of the coffee shop. Above the row of cottages across the street, the sun was low, dipping below the emerald sheep pasture in the distance. As was often the case, gazing west through an amber sky brought melancholy thoughts of April.

He hadn't heard from her in nearly two months. Other than bills, in his ten years in Tetbury, he'd only received mail from her.

It'd been against the strict advice of his advisor, of course, but there were limits to his sacrifices. Just as they'd planned on their last night together, he'd waited six months before writing. Since then, they'd corresponded faithfully every three weeks, her letters pabulum for his soul.

April letter days were Owen's best. He wouldn't open them right away, sometimes even waiting a few days, his mind luxuriating in the comfort that he was in her thoughts and savoring the anticipation of her words. Then, he'd pour a beer—on his stone patio if it was sunny—and carefully open the letter, pressing the pages against his nose for a hint of her scent. He'd close his eyes and she'd appear next to him, her soft lips forming the words on the paper.

By mutual unspoken agreement, there were no protestations of love or reminiscences of good times. There were no references to a future together, no matter how oblique. So far, she'd omitted news of other suitors, and if and when the time came, he'd do her the same courtesy. With those restrictions, they'd shared their lives on paper, every three weeks for ten years.

"Hi. Do you have black currant tea?" Margo's cheerful voice at the counter stirred Owen from his thoughts. She was sleek and fit in a black sweater and matching leggings. Her straight brown hair, tinged in auburn, was cropped severely at her neck and angled forward, veiling her profile. "And a banana, please."

Owen looked over at Tommy, who glanced his way and smiled. "Is something funny," his customer asked? Owen heard an American accent softened from some time in the UK—probably something like how he sounded.

"Well, it's just that you've asked for exactly what Ancil, over there, orders nearly every day." Margo turned toward Owen, revealing high cheekbones and a playful smile.

"Then I'd say Ancil has excellent taste," she said, with a nod his way. After collecting her tea and banana, Margo left, pretty sure Owen was watching her leggings walk away. She'd been patient and now knew his routine well enough to plan another chance meeting soon.

"What was happening in Tetbury?" Owen mused, as he packed up his computer. He'd scarcely noticed more than a few attractive women in the past decade, and now, to borrow from Brodie Dundas, "you couldn't swing a dead cat…"

It occurred to him, as he turned up the collar of his jacket, bracing against the freshening breeze on his walk home, that he was finally bothering to notice members of the opposite sex. He didn't want to admit it, but April was slipping away. Surely now she'd found someone and probably felt wrong about staying in touch.

Arriving at his cottage in the gloaming, he shivered away a chill as he approached his letter box on the street. He stood before it for a moment before opening the hinged door to reveal an empty box of cold metal.

It had been fifty-seven days, and as he trudged toward his front door, his heels dragging on cobblestone with each step, Owen resigned himself to the end of April. The tether to her soul had snapped and now its frayed end fluttered alone in the chilly breeze.

CHAPTER 29

Boston 2013

Professor Anendale was up early, padding out in his driveway in slippers to collect his paper before first light. He smiled to himself as he brought it into his study, fumbling for his reading glasses in the pocket of his robe. Sure, Prescott was the darling of the media now, but he still had a few well-placed friends.

He opened the Arts section and saw himself on page one, above the fold. Not the most flattering of photos—he appeared tired to his eye—but looking smart in his cardigan and spectacles, next to the headline that read *Professor Claims Prescott Stole Best-Seller.*

Across town, a flurry of texts had Owen's phone vibrating across his nightstand. He awoke suddenly, surprised not to feel April next to him before getting his bearings. She was away visiting her parents, their first night apart in five blissful days. She'd taken a week of vacation days and they'd been inseparable—hiking, golfing, and lovemaking. He'd even taken her to lunch with his mom yesterday. Within ten minutes, mother and son had exchanged knowing smiles.

Now, he rubbed his eyes and picked up his phone just as April's name appeared on its screen.

"Hi there. What am I missing? My phone's been blowing up."

"Yeah, so, it's not good, babe. Front page of the Arts section. It's about the Professor What's His Name's lawsuit."

"Fuck. How can they print that?"

"I'll send you the link right now. I miss you, by the way. And this will be fine."

"Thanks, I miss you too. I'll call you later."

Owen opened the link to the article.

In a lawsuit filed last week, esteemed author and professor at Breastwing College, Norvel Anendale claims that he and Owen Prescott co-wrote the award winning and best-selling novel, Orchards of Grace, which has catapulted Prescott from obscurity to among the country's literary elite…

Owen could hardly believe his eyes. When he'd first heard rumors about Anendale's claims, he'd dismissed them as the sad prevarications of a washed-up author. A former classmate had heard it first as part of the professor's liquor-fueled diatribe at an English Department mixer. In disparaging young authors at the school, Anendale had commented that he'd "basically written Prescott's novel for him." The outlandish remark had barely registered with Owen.

Even when the rumors persisted, based on more vague allegations by the professor, the truth had shielded Owen from any real concern. There was not a single kernel of merit to Anendale's claim. He had not written, edited, or consulted even once on a single sentence of his novel. Given that, Owen couldn't imagine the professor actually formalizing his allegation. What kind of lunatic would fabricate a lie out of whole cloth and then attempt to prove it?

Apparently, a lunatic named Norvel Anendale. But even as he read the article, clearly written by someone sympathetic to the professor, Owen was surprised by his inner calm. It wasn't just that he knew Anendale had no proof. Clearly, that hadn't deterred him so far. Deep down, Owen knew that April was the source of his piece of mind. No matter what lay ahead he wouldn't be left to face it alone. More than anything, no matter what happened, his happiness was secured.

His phone buzzed again in his hand. "Joe, talk to me."

"Hey, I've got this under control. We have a press conference scheduled for noon at the conference room at the Copley. I'm already feeding a contact with the *Post* some background on this clown. Also, our lawyers are filing for dismissal later this week."

"Okay, Joe," Owen said, mild surprise in his voice. "It sounds like you're actually on top of this. For a criminal defense hack, that is."

"Yeah, thanks. And don't act so surprised. Bad publicity is right up my alley. And I'd say any publicity is good publicity, but this is testing that theory. I'll see you soon."

CHAPTER 30

Not long after Owen left his cottage for Bunson's Nook, Mrs. Pembroke knocked on his door to borrow a bottle of beer for a picnic she was arranging with Mr. Boles. Surprised by his absence at such an early hour, she let herself in and walked to the kitchen, stopping to close an open window in the front room. A cold front was moving in and it was unlike Owen to be so careless.

As she opened the fridge, she heard a noise coming from his bedroom, or at least, she thought she had. "Ancil," she called, moving to the front room. "Ancil, are you there?" Cautiously, she walked toward his bedroom. The door was ajar and the lights were off.

She stood for several moments, listening, unsure of what to do. Letting herself in his home was one thing, but entering his bedroom was quite another. On the other hand—her active imagination now in overdrive—what if Ancil was injured or paralyzed? Finally, she reached out and nudged the door. It swung open slowly, creaking on its hinge.

Owen's room was arranged much the way Mrs. Pembroke had imagined it. Her old chest of drawers and Welch dresser to her right, his bed to her left with his nightstand behind it on the far wall. Like the rest of the cottage, the room was as neat as a pin, save for the ruffled comforter and pillow at the head of the bed. She breathed a sigh of relief, and out of habit, approached and tidied the bed. As she straightened the covers and fluffed the pillow, a distinctive flowery fragrance floated from the bed. And was that a lipstick smudge on the pillow?

Feeling most uneasy for her snooping, she backpedaled out of the bedroom, careful to leave the door as she'd found it, nearly closed but ajar. Her mind was swimming as she reached the front door. That cheeky devil, Ancil Bradford. Shagging someone on the sly, right under her nose. He had loads of secrets, this one.

Unsettled, she opened the front door, then shut it, remembering the beer. Just then, she heard another noise from the bedroom. She was sure of it this time. She froze, her eyes locked on the bedroom door for what seemed a full minute. Then, the door moved ever so slightly. At least, she thought it had. Presently, out walked Guildy, pausing to meow on her way to the kitchen and her bowl. Completely flustered, Mrs. Pembroke forgot the beer and beat a hasty retreat to her home, not at all sure what had happened.

CHAPTER 31

Boston 2013

Owen stared behind the bar, its rows of bottles distorted through the bottom of his glass as he fished an ice cube from his empty drink. He wasn't sure exactly when his day had turned to shit, but it had. Obviously, his wake-up alarm sounding the lawsuit hadn't been an ideal start. Then scrolling through the texts from friends, he'd detected a certain amount of reveling in his misery. Not full schadenfreude, but maybe hints from his struggling writer friends that they wouldn't mind him returning to their ranks.

Everything about the press conference had been irritating. Joe insisting on referring to it as a "presser" for one thing. He'd also pointed out a coffee stain on his shirt, and Owen had spent much of the time at the podium trying to hide it, feeling like George Washington with his hand in his waistcoat. Then April had called in the middle of the fiasco and he'd missed his chance to talk to her.

Also, the whole point of the press conference seemed defensive. No, he did not plagiarize his best-selling novel. As if that doddering, lying lush had as much of a claim to *Orchards* as he did. If anything, he felt like his attendance was legitimizing Anendale's claim.

But he'd patiently answered all the questions. No, he'd never asked the professor to edit or even read his novel. They'd never exchanged words about the book or anything remotely related to its subject matter. And fuck no, he'd wanted to say, he had no idea what had given Anendale the idea that they had collaborated on the book.

It had been a day to forget in every respect and Owen was well on his way to a valiant attempt, sitting on a familiar stool at Lefty's, Breastwing's unofficial pub. Another gin and tonic was fizzing before him, its torrent of tiny bubbles swirling around the glistening slice of lime. His gums tasted the tartness before he raised his glass, the light froth tickling his nose just before his sip.

But even as his face began to feel melty and his senses fogged, Owen couldn't escape thoughts of the lawsuit. Not that he feared its ultimate result. He'd already made it clear to Joe that there was to be no settlement. Unless that conniving fraud was ready to admit his lie, he would take him to trial.

"Hey, Owen. Tough day for you." A former classmate took a seat on the stool to his right.

As he drank, he began to feel much more inebriated than the night's moderate intake warranted. Sipping cautiously, he realized the source of his growing anger was his emotional attachment to his book. He recalled the late nights at his computer, channeling his own militaristic upbringing, letting himself leak out onto the pages. This waste of human flesh, Anendale, was telling the world that this never happened. The professor's gambit was more than a money grab, it was an attempted theft of his soul.

Owen felt the rage building even before the question was asked, roiling up within him. "So, I assume there's nothing to the lawsuit. Can you think of anything…"

"No!" Owen heard himself yell, shattering his glass on the bar as customers around him scattered. The rest had been a blur of scattered images. Firm hands at his elbows, whisking him out of the bar, his bloody hand wrapped in his shirttail, and his slow stagger over the six blocks home.

Now, as he lay on his couch, covered in a spare comforter, Owen began to piece together the evening. He recalled two, maybe three drinks at the most, and yet he'd blacked out. Apart from the obvious glass smashing incident in the bar, something had gone very wrong. Slowly, a sickening feeling of dread washed over him.

As he'd felt his way home, propping himself on front stoops and car hoods, he recalled the distinct impression of someone behind him, even steadying him a few times on the way. Also, there was his current state of undress. He was surprised to find himself stark naked.

Owen pulled the comforter to his chin, realizing it was the one he kept in the spare bedroom. He rubbed his eyes. And what was this? His hand was wrapped and bandaged with gauze and tape from his bathroom. He knew he couldn't have dressed his wound himself with one hand, especially in his condition.

Panicking, he sat up, desperate to recall the evening. Soon, a vague and horrible memory took shape. He was on his back on the couch, unable to move. And…oh, God. Someone—another person—was in his house, standing near him, holding the ends of his pant legs, pulling off his pants. He saw flashes of a woman's form and lots of blonde curly hair. He groaned, a familiar wave of nausea taking hold.

Fuck! What was this woman capable of? Owen stood, wrapping himself with the comforter as he walked to the kitchen sink, his head pounding with every step. He splashed water on his face, certain now he'd been drugged. He headed toward his bedroom, peaking in the dining room on the way. No place settings this time. He paused at his bedroom door before pushing it open, half-expecting to find her inside.

One of his father's many asinine military habits drilled into Owen as a youth was the importance of precision bedmaking. Owen hated that it had taken hold, but now he was a slave to the morning ritual. Sheets were creased and double-tucked, covers squared away, and pillows perfectly stacked. He walked slowly to his bed where the covers were turned down and twisted with the sheets. A single strand of curly blonde hair lay across his pillows.

CHAPTER 32

Walking back to the Piper's Arms for another writing session, Owen saw the buxom form of Mrs. Pembroke's black-haired spy walk into Balfry's Bakery ahead of him on the sidewalk. He had to admit that her appearances around the village had him curious. He'd seen her on two previous occasions ducking into various businesses, both times in the early morning.

Settling in at his familiar table in the pub, Owen admitted to himself that he had been thinking about another woman—the sleek and stylish one who'd ordered the black currant tea at Bunson's. He'd purposely avoided the coffee shop for a few days, partly out of loyalty to April, although he knew that was silly.

Mostly, though, it was because he didn't want to appear too eager. It had been a decade and he was leery of current dating norms. His anxiety was heightened by the woman's presence and poise. "Then I'd say Ancil has excellent taste," she'd said without missing a beat. It was almost as if she'd been waiting to use a prepared line.

At their next encounter in the coffee shop, he'd have to step up his game, maybe have a line ready. Something sharp with no risk to offend. A line that didn't sound rehearsed and was easy to remember. He'd have time to think of just the thing.

"I didn't know they served bananas in here." Owen followed the velvety voice above his laptop screen to the crimson lips of black currant tea herself, who seemed to have materialized out of nowhere.

Owen stood awkwardly. "Hello again," he said, clasping his hands together for no reason, feeling time slip away before he spoke again. He could feel his palms warming. "Actually," he finally said, "I come for the black currant IPA."

"Really," Margo said, smiling, "I hadn't pegged Brodie for a brewer of fruity beer."

A faint tone of familiarity fluttered through Owen's mind. Perhaps something about her voice. "Oh, yes," he said, feeling better about himself, "Tuesday's special is haggis paired with a tangerine white ale. It's quite delicious."

"I'm Margo Cummings," she said, extending a hand. She lied about her last name on the off chance an online search would turn up one of her freelance articles.

"Pleasure. Ancil Bradford," he said, happy to hear his mother's first name and returning the lie.

Margo subtly wiped Owen's sweat from her palms on her pant legs. "Well…" she said, pausing, "I'll let you get back to it then." She walked to a nearby table and sat alone.

Owen cursed himself. He'd noticed the pause—the perfect time to ask her to join him—but had frozen. Truth be told, he'd been so proud of his spontaneous banter, the moment had snuck up on him. Also, he'd become acutely aware, as she stood there across from him, in a t-shirt that hung vertically from her small breasts, not quite reaching her belt, that he had not fully appreciated her body in the coffee shop. She was extremely fit, from toned arms to tiny waist, to beautiful, rounded ass and athletic legs. This wasn't the product of a daily run to fight the love handles. This represented a serious commitment.

Owen sketched out in his mind a new fitness routine that he knew was unrealistic. Then he modified it. Still a pipe dream. Seeing Margo looking at the menu, he ordered another beer and chips. Rome wasn't built in a day, after all. There'd be plenty of time for exercise.

Presently, he settled back to his writing, sneaking peaks at her from time to time. April flashed in his mind once—their first meeting at the book signing, then skinny dipping in the hotel pool. He also thought of the family advisor's words of caution. This stranger was an American, after all, and statistically, most Yanks in Europe were from the northeast, making her more likely to have known of him.

Sometimes, though, like now, Owen had wondered what his freedom meant if his life itself was a prison. Over the past decade, he'd learned a lot about his wants and needs. Mostly, he'd been surprised by what he could happily do without. Most were modern conveniences. He'd gotten on fine without a cell phone, a reliable car, and a giant supermarket. Not to mention all the human services that had turned out to be quintessentially nonessential—agents, house cleaners, laundromats, and interns. Even socially, while he sometimes missed the collegial company of his fellow writers, he could do without the overwrought social scene he'd left behind.

But matters of the heart were different. In the past month, without April's letters providing, at least, the illusion of a partner, he'd felt empty. A void in his soul had opened, and an icy wind whipped through. He had no interest in trying to replace her. She would always reside with him, a warm place in his mind to visit.

But he missed women—the thrill of a subtle glance or the brush of a sweater, teetering through the intricate dance of courtship. He missed his mind wandering to a recent memory, the ache for physical pleasure, and the comfort of a familiar scent on his clothing or in his bed. Most of all, he missed the luxurious ease of a true companion, when every secret and private thought could be released. That was true freedom.

While he was finishing up his chips, Brodie came over, eyeing him scornfully as he set down a fresh pint. The proprietor stared at him hard, then turned and looked pointedly in the direction of Margo, then back to Owen. "Be happy while yer livin,' Ancil Bradford," he said, adding flare to his heavy brogue, "for yer a long time deid."

Owen downed a gulp of beer, stood, and walked to Margo's table. "Would you like to go out some time, Margo Cummings?" he said, surprised he hadn't stuttered.

She smiled up at him. "As a matter of fact, Ancil Bradford, I would like that very much."

A short time later, Margo walked up the stairs to her apartment. Its location was proving so useful for her purposes. She sat at the rolltop desk and opened a file labeled Prescott. She'd scoured the internet for articles about the murder, piecing together a timeline of the killing, the charges, and Owen's flight. Continuing the narrative, the journalist opened her laptop and began to type.

CHAPTER 33

When she thought about it, Alyssa didn't know why British law enforcement should be any less bound by red tape than the FBI. Her phone call had triggered an avalanche of forms, verifications and inter-agency memorandums that had buried the pursuit of her fugitive in a mountain of paper. It had been three weeks since her call to Scotland Yard and she was still waiting.

The problem had been calmly explained to her by a chief inspector in the soft and refined accent of a BBC reporter that would have made reading the phone book sound intelligent. Save for a digital imprint of Prescott's face, there was precious little known about his new identity. Despite the close call in Rotterdam, the police didn't have a phone, IP address, alias, credit card or partial license plate. They had no knowledge of his associates, current occupation, or frequented areas. Despite Agent Wagner's brilliant deductions about his likely residence in the Cotswolds, the task would be difficult. The region spanned eight hundred square miles and was home to nearly 200,000 people, so success would likely have to rely on a chance sighting.

Within the bureau, Alyssa's Cyclops application had earned grand reviews and a commendation for the director. While she took solace that her code was being used to track down bad people all over the world, Owen Prescott's freedom still stuck in her craw.

Not surprisingly, there'd been no Cyclops sightings since Rotterdam and she expected he'd been scared back into his hole for a while. Still, Alyssa was convinced that some old-fashioned detective work could do the trick.

Diving back into Prescott's background, a rift with his powerful father began to take shape. While the author was quick to thank his mother for her support in interviews, mentions of his dad had been conspicuously absent. When asked about his son's success, the steel and aerospace magnate had managed only a few curt words. "His success has been surprising," he had bluntly said in a feature in the *Post* and had refused to elaborate.

To Alyssa, this meant Prescott loved to write. To forego an easy stroll in his father's footsteps, he would have to be passionate about his craft. And this meant he was out there somewhere, writing. In an interview with *Literary World* in 2011, Prescott spoke of his creative process. "Some authors like to isolate," he had said. "I'm quite the opposite. I draw inspiration from observing people—their actions and various eccentricities. I love to spend a day in a coffee shop with my laptop, my eyes and ears open."

The agent's fingers rattled her keyboard. There were fifty-five million people in England and an estimated twenty-one thousand coffee shops. So, in the Cotswolds, that meant approximately seventy-five coffee houses. Alyssa bet he was in one of them now.

Prescott's father owned a few racehorses, so he also might frequent Cheltenham Racecourse, a short train ride from most of the Cotswold villages. On the other hand, he didn't seem like the horse racing type, and he'd likely avoid large gatherings.

To Alyssa, her fugitive's precautions had all the earmarks of a professional advisor. His changing appearance, lack of digital imprint and calculated travel all pointed to a mastermind with a background in espionage. His father certainly had the resources to secure such expertise. Also, he'd likely been motivated to get his son out of town and avoid prolonging the family scandal with a lengthy trial.

"Sam, how would you choose a village?" she called over the cubicle wall.

"Prescott again? Well, I would avoid people, especially American tourists. So, I'd choose small villages, not on a major highway or railway."

"Not bad." Alyssa pulled up a map. There appeared to be about twenty-six villages in the region. Half were on railway lines, and four others were featured on a popular bus tour of the region. Down to nine villages and roughly twenty-seven coffee shops. The young agent smiled at her progress. Prescott's grounds for hide and seek were shrinking.

Alyssa had also learned that the police services available to the villages varied greatly. The larger municipalities had their own police forces. These would be avoided by Prescott, as would the unincorporated areas between the villages that were patrolled by the well-funded Non-Metropolitan Police Force. The seven smaller villages, however, were jointly served by the Village Constabulary, which appeared to be spread thin. She cross-referenced. Four villages, twelve coffee shops.

Over the next two hours, Alyssa continued to dig, learning more about Owen Prescott, narrowing her focus in the Cotswolds and magnifying its landscape. Finally, just before 6:00 p.m., a call came through from Chief Inspector Ramsey her liaison at Scotland Yard. The paperwork had been approved. There wouldn't be a full-time agent on the case, nor had she expected one. The case would be assigned as a secondary area of inquiry.

Ramsey explained that Inspector Yancy Norich was already ensconced in the Cotswolds, working undercover on an auto insurance scam. Alyssa could forward her materials directly to him. In the meantime, Prescott's photo would be up in the local post offices. Also, the few Cotswold businesses with video cameras would be encouraged to allow transmission to the Cyclops network.

"Special Agent Wagner, a slight word of caution, if I may?" asked the chief inspector.

"Of course." These Brits were so polite.

"Our man, over here, Norich. I know you're a champ with the technology. I'm afraid he's a bit of an old dog. Good at his job, mind you, but he hasn't exactly adapted with the times, if you get my meaning."

"Understood, sir. I look forward to working with him."

Alyssa was so elated with the news she would take anyone who could fog a mirror. No more waiting for Prescott to appear in front of a camera. Now, the search would be taken to him.

She looked at her cubicle wall. "Sam?" she called. It was finally time to give Sam a try. Who knows, she thought, maybe he'd relax with a few drinks in him. But his cubicle was empty.

Alyssa stood and sighed, throwing her backpack over her shoulder. Two lists appeared on her computer screen as she left for the night. The third village on the list was Tetbury, the ninth coffee shop, Bunson's Nook.

CHAPTER 34

Boston 2013

"Come to order, Ladies and Gentlemen." Judge Leonard Nixon banged his gavel as he spoke, his raspy voice squawking above the hum of conversation in the crowded courtroom. "Calling the case of Owen Nathaniel Prescott versus Desiree Richins."

Attorney Adam Everett, looking overdressed for the drab courtroom in his blue pin-striped suit, ushered Owen to the right side of the counsel table. The attorney had met Owen at the courthouse.

Owen was a wreck. He hadn't slept, dreading the confrontation with his stalker. He'd even considered just not showing up. His eyes scanned the crowd. Having caught only glimpses of her, part of him was eager to see his alleged spirit-mate. A full minute after he'd taken a seat next to his attorney, a washed-out woman with frizzy, untamed blonde hair slowly strolled down the center aisle of the courtroom. Draped in a tie-died sarape, she seemed unsteady on her feet, feeling for the floor with each step.

"Appearances," barked the judge, when she'd finally reached the counsel table.

"Adam Wayne Everett for the Petitioner, Your Honor."

The judge waited several seconds, then peered down over his reading glasses at Ms. Richins, who was smiling and gazing around the courtroom as if seeing it for the first time.

"Ma'am, are you Desiree Richins?" the judge asked, as if speaking to a child.

The silence continued as her glassy, pale blue eyes took in her surroundings with a faraway stare. Finally, as the Judge was about to speak again, a throaty whisper came through the microphone on the table. "May it please the Court, Your Honor. Indeed," she said calmly, a warm smile spreading over her face as she turned toward Owen, who stared straight ahead. "I am Desiree Marie Richins," she said, in the haughty trans-Atlantic accent of the upper crust. "I believe I am referred to as the Respondent in these proceedings." She spoke with her mouth close into the microphone, the echo lending a celestial air to her presence.

The judge returned a wry smile. "Ms. Richins, Mr. Prescott has requested a restraining order. Will you be contesting this order?"

Another pause, as she considered the question, smile in place. "Oh, I would never oppose Mr. Prescott's wishes," she said, this time catching Owen's eye with her vacant stare.

"Very well, Ms. Richins, I am ordering you not to have any contact with Owen Bradley Prescott, be it written or telephonic or by any means, including a third party, and to stay one hundred and fifty yards away from him. Do you understand and agree, Ms. Richins?" The Judge, not in the mood to wait again, recited the script rapidly from memory while he signed the order. "Ms. Richins, will you comply with the order?"

"Of course," she said, as if the question was absurd. "I have absolutely no problem with the order."

Owen watched her take her copy of the order from the bailiff and slowly make her way out of the courtroom with a carefree and wobbly saunter. Afterwards, as Owen walked to his car, he thought to himself that Desiree Richins had absolutely no problem with the restraining order because she had absolutely no intention of following it.

"Hi Pril," Owen said, pulling out of the court parking lot. After hearing the latest stalker tale, April had made him promise to call.

"Ooh, Pril," she said cheerfully. "I like that, I think. How'd it go?"

"Restraining order granted."

"Thank God. She should be in jail. What was she like?"

"Not that weird, really. We talked it out and I think I might be her spirit-mate after all. We're going to see each other for coffee tomorrow. You know, take it slow."

"Hilarious, Prescott. Seriously, did she seem scary?"

"Honestly, every bit as scary as you might think. A bit of the crazy eyes. Also, she spoke as if she were addressing the House of Lords. Complete wack-a-doodle."

"Well, be careful. What are your plans besides pining for my return?"

"Staying in tonight, meeting Joe for a drink tomorrow. You're home Friday, right?"

"Yes. I can't wait to see you. Can you pick me up at the airport?"

"Of course. They'll be a fee of course, made payable upon arrival."

"Oh, not until arrival? I was planning to test your powers of concentration on the ride home."

"Um, did I mention you were on speaker with my mom?" A few seconds passed before Owen broke into laughter.

"Oh! Owen Prescott! So mean!" she said, laughing. "Good luck getting laid now."

They said their goodbyes and Owen resumed his uncomfortable thoughts of Desiree Richins, the court-stamped document on the seat next to him doing little to ease his mind.

CHAPTER 35

Owen arose early for his morning run after a restless night's sleep. He was excited about meeting Margo. Even with no idea what was to come, the prospect of any female companionship was thrilling. Still, as he jogged along a country lane on the outskirts of Tetbury, thoughts of April floated through his mind, clouding the image of his new friend.

Back at his desk for a morning writing session with Guildy curled on his lap, he stared idly at his computer, knowing he would accomplish nothing. Finally deciding on a course, he rose quickly, softly deposited his cat on his chair and headed to his shed for an excursion in the Rover.

Mrs. Pembroke, just leaving her home, waved him over. "Good morning, Owen. Would you mind toting a sack of briquettes to my garage?"

"I'd be happy to," he said, and walked to the trunk of her roomy, black sedan.

"You know," she said, mischievously, as he hoisted the sack on his shoulder, "there's been a fair amount of scuttlebutt in the village about you and a certain someone."

Owen stopped in mid-stride and turned to face her, incomprehension on his face. "Excuse me, Mrs. Pembroke? Who could possibly…I don't understand," he stammered.

"I'm just reporting what I've heard," she said with palms up, walking ahead of him to the garage.

Owen followed, set down the sack, and spoke quietly. "Mrs. Pembroke, as a matter of fact, I've only just met someone. As you know, given my situation, I'm never thrilled to have anyone in the village paying attention to me."

"Oh, it's just been idle musings, really. Nothing to jeopardize your identity," she said, trying to sound casual. "And who is this mystery woman?"

"That's the thing. We haven't even gotten to know each other."

I'd say you've jolly well gotten to know each other, Mrs. Pembroke thought to herself. "Well, don't pay it any mind," she said, heading into her house. "And thanks for the help."

Owen was confused and a bit shaken. Who could have possibly taken any notice of his two innocuous exchanges with Margo? Aside from Mrs. Pembroke, there were only a handful of shop owners in the village who knew his name. These thoughts swirled in his head as he guided his Rover out of its shed and through the village, turning east on Road A4135.

Upon his arrival in England, on the advice of the advisor, Owen had used a fictitious company name to obtain a post office box where he received all his mail. Because Tetbury didn't have a post office, he'd gotten it in the neighboring village of Nailsworth. Eventually though, the bi-weekly ten-minute drive had become tiresome and unnecessary, and he'd been receiving all his mail at his cottage for several years.

Owen told himself that this final trip to check the deposit box for a letter from April would finally allow him to turn the page. Even though he was sure the box would be empty, as she hadn't mailed anything there in years, he needed to see it for peace of mind. He parked on the street outside, and soon he was staring at the inside of the empty box. Breathing a sigh of resignation, he walked down the hallway toward the exit, its wall lined with face shots of surly fugitives. Just before the exit, he stopped cold, face-to-face with his own, labeled Owen Prescott: Murder.

Owen covered his face with one hand and tried not to run to his car, his heart racing as he fumbled with his keys. He looked down the street. Shit! A cop on foot patrol was a half block away and walking toward him on the sidewalk. He ducked inside the Rover and pulled a knit cap down over his ears. He turned the key and heard the lurching groan. "C'mon, c'mon," he whispered, pleading the engine to turn over. It wouldn't.

He glanced up at the approaching officer. Not more than fifteen yards from him, now. Struggling to control his breathing, Owen tapped lightly on the gas pedal and turned the key again. More groaning, then finally, he heard the glorious sound of the sputtering engine.

The bobby was nearly upon him now, still strolling toward him on the sidewalk, as Owen shifted into drive. He snuck a final glance. Fuck! The officer was approaching his car with a raised hand. Owen's mind raced. Should he drive away, maybe pretend to not have seen him? He froze. Too late now.

Reaching the car, the bobby bent at the waist, sizing up Owen for what seemed like an eternity. "You know," he said deliberately, adjusting his cap, "you would do well to have a look at the crankshaft." Left without the power of speech, Owen could manage only a thumbs up signal. His stomach churned as he eased the Rover away from the curb. The bobby noted that the driver certainly looked guilty of something. Oh well, he thought to himself, watching the Rover head for the highway. Whatever his game was, it would be a problem for another village.

Once out of Nailsworth, Owen took a random lane off the main road. After a mile of driving, he pulled over, his hands still shaking on the wheel. Something about seeing his face was jarring. It wasn't a photo, but a digitally created image, and it was spot on. He hadn't seen a likeness of himself in more than ten years.

The murder label was equally traumatic. It was his own given name, not the Ancil Bradford character he'd been portraying. After all, it would be him—Owen Bradley Prescott—who would be in prison for the rest of his life if things went south.

He breathed deeply, collecting his thoughts, wondering what about the image of himself on the wall of the post office haunted him. Then it came to him all at once, a clear chime piercing the fog. He realized that in the image, his face appeared exactly as it looked now, with short hair and a trimmed beard. He had lost his game of rock, paper, scissors decisively, and whoever was tracking him was smart as hell.

CHAPTER 36

Boston, September 22, 2013

Owen had spent his Thursday afternoon at a mansion near the idyllic coastal village of Padanaram, Massachusetts, as guest of honor at a millionaire's book club. For his troubles, Joe was given the opportunity to pay an exorbitant price for two of the hottest tickets in town.

The Red Sox were on the verge of a World Series championship, and Boston was about to erupt. The tickets for game six hardly seemed worth it, but Owen knew Joe would appreciate it.

After a ninety-minute drive, he was back in Boston by 6:00 p.m. and ready for a drink. Joe had agreed to meet him at a tavern a block from his home. He was seated at a table when Owen arrived.

"Book clubs suck, Joe."

"Yeah, it must be awful to be fawned over by adoring fans while you rake in cash."

"Right. How much do I make on each book again? Eighty cents?"

"About a dollar for hardcovers, and online sales are killing it. The appearances are just…"

"Yeah, I know, just to get my name out there. Any news on the lawsuit front? Like, you know, Professor Assdale stepped in front of a bus?"

"No. The wheels of justice turn slowly. Any sign of the stalker? Your description of her was frightening. You should write her into your next book?"

"Wouldn't be difficult. Should we get a pitcher?"

"Sorry, I only have time for a quick beer." Joe took a sip and averted his eyes, trying to look casually around the bar. "What?" he asked defensively, his eyes finally resting on Owen's fixed stare. I just happen to have plans," he said, smiling sheepishly.

"Holy shit." Owen smiled, pausing to watch Joe squirm. "You have a date."

"It's not really a date. It's just..."

"No, don't ruin it for me. This is awesome, Joe. And what are you doing here? I'll get your beer. You need as much prep time as possible."

"Thanks for the vote of confidence," he said, standing to leave.

"I expect a full report tomorrow," Owen called after him.

After a slice of pizza and a beer, Owen decided to go home and write. April would be home tomorrow, he thought playfully, and he wanted to be rested. He caught himself looking furtively behind him on the short walk home and was happy to see the light on in Will's room when he arrived. He smelled chocolate chip cookies, which meant Will's girlfriend was also there.

Owen settled himself in front of his computer with a cup of tea and turned off his phone, prepared to lose himself in his writing. Across the street, a brilliant sunset backlit the sprawling oak tree. Still, as he gazed out his window into the night, he couldn't shake the sensation that he was being watched.

. . .

On the north side of the city, a few blocks from the Breastwing campus, promptly at 4:00 p.m., Professor Anendale had just finished making his first drink of the evening. He paused, catching sight of himself in the oven door. He looked good, having just showered and shaved in preparation for his visitor. Another phone call had clarified the nature of the mysterious documents, and the professor could hardly contain his excitement. What time was he coming? He unzipped his leather daily planner Lydia had given him decades ago and squinted at his shaky handwriting. It looked like 5:00 p.m.

It had been a while since he'd had a visitor, especially one so important to his resurgence. He and Lydia used to entertain frequently. They would pour expensive wine and she would make hors d'oeuvres and look beautiful in a fancy dress. Back then, his fellow professors—contemporaries—would hang on his every word. That was before the wave of young professors had arrived, diluting the college's excellence, softening its academic rigor.

Lately, his memory of the specifics of his collaboration with young Owen Prescott had been coming back to him, usually while relaxing after a drink or two. Prescott had approached him one day after class—or was it during his office hours. Anyway, the student had asked him to read his manuscript, which he planned to submit for his senior writing project. It was passable compared to the drivel of most of the students, so the professor had made some suggestions. Then Prescott had come back to him over and over, lapping up his input, and even asking for guidance on how to write particular scenes.

Eventually, as more and more of Anendale's prose found its way onto the pages, he'd told Owen that he felt uncomfortable with the extent of his contribution to an assigned writing. It was then that Prescott told him that he would not submit the story for his senior project, but instead wanted the professor to co-write the book. It had gone something like that, anyway. The details were hazy, but it was unthinkable that Prescott wouldn't solicit his expertise.

Anendale sat on his chesterfield, swirling his drink, letting his imagination merge with his memory. Prescott, he recalled, was just one of the many fawning students who had come to him, hoping to tap into his genius. What they all failed to understand was what he had couldn't be taught.

They had no grasp of the true creative process that could produce something like his *Cake Batter Blues*. Inspiration like that came from your bones. You didn't sketch out a plot on a napkin and start writing unless you wanted to end up with something like *Orchards of* whatever-the-fuck. That was the twisted irony, really. While he would reluctantly admit basically writing the damn thing for Prescott, he wasn't the least bit proud of it. Clearly, though, it was the spark Prescott's career needed.

Anendale stood and ambled to the kitchen to freshen his drink. His company wouldn't be here for another half an hour. Back in the living room, he lowered himself again to his chair, luxuriating in his future. Soon, the lawsuit would restore his reputation and he'd be back in his rightful place at Breastwing. If he concentrated, he could feel it already happening. He hadn't started actually writing yet, but he could feel the sparks flickering within him, heating the embers of his literary fire. He drank to his future. His mind was limber now, bending to accommodate his imagination.

His eyes wandered behind his desk, where his Cupcarthe Pyramid sat in ignominy, collecting dust. Soon he would put it back on the mantle above his fireplace, where it belonged. He only wished his Lydia could be here to see his resurrection.

Anendale looked again at the foot-high statuette. Why should he wait? The pyramid deserved its rightful place of honor and it would impress his visitor. He rose and walked to it, took it off the shelf, leaving behind a perfect, dustless square. He wiped the pyramid on his cardigan, caressing the black onyx, moving a finger over his name, etched in its base. Then, drink in one hand, prized pyramid in the other, Norvel Lambeth Anendale set out for the mantel to restore his dignity. He heard someone on his porch. Perhaps his guest was early.

CHAPTER 37

Back at his cottage after his traumatic trip to the post office, Owen unscrewed the cap off his whiskey bottle and poured himself a shot. He would be meeting Margo in an hour. Thank goodness she'd suggested an afternoon hike and not dinner in Oxford.

He sat at his desk and breathed deeply. There was a private shipping office in Tetbury, but he was sure at least some of the residents used the post offices in neighboring villages. If his photo was up in the post office in sleepy Nailsworth, it would be in all of them. He pushed aside thoughts of how in God's name he'd been tracked to the Cotswolds. It didn't matter now.

First things first. His appearance had to change. As he began to shave, Owen considered relocation. He knew that bald-headed toady would be in favor of it. He thought back to the meetings with his father's team of sycophants. They'd walked around with rods up their asses and had spoken in the affected language of the paramilitary that Owen despised—threat-level black, def con two and all that crap.

Moving from Tetbury—starting over for a second time without a soul in his life—was out of the question. It had taken years of living like a hermit to slowly cultivate the reality of Ancil Bradford. Examining his freshly shorn face in the mirror, he recalled the monotony of the first four or five years, living under the strict rules of the advisor. He'd only gone outside to get sun on his back patio, to tend his garden and for nighttime runs. He'd shopped every six months, living on canned food and fresh vegetables. In some ways, the disciplined, spartan lifestyle had brought back memories of his childhood home. Owen pressed a warm washcloth to his face, soothing the razor's sting.

Unveiling his face in the mirror, Owen saw a pale, slightly older version of himself. The beard had obscured some wrinkles, and his weight loss had left behind a more angular countenance. His change in appearance would have to do. He knew he didn't have another relocation in him.

He pulled on jeans and a sweatshirt and found some unopened deodorant in the bottom of his bathroom drawer. He'd decided against shaving his head, the choice the result of a coin flip. He'd let his hair grow out again and until then, wear a hat when out in public.

It was a half-mile walk to the hiking trail outside the village, and Owen managed to clear his head of paranoia of being recognized on the way. As was her habit, Margo seemed to appear out of nowhere, looking fit in a black tracksuit.

"Hi Margo, you look serious about this hike," he said, sizing up her outfit.

"Hi yourself. Would you have preferred a skirt and heels?" she joked.

"No, I'm just laying the foundation for an excuse if you leave me behind. As you can see, I'm not dressed for an athletic endeavor."

"Right. And let me guess, your hamstring's been acting up?"

"Ankle, actually. But luckily, I have an incredibly high pain threshold."

"I see." She flashed an easy smile. There was something very soothing about her face that put Owen at ease. "And you shaved. I like it."

Luckily, what with his stress about being captured and spending the rest of his life in prison, Owen hadn't worried about his first date in years. They talked about themselves—or rather, their backstories—in comfortable conversation, each one none the wiser. Margo mentioned her pending divorce and spoke vaguely of her career as a journalist. She told him she was currently on assignment for a travel magazine and didn't pry when Owen sidestepped questions about his career as a writer.

"So, are you a sports fan?" she asked, casually.

"I suppose I am, yes." He assumed that was the correct answer.

"Casually, or one of those guys whose day is ruined if their team loses?"

"No, very casual," Owen said, gambling with the truth. "I take it you are as well?"

"Yes, my dad and brothers are absolutely maniacal sports fans. They absolutely live and die with their teams, and if they lose, they can be quite unpleasant to be around. My dad doesn't need an excuse to be unpleasant, but that's another story."

"Interesting," Owen said, knowing exactly what she meant.

Margo, grimaced, as if regretting what she was about to say. "I only follow English professional soccer, actually."

"You're kidding?" Owen asked, her answer stopping him in his tracks.

"No, why?" She walked back to where he'd stopped. Owen considered not answering, for fear she would think he was making it up.

"English soccer is the only sport I follow!"

"Wow, that's pretty weird." Her brown eyes met his as she moved toward him. "Black currant tea, bananas, and now this? We could be on to something here, Ancil Bradford." Owen thought she may have paused for a kiss, but he hesitated, and they resumed their hike.

"Next, I suppose you're going to tell me your favorite author is…" Owen paused, waiting for her response.

"Present company excluded, of course—that is, once I've actually read one of yours," she laughed. "But I'm afraid the streak stops here. I like this very obscure writer named Annabelle Steves. She writes…"

"Oh my God. Totally freaky and twisted thrillers! I know her well!" Owen interrupted, dumbfounded.

"That's unbelievable," she said. "But I disagree completely," she said in mock seriousness. "What's twisted and freaky about torture and mutilation?" Owen laughed. Who was this woman who had magically materialized in his life?

They shared more about each other, amazed at their similar tastes in food, drink, and recreation. Their birthdays were even just a day apart. "And I haven't mentioned it," Owen said, "and at the risk of sounding creepy, my mom goes by Margo."

"Wow! Well, I hope you don't have mommy issues," she joked.

"Not that I know of, no."

"This is crazy!" she said, moving closer again when they'd stopped to enjoy a view. And now there was no mistake. Their lips met, a quick kiss, and then again, lingering and tasting as they embraced. Finally parting, they locked eyes, smiling and sharing the same thought. She began to nod.

"Yep," he said, nodding back.

"Oh yeah," she sighed, as they continued down the trail, arm in arm. Owen's life as a fugitive was the furthest thing from his mind, and Margo knew she wouldn't be writing tonight. Some days just needed to be lived.

CHAPTER 38

Boston, September 23, 2013

Detectives Lew Sevilla and Pete Jepson squatted near the body, handkerchiefs over their noses, as the techs took photos of the scene. It was 4:30 a.m. on Friday morning. They had been dispatched to the scene after a patrol unit responded to a jogger's report that the front door of the home was wide open.

Norvel Anendale was on his back, his mouth contorted and eyes bulging in a grotesque expression of pain and disbelief. The base of the Cupcarthe Pyramid protruded from his blood-soaked cardigan sweater, just below his ribcage. A strip of material—perhaps a thin scarf or narrow men's tie—was cinched around his neck, its edges tinged with crimson where it had cut into the skin. There was an angry gash on the bridge of his nose. To the victim's right, on the tile floor, just outside the pool of blood, a well-worn spiral binder lay open, its pages filled with hand-written notes. Some of the pages had been ripped from the notebook and lay scattered on the tile floor.

Sevilla pushed up one of Anendale's eyelids with the end of his pen, peering under it. "What do you think, P?" he asked, in his best hard-boiled detective voice. "It seems quiet. Maybe a little too quiet?"

"Garroted and bludgeoned? Who knew an ugly cardigan could inspire so much passion?" quipped Jepson. For the veteran duo, the more gruesome the murder scene, the more essential the humor.

"Classic pyramid scheme," Sevilla added, standing to speak to the patrol units.

Norvel Anendale's death had not been an easy passing over. After the initial shock, he'd panicked as blood flowed freely from his wound, oozing from the base of the pyramid, surrounding him in a sticky pool. Entering the early stages of hypovolemic shock, he'd begun to sweat profusely and had felt his chest pound as his heart struggled to maintain blood flow to his vital organs.

Angling his head, he'd caught a glimpse of Lydia, looking down at him from the side table. She shouldn't have to see this. He'd felt the chill of death as his body shunted blood from his extremities. Soon after, he panicked, his brain deprived of oxygen. His last thoughts were jumbled before his heart spasmed and stopped— the lawsuit, his pyramid, his Lydia.

The detectives stepped under the police tape and supervised the standard crime scene protocol. Officers canvassed the neighborhood for witnesses and the room was dusted for prints. The professor's clothing and the garrote were cut off him with scissors and collected for DNA testing.

A uniformed officer approached the detectives. "Neighbor says the vic is a fancy literary professor at Breastwing. Won something called a Cupcarthe Pyramid years ago."

The detectives looked at each other. "An award like that will stay with you, huh, Pete?"

"A Cupcarthe, wow," deadpanned Sevilla, "I didn't know he had it in him?"

Jepson laughed and shook his head. "Wager on cause of death?"

Sevilla took a moment to consider. "Well, no petechiae," he began, referring to the specks of blood in the eyes—the result of burst capillaries—commonly found in victims of strangulation. "No swollen tongue either, from what I could see. Flushed face but that could have been from the alcohol. Looks like he'd made a few cocktails in the kitchen. I'm going with the rather obvious pyramid sticking out of his gut."

Jepson looked dubious. "So, the perp impales him. Then, as the vic lies there, bleeding out, with a foot-long pyramid sticking out of his chest, he decides to strangle him? A beer says it's a strangulation, then the impalement out of rage, apparently because he felt strongly that the book he wrote should have had a stronger ending."

"First, I'm not sure impalement is a word. But even so, hear me out. The victim is old and drunk and doesn't hear the perp approaching from the rear. The perp loops the garrote around his neck and strangles him. The blood to the victim's brain is cut off so he passes out. Ten seconds later, when he comes around, the perp decides to leave no doubt and impales him."

A young officer, who looked to be fresh out of the academy, approached the detectives. "Um, sirs, er detectives," he said tentatively, "I was just collecting this notebook, logging it in, and I think I might have some information that might be impor…that is, it may be pertinent to, uh…"

"Officer, Dietrick, is it?" asked Jepson, interrupting. "Try not to piss yourself, son. Just relax and tell us what you know."

"Okay, so I'm a big reader, and I was just noticing that the notebook is labeled 'Orchards of Grace' and it contains, like, an author's notes on the book."

The detectives looked at each other and shrugged. "The author is Owen Prescott?" the officer said, waiting with raised eyebrows.

"Dietrick, I'm afraid you're dealing with a couple of illiterates here. Should that mean something to us."

"Wait," said Sevilla, "that name's been in the news lately. Isn't he being sued over a book?"

"Yes, *Orchards of Grace*," Dietrick continued. "Your victim, here, was claiming that he stole the book from him."

"Well, shit, Dietrick. Do you make a habit of solving murders on the first day?" asked Sevilla.

"No, sir, I just…"

"That was what we call a rhetorical question, Dietrick. You'll know that, because you're a big reader, am I right?"

"Yes, sir," said the officer, smiling.

"Helluva job, kid," added Jepson. "We'll make sure you get a mention in our reports. And once the photos are taken, let's open some windows. This place smells worse than a vegan fart."

The detectives made some final notes and headed to their car. They would spend the day in the precinct, writing reports and speaking to Anendale's family, if any were around. Then after the autopsy, they'd conference with the pathologist to see who'd buy drinks.

"I feel like we need one more line, Lew," his partner said, before they pulled away. "You know, for the sign-off scene."

Sevilla thought for a while, then smiled at his partner. "Looks like this author found the road death traveled," he said, failing to conceal his pride.

"Partner, you never disappoint."

CHAPTER 39

Seated at his desk the evening after his kiss—more accurately, the evening after his hike, but that's the way he thought about it— Owen set about writing a sex scene. Understandably, it had been a while since he'd been so inspired.

Closing his eyes, he lost himself in the memory of his kiss with Margo and soon his fingers were moving across the keyboard, as if powered up by his mind. The kiss had been one of those rare moments when an avalanche of thoughts was exchanged in a moment's time. Their mouths slid together in a warm seal, sending a current humming through their bodies.

In one kiss, they'd tugged on loose threads from their bodies' tapestries and watched as they unraveled for each other. Each pull of the thread more hungry than the last, sending lines streaking across their fabric, unexpected ripples of pleasure revealing more of their bodies—a collarbone here, a biceps there. They tore at their threads now, one shared ache surging within their half-naked forms.

Something like that, anyway, Owen thought to himself.

Yesterday, parting with Margo back at the trailhead, neither had suggested seeing each other the following day. It had just been assumed. "There are lots of great trails in this park," she'd said, and they'd agreed on another hike. Owen hoped it wasn't a subtle hint that he needed to get in shape to match her fitness level, but for once the thought hadn't lingered. Margo's easy confidence was infectious. She had an almost prescient way about her—an outward assurance that all would be well—that soothed Owen's mind.

Owen, after all, had been living under anything but soothing conditions. Despite his eventual assimilation into the country life in the Cotswolds, he lived on edge. Lately, he'd wondered when the bobby in Nailsworth would next wander into the post office and remember the guy with the bad crankshaft.

Never mind the recent harrowing experiences there and in Rotterdam, his everyday life was lived on high alert. Every day he awoke with a wonder if this would be the day—the day a tourist would place his face or his pursuers would track him down. Every trip outside his cottage was a risk, every passerby a threat. So Owen found Margo's quiet confidence comforting, her dreamy aura a sensual distraction from reality.

Owen wrote well into the night and awoke to the sound of the weekly garbage pickup. After coffee and toast, with thoughts of Margo's hard body in his head, he lowered himself to the rug in front of his fireplace for what he reckoned would be his first pushups in twenty years. He thought three sets of ten was reasonable, starting small to build a base. He'd heard some muscle head use that phrase.

After the fifth quivering trip from the floor, Owen collapsed onto his stomach. Three sets of three, perhaps, starting tomorrow. Next were sit-ups, which he could only accomplish by hooking his toes under his couch for leverage. Only three complete before the nausea brought on by the rapid head movement reminded him of why he hated the exercise. He laid on his back, telling himself that however pathetic his attempts, he'd be back at it tomorrow.

After a shower, which seemed strange before a hike, he was on his way to the trailhead wearing sweatpants this time. Arriving early, he stretched and ate a nutrition bar. Soon, Margo's lithesome form was bounding toward him and into his arms. "Hi there," she said after a kiss. It surprised Owen but at the same time felt very natural.

"Hi, there, yourself," Owen said, beaming.

"I see you're dressed appropriately. Ready for a challenging hike, Bradford?" Owen hesitated, mainly because it was the first time he'd heard anyone refer to him solely by his last name alias.

"Uh, sure. Of course, with the caveat that my hamstring could flare up at any time."

"Of course," she said facetiously, "but I thought it was your ankle."

"It's more of a hammy slash ankle issue," he said, grinning. "Slash I'm afraid you'll leave me behind."

"I promise not to," she said, and they were off, heading up a steeper trail than the day before. Again, conversation came easy, the couple content with each other's vague answers as they navigated through their own false identities. Owen wanted to know more about this woman who had magically appeared in his life. She'd outlined a life growing up in a big family in Connecticut and told him that she'd recently separated from her husband, but he'd noticed a reticence to speak of her recent past.

For her part, while Margo wanted a complete picture of his fugitive life, she was thrilled with their blossoming relationship. For now, she was satisfied with teasing details from their flirting conversations.

In the back of their minds, both knew there would be a shelf life for their relationship unless all was revealed. But this was only their second date and for now, both were happy to live in the moment and kick that unpleasant can down the road.

"How's your hammy slash ankle," she asked, squeezing his hand as they reached the peak of the climb.

"Great," he said, between breaths, gazing at the view. Verdant hills lay before them, dotted with barns and striped with hedges. "Again, my pain threshold is off the charts. Most men would have to be airlifted out."

"Well, thank you for your sacrifice. When the bone pushes through the skin, though, I must insist we call it a day." They laughed, kissed and took in the scenery before heading downhill.

"What would you say to dinner at Piper's Arms?" she asked as they arrived back at the trailhead. "I hear they make a mean boiled cabbage."

"Ah, the secret to your figure is revealed. I wouldn't miss it."

Owen walked back to the village to grab a latte from Bunson's, stopping by his cottage first to grab a sweatshirt. He checked the empty letterbox on his door out of habit, but April was only a fleeting thought as he pulled a hood over his head for his trip into the village.

While in line at Bunson's, he saw Mrs. Pembroke, facing away from him, seated across from a man who could only be her Mr. Boles. As Owen stood in the queue, Boles rose to retrieve napkins from a nearby counter. He was a large, well-dressed man who moved with surprising grace, suggesting a former athlete.

Something about him made Owen uncomfortable. For one, he seemed acutely aware of his surroundings. Even while engaged with Mrs. Pembroke, his eyes darted vigilantly around the coffeehouse. Also, there was a formality in the way he carried himself—his perfect posture perhaps—that reminded Owen of his father and his military friends.

Instinctively, Owen pulled the edges of his hood forward and left, deciding in favor of a cup of tea at home. He would make the acquaintance of Boles sometime, but maybe another day.

CHAPTER 40

Boston, September 23, 2013

Owen's phone buzzed on the console of his car. "Hey, did you hear about Professor Anendale?"

"No, but don't ruin my day, Joe. I'm on my way to pick up April."

"Wow, the airport pickup. This is getting serious."

"Yes, the airport pickup, followed by nooky, I hope."

"I'm pretty sure sex after an airport run is state law. But this shouldn't ruin your day. Anendale is dead. Murdered last night."

Owen paused, taking it in. "What? Really? Wow."

"I know, right? How bizarre is that?"

Owen felt a pit in his stomach. He had definitely wished ill on Anendale but hadn't really meant it. Joe was droning on about an upcoming homicide trial, but he wasn't listening. "That's horrible," he mumbled to himself, as he took the exit for the airport. He hung up, forgetting to ask Joe how his date had gone.

Soon, though, he was curbside at the airport, and April was in his arms and on his lips. "So much better in person," she whispered in his ear.

"Is that another knock on my phone skills?" he quipped, loading her suitcase in the trunk.

"Who me? Never."

Their easy conversation on the way home was a welcome distraction, but soon Owen's thoughts drifted back to Anendale.

April squeezed his hand as he parked on the street near her apartment. "You're lost in thought. Is everything okay?"

"Yeah, sorry. I just got off the phone with Joe."

"Any news about the lawsuit?"

"Professor Anendale was murdered last night," he said, turning off the engine.

She sat with mouth agape for several seconds. "You're kidding? That's awful."

"Yeah."

"I guess no more lawsuit," she said with a wary grimace.

Owen sighed. "Yeah," he said, quietly, acknowledging the awkwardness.

"And kinda joking, but kinda not, I'm glad you have an alibi."

"What?" asked Owen, as April's words and all their meaning slowly registered in his mind.

"You were out with Joe, right?"

Over the years since, Owen would think back to this moment many times. The news of Anendale's murder had shaken him from the start, more than he'd expected. He'd assumed it was the shock that his private wish for the worst for Anendale had come true. To be sure, he felt guilty about it.

Somewhere, though, deep in the chasms of Owen's mind, news of the murder had brought a faint echo of dread. On some level, even before April's comment had brought it to the fore, he'd thought about his obvious motive and his explosion of anger in the bar. "Joe blew me off," he said, expressionless, staring straight ahead. "He had a date."

Holding hands, they walked in silence toward her apartment, each thinking about the murder. Owen was staring down at the sidewalk as they approached her stoop. Suddenly, April gasped and released her grip, covering her face with two hands as she stared up at her front door.

The image was jarring. In the middle of the wooden door painted yellow, a note, written in black stenciled letters on white construction paper read "Stay Away, Slut. He's Mine." Behind the note appeared to be some sort of plaid cloth. The note and cloth were held in place by a large dagger, stabbed into the door.

As April stood, frozen in place, shaking, Owen slowly approached the door. Up close, he recognized the plaid cloth as a pair of his boxer shorts. The blade of the dagger dripped with fresh blood.

CHAPTER 41

"I see this dinner as a potential pitfall for us," Owen said, looking across the table at Margo with a poker face, his voice dripping with exaggerated concern.

"Is that right?" she asked, frowning to play along. "So, you've heard about my penchant for projectile vomiting?" Owen laughed, breaking character.

"No?" she asked. "What then?"

"Well, for starters, there's the activity of eating itself, fraught with opportunities for embarrassment. You know, spilling, using the wrong utensil, mispronouncing something on the menu, not realizing you have lettuce in your teeth. The list is endless."

"As far as the utensils and the menu, you're probably on safe ground here at Piper's Arms. Not exactly an international flare."

"You'd be surprised. I think I was twenty before I realized how to pronounce ragout. I kept picturing a smelly dish towel."

"I see your point. Maybe we should leave."

"And even if everything goes well, there's always the looming possibility that you'll find me annoying—the way I chew or the way I like to keep my food separate from each other."

"So, you're a keep separate person?"

"Of course. I'm not insane," he deadpanned.

"Oh, by all means, you've never seemed more sane," she said sarcastically, miming a request for the check.

"Well, welcome to O..." Owen caught himself. "Welcome to Ancil Bradford's wonderful world of neuroses."

The reality was that Owen couldn't recall the last time he felt so relaxed. Not only was Margo a certified eight point five, she laughed at his jokes and had a wicked sense of humor herself. But it remained her indefinably mesmerizing presence that had Owen nearly speaking his own name.

Greeted by Brodie, who gave Owen a wink and an especially hearty handshake, they ordered a bottle of Chardonnay and fish and chips. "I would have thought your nerves about tonight would have centered on something else?" Margo said with a sly smile. "Perhaps something to do with certain third-date expectations."

Owen stared across the table, recognition slowly washing over his face. "Oh..." he said, with raised eyebrows, "Sorry, it's been quite some time since I dated. No, actually, I'm quite comfortable with Monopoly."

"Excuse me?"

"Well, I assume you're referring to the traditional third-date tradition of a late-night Monopoly game." They laughed, both happy she had brought it up.

"Well, here's to a good game tonight," she said, after the wine had arrived. They toasted, then set down their glasses wearing similar wry smiles. "Ice?" she asked.

"Definitely ice. I've come to enjoy tepid beer, but definitely not white wine."

"So," she said, "Tell me about your writing. Do you write every day? What's your creative process?"

"Ah, my creative process. That's always been a bit of a bugaboo for me. I don't really have one."

"Really?"

"Well, at some point, I said I didn't, and my agent told me to stick to that explanation. He wanted to cultivate a brand. He called it 'the every-man's writer.' To be honest, I thought it made me sound stupid."

"Interesting. But you write a lot in public. Does that help?"

"Definitely. I watch people to help develop characters. Sometimes for plot lines."

"So, you're sort of eavesdropping on these people?"

"Not necessarily listening in. Just imagining."

"Okay," she said, scanning the pub. "How about that couple over there?" she asked, pointing at a young couple sitting across from each other. "First date?"

"Oh, no," Owen said confidently. "He's just told her she wouldn't survive the night."

"Wow. Hopefully, it won't be the fish and chips," she said, laughing.

"Try not to ruin my creative process," he deadpanned. "He's strapped explosives to her and its curtains unless she talks."

"What's he after?"

"The codes to the missile de-activation. What else?"

"Well, that's quite dark, Ancil."

"What can I say? I'm presently writing a spy novel. Your turn. How about the woman at the end of the bar?"

"Ah, I'm glad you asked. She is currently plotting the overthrow of the Sultans of Sakaria."

"Really, from right here in the Piper's Arms. That's quite ambitious."

"Well, the Sultans, obviously, live in the future, and specialize in germ warfare. She is taking a respite to work on a vaccine."

"Fascinating," Owen said, beaming at his date. "I should have known you'd be a fantasy fan. So, what's the vaccine for?"

"The common cold," she said, and Owen snort-laughed.

"I guess if your entire army is sniffling constantly..." he said, still laughing.

"Exactly, blowing their noses..."

"Hello Ancil," came a voice from behind him, interrupting their giggling. It was the familiar high-pitched and somewhat snooty tone of Mrs. Pembroke. Owen stood and greeted her. "This is

George Boles. George, Ancil Bradford." The men shook hands and Owen introduced Margo as his friend, earning a smirk from Mrs. Pembroke.

"Glad to meet you, George."

"As am I, Ancil. I've heard a lot about you," Boles said, cordially. "I understand you've found a permanent home here in England." Ancil shot a look at Mrs. Pembroke.

"Well," she said, hurriedly, "we'll leave you two to have your fun," and led her date to a table by the window.

"I don't think she likes me," Margo said, once they were out of earshot.

"Really? Why?"

"No idea, but I got a distinctly cold vibe. Maybe she's jealous," she said, winking.

Soon, Margo was leading Owen up the stairs to her room.

"Nice view," he said, following her faded jeans to the window. "The view of the street isn't bad, either." Looking out the window, she leaned back into him, holding his hands in front of her. He pressed into her, his hot breath finding her neck through soft hair. She murmured a sound of pleasure then turned to face him, her nails lightly scratching his stomach as she played with his belt buckle.

"So, was Mr. Boles right, Ancil Bradford? Are you here permanently?" She whispered the question with searching brown eyes.

Owen's breath began to shorten as her fingers roamed. "I hope not," he said, with a dampened smile. He didn't know it, but Margo knew exactly what he meant.

"C'mon," she said, leading him away from the window. "Time to play Monopoly."

CHAPTER 42

Boston 2013

"Okay, time to settle the bet," Jepson said, as the detectives arrived at the county coroner's lab. They had spent the day writing reports and briefing the sergeant. News that Owen Prescott was a potential suspect was to be kept under wraps for now. Any charges would bring media attention, so orders were to build an airtight case before bringing it to the District Attorney.

Also, they didn't want to spook their suspect. Given his family's wealth, he would surely lawyer up at the first sign of trouble.

The detectives had read about Anendale's lawsuit and had contacted his attorney. Predictably, he'd had no contact with Prescott directly, only communicating through his attorney. Canvassing the neighborhood had come up empty and the shoe print had been a popular brand and too smeared to assign a size. The lab was processing a strand of hair and fibers from the clothing, and the DNA testing would take at least a week.

"What's the word, Lumps?" Jepson asked, as the detectives stepped inside the office of Deputy Coroner, Artie Lumpkin. Tucked away in the lab's basement, the doctor's cramped quarters resembled a hoarder's lair, with boxes of files stacked in various heights and mounds of old files obscuring furniture.

The pathologist's filing system was a running joke among cops, and his appearance did little to inspire confidence. Short and rotund, he was constantly wiping his sweaty brow with a handkerchief and appeared forever overwhelmed by his workload.

As Detective Sevilla had remarked on the ride over, "Someone had to finish at the bottom of the class in med school."

"Hey guys," Lumpkin said, popping in the last bite of a hot dog, "you're here about that Daulton homicide, right?"

Detective Sevilla exhaled and blinked slowly. "No, Lumps, we're here about the Anendale case. Please focus. This is our office's only priority at the moment."

"Of course, of course," the doctor said hurriedly, wiping mustard from his fingers on his lab coat. He dug a file from a heap on his desk. "Yes, yes, Anendale. Let's see, I calculated the time of death. As for the cause, let's see," he said, paging through the file. "Oh yes, the strangulation bludgeoning case. Sorry, guys, I've been swamped."

The detectives traded glances of derision before Lumpkin spoke again. "So first of all, the victim's body was not healthy. I haven't seen the lab report on his blood-alcohol level yet but given the state of his liver, I'd bet you guys a hot dog he was drunk."

The doctor paused to wipe his forehead. "There were obvious ligature marks on the neck. He was clearly garroted. However, there weren't the other injuries that we typically see in strangulations. No bleeding in the ear, no petechiae. Not even bruises or scratches that would suggest a struggle."

"So, he bled to death, Doc?" asked Sevilla.

"Technically, hemorrhagic shock. But yeah, the injury to his abdomen was the cause of death."

"Now, if you'll excuse me, guys, I have another autopsy to attend. Gotta love Southie, right? Three murders last night," the pathologist said, and began rummaging through files on his desk.

"You know, Pete, chances are, if there's DNA evidence, Prescott probably isn't in the system," Sevilla remarked as they left the office. "We might have to do some old-fashioned sleuthing, partner."

"Yep," answered Jepson, "but now it's time for some old-fashioned drinking. I'm buying."

CHAPTER 43

Owen awoke in Margo's bed to the sound of the sink in her bathroom, his body happily sore from an intense night of surprisingly physical sex. It'd been his first in more than ten years, and given his anxiety leading up to it, he thought it had gone reasonably well.

Although Owen was aware Margo was very fit, her naked body had been striking. While her arms and legs were toned and defined, her sculpted abs were other-worldly, porcelain skin stretching tight over a chiseled six pack. She'd shaved every inch of her body, which added to the impression of a mannequin carved from hard plastic. Owen had read that shaving had become the new norm, but still her smooth musculature had taken his breath away.

Sensing his caution, she had taken control of the bed, guiding him with confident persistence and firmness while her face remained serene and relaxed. Nervous, he'd started slowly, but soon, the intense physicality below her placid confidence had him panting, then gasping for her, matching her fervor before their climax.

Owen sat up, rubbed his eyes, then collapsed back on the pillows, replaying the night in his mind. He would ask if she preferred he shave his body, and he definitely needed to step up his exercise routine. He rolled to his side, facing the rolltop desk across the room, its writing surface just above eye level. Margo's stomach flashed across his mind again, its intricate lines defined by the moonlight through the window as she writhed atop him. He thought back to his failed sit-ups and wondered how many she must do daily.

A yoga mat lay rolled on the floor below a pull-up bar. He looked back at the desk. Its cover was pulled down to within an inch of the desktop. He stared lazily through the crack, his mind still on Margo's exquisite body. It was several seconds before his brain registered the object in his vision.

If it hadn't been for the orange book jacket, he wouldn't have noticed it. Over his mild objection, his editor in the states had insisted on the tangerine cover for his debut novel, *Cauldron in the Streets*. Published while he was still in college, the book had not sold well. The bright orange book lay on the writing surface of the desk, barely visible through the opening. He squinted but couldn't quite make out the lettering on the spine. A wave of tepid nausea washed over him. It couldn't be.

Panicked, he glanced at the bathroom door. He rolled out of bed and stood. The desk was fifteen feet away. Naked, he crept toward it, bending at the waist to see inside the crack. Just then, the water in the bathroom shut off; the light under the door, extinguished. With one step and a leap, he was back in bed as the bathroom door swung open.

Margo walked toward him wearing only his blue shirt that hung loose and unbuttoned from her shoulders. "Morning darling," she said, sliding into bed. "Like my shirt?" she asked, pressing into him, resting her head on his chest.

"Sure," Owen heard himself say, happy, at least, to have the power of speech. "Traditionally, of course, it's worn buttoned." His mind raced. *Please, Margo, don't want sex.* He was sure he wasn't up to it now.

"Oh, would you prefer I button it?" she asked, her hand dragging up from his thigh for a gentle squeeze. *Then again, maybe the orange book was a coincidence.*

She kissed his lips gently. "No fair, you've brushed your teeth," he said feebly.

"Oh, do you want to go brush," she asked with a coy whisper, her hand massaging rhythmically now. "Go ahead, Ancil," she teased, "get out of bed."

"No, I'm good, thanks," he said, breathing heavily. *There must be hundreds of books with orange covers.*

"No, really. You get out of bed now and I'll button my shirt?" She giggled, then kissed him again deeply, sucking his bottom lip as she pulled away. "No?" she asked, in a pouty voice, her hot breath in his ear as she climbed atop him, guiding him to her. "That's what I thought," she said, pressing on his chest as she arched into him.

No way that was my book.

. . .

Walking home through the village in the sunshine, Owen sipped a coffee from Bunson's and tried to make sense of the latest revelation. After this morning's round of passion, he and Margo had dozed together, chatting about literature, the orange book in her desk long since flushed from his mind.

Later though, hearing Margo's shower from the bathroom, he had unfolded his body—by then he was officially sore—pulled on his boxers and ambled to the desk. He had looked through the crack, knowing deep down what he was about to see. *Cauldron in the Streets.* Owen Prescott.

In the light of day and, more importantly, out of bed, an innocent explanation was nearly out of the question. Were it not for so many shared interests and favorites between them, Owen would have dismissed the possibility of a coincidence entirely. There'd definitely been a spike in the book's sales after the success of *Orchards of Grace.* Still, it seemed a long shot.

Across the street, the sight of the mysterious and well-endowed woman with long black hair interrupted his thoughts. What was she doing entering Rooster's Arms at 2pm? Lunch perhaps, but it was a bit early for a pint. She certainly called upon a lot of businesses in Tetbury.

Owen arrived at his cottage to find an irate Guildy meowing at his door. "You women are nothing but trouble, Guildy," he said, filling her bowl. He opened the cupboard, brought down a bottle and poured himself three fingers of scotch.

The real question, as he saw it, was when Margo Cummings had obtained his book. It was possible that she'd purchased it after they'd met, after figuring out his identity. This was not likely but at least possible, as it could be found in Birnam's Books on the far end of Sibley Lane or perhaps in the local library. But if this were the case, she hadn't mentioned it. On the other hand, if she'd had it before meeting him, as Mrs. Pembroke would say, that was another kettle of fish.

He took a healthy sip, feeling the burn in this throat. One thing was certain, he could ill-afford to wait to find out the answer. For once, he agreed with his father and his militaristic friends. He needed to go on the offensive.

CHAPTER 44

Boston 2013

"So, where were you? You know, the night it happened?" Owen looked away as April's question floated across the table from her angelic face and hung in the air like a thought balloon between them, ready to burst with the slightest prick.

They had spent most of April's first day back dealing with her housewarming gift. They'd filed a police report—it had to be Owen's stalker, Desiree Richins—and April's father, the police commissioner, had pulled some strings to increase patrols in the neighborhood. For the time being, though, they decided April would stay at Owen's. They'd moved some of her belongings in, then began a wonderful reunion, talking and love making deep into the night.

In April's absence, a part of Owen had wondered if he'd somehow exaggerated her qualities in his mind. Now, he was beyond reassured. If anything, he had forgotten so much of what made her beautiful, fun, and exquisitely perfect.

He'd never felt the least bit self-conscious around her. Her smile seemed to free his desires, fears, and dreams, easing them from him in waves of relief. Her chestnut brown eyes saw deep within him, sparking embers that warmed his soul. He hung on every word formed by her perfect mouth, desperate for every morsel while relaxing in her free and easy spirit. Physically, she was his type—he hadn't known it before—packaged in rounded curves that swayed before him and enveloped him in long undulations of blinding ecstasy.

They had stirred only briefly for more sex before drifting off again in each other's arms. At 11:00 a.m. they had awakened, tangled in the sheets and famished. Owen had made cheesy omelets before they played nine holes of golf at a par-three course in the suburbs.

Until now, sitting across from her at Owen's favorite coffee shop, he had scarcely thought of anything outside their wonderful world for two, but now April's question hovered, its answer threatening to pierce their bubble of bliss.

"After Joe left, I decided just to walk home and write," he answered, trying to sound casual.

"Was Will home?"

"Yeah, in his room, I guess."

"So, he didn't see you?"

"I don't know," he said, failing to disguise the concern in this voice. "I don't think so."

"I mean, did you see anyone? Make a call?"

"I don't remember, April," he said defensively. He sighed, staring above her head, recounting the evening in his head. "I met Joe at 6:00 p.m. Was home by 6:45 p.m. Then I turned my phone off to write."

"Sorry for all the questions. I don't want to worry you. It's just that you may want to think about firming up that alibi?"

"An alibi? Are you serious?" he asked, looking around, whispering across the table.

"I'm sorry, Owen. It's probably all the stories my dad tells me about. Forget I brought it up," she said, holding his hand in the middle of the table. "I just freaked out there for a minute. I guess I imagined you being taken away from me. For all I know, the murderer has already been arrested." They moved on to happier topics, but Anendale's murder lurked at the edges of their minds.

Parked across the street from the coffee shop, detectives Sevilla and Jepson sat in their four-door sedan, stewing in their boredom.

"Typical politicians," grumbled Sevilla in the driver's seat, tossing the wrapper of a nutrition bar onto the floorboard and pulling another from his pocket.

"Yeah, 'do a very thorough, deliberate job, and do it in a hurry.' This is stupid. He'll probably take his cup with him. By the way, I think the idea is those bars replace a meal. You've had three since we left the precinct."

"The ancestry website would have gotten back to us in a week, tops," Sevilla continued with a full mouth, ignoring the comment. "Instead, we're out here chasing leftovers like a couple of scavengers. By the way, it's your turn to go garbage diving."

"Don't remind me," muttered Jepson.

Lately, the detectives had adopted the practice of comparing a DNA sample from a crime scene to the millions stored in ancestry databases that sold family histories. Even if the killer hadn't used the ancestry service, the police used the method to identify distant relatives, then narrowed the search through traditional police work. The tactic had solved several cold cases and was credited with the arrest of the infamous Zodiac Killer in California.

In cases like theirs, where there was a known suspect, the technique would be even more useful. If there was a positive hit on one of Prescott's relatives, together with the motive and papers found at the scene, it would be enough for an arrest warrant. Then, the confirming DNA sample could be taken from the controlled confines of the jail.

But due to time constraints imposed by their boss, the detectives had been ordered to compare Prescott's directly with the crime scene sample. This meant obtaining his DNA without violating his right to privacy, which usually meant collecting his discarded paper cups.

"You know, Pete," Sevilla said, crumpling another wrapper, "it used to be that if someone didn't like a book, do you know what they would do?"

"Something tells me you have the answer."

"They would skewer the book, Pete, not the actual author."

"You won't stop, will you? By the way, I subpoenaed our boy's cell phone records. Maybe we can place him near the scene."

"Good. And I was thinking, with apologies to our resident literary scholar in the patrol division…"

"Dietrick."

"Yeah, Dietrick. Anyway," continued Jepson, "I'm sure the kid knows his stuff and I think Prescott's name was even in the notebook. Still, we should probably have a handwriting expert look at it."

"Good idea. The Sergeant will like that idea."

"Even though, if you ask me, handwriting analysis is…"

"Total made up science," Sevilla cut in.

"Yes! Complete and utter bullshit! Have you ever heard one of those blowhards testify? They don't take measurements or analyze pen pressure—nothing. They're like, 'Do you see how this loop in the L is similar to this L? And do you see how the E dips slightly below the line.' What a bunch of hooey."

"But yes," Jepson agreed, laughing, "we should definitely use one. Hey," he said, changing his tone, "they're leaving."

Owen followed April out of the coffee shop's main doors into the bright sunshine of early fall, tossing their tall paper cups into the garbage on their way out. Jepson hustled in a side door, keeping eyes on them as he went. Approaching the trash, he let out a disgusted sigh. The large, round plastic barrel was positioned in a corner. Four feet in diameter, it was three quarters filled with hundreds of identical white and green cups. "Shit," muttered the detective, knowing there was no way to determine which one had been Prescott's.

Sevilla had made his way inside and patted his partner on the back. "C'mon, Pete," he said, suppressing a smile, "we'll get 'em next time."

CHAPTER 45

Owen arrived at Balfrey's Bakery when it opened at 6:00 a.m. and chose a table in the back that faced the front window with a clear view of the Piper's Arms. Margo had told him that she did her strength training at night—just a few crunches, she'd said, obviously underselling her routine. This meant she took her run in the early morning.

On his walk to the bakery, Owen had seen buxom black hair again, continuing her tour of Tetbury's small businesses. This time he'd spied her entering Bunson's from a few blocks away and leaving soon after empty-handed. He had to admit that he found the woman's early morning pop-ins around the village confounding. She didn't appear to be carrying anything to sell. Also, there was something about her quick walk and overall demeanor that suggested secrecy. Owen was also aware that given recent events, his suspicion could very well be the product of his paranoia.

He sipped his coffee, his stomach in knots, eyes trained on the front door of the pub. If Margo used the back entrance, he'd likely miss her, but she always left from the pub. Twenty minutes later, she walked out of the pub's front door. After a few stretches, she set off running, headed toward the park where the couple had hiked.

Owen's heart pounded as he crossed the street and walked down the alley behind the pub where a short wooden staircase led to the entrance of Margo's apartment. He jogged up the stairs to a small porch, its railing lined with various potted plants. He moved to the railing where he'd seen Margo stash the spare key, finding it on his third try hidden below a pot of tulips.

He breathed deeply, looking back at the alley behind him before unlocking the door. Owen figured he had at least thirty minutes but he didn't want to waste time. He was committing a burglary, after all. He unlocked the door. Then, walking on eggshells, he stepped outside and replaced the key under the tulip pot before entering. Inside, as usual, the apartment was tidy. A kettle of tea rested on the spotless stove top, a clean cup on the kitchen counter. Over on the wall, a towel was folded neatly over the pull-up bar.

Owen hurried to the rolltop desk, sat down and peeled it open. *Cauldron in the Streets*, by Owen Prescott, lay where he'd seen it the day before. The book looked newly purchased, but it was impossible to tell for sure. He thumbed through it briefly. No notes in the margins, no dog-eared pages.

On a shelf at eye level was a framed photograph of Margo and a man in his late fifties, presumably her much older ex-husband. Who knows, maybe current husband, he thought to himself. He opened the drawers quickly, conscious of the time. Most were empty, save for pens, pencils and other supplies that had the look of being there well before Margo's arrival.

As Owen checked the last drawer—a deep one next to the floor on the left—he thought he heard the faintest of hissing sounds behind him, but ignored it once he looked inside. There, in the front of the drawer, were copies of his latest three books. His stomach lurched.

Frantically, he pulled the drawer out further. Behind the books, deep inside was an accordion file bulging with papers. A copy of a newspaper clipping protruded from the file and lay across its top, part of a headline facing Owen upside down. Prescott Flees the Coun....

Owen's face suddenly pulsed with heat. He dug down into the folder. More clippings about him, the lawsuit and the murder, a handwritten list of his books, and a program from the lecture at Oxford. His galloping mind stopped on a dime in front of Margo's face, wrapped in a scarf, looking up at him in the middle of the street in Oxford. Who was this woman?

He shut the drawer and wiped his face, already slick with sweat. There was a building whistle in his ears and he felt dizzy. He sat back and swiveled in the chair to face the room, desperate to get his bearings. He scanned the room as the shrill whistle grew louder. His eyes fell on the kettle on the stove. Fuck! He raced toward it and took it off the burner. It had been left on a low setting and had obviously reached a boil. He turned it off, his addled brain slowly recognizing the danger. What if she remembers...

Just then, Owen heard the thuds of bounding footsteps coming up the stairs from the pub. Owen leaped to a sofa, his foot landing on a cushion, and vaulted over it, landing awkwardly on his side as the front door opened. Numbed to any pain, he flattened himself against the floor, desperate to control his breathing.

Margo's trainers bounced to the stove. "Damn!" she said aloud, seeing the kettle safely off the stove. Owen froze, willing her to resume her run. She caught sight of the oven light on the stove top, indicating heat, and frowned. She started to check the temperature of the kettle but waved at the air in frustration and headed toward the front door.

Hearing the door latch, Owen's body collapsed in relief on the floor. Soon, he pressed himself to his knees and stood on rubbery legs, shaking his mind from wondering about Margo and why she'd been hunting him. He would have time for that later.

Breathing deeply, he returned to the desk and arranged the accordion file as he'd found it, then closed the rolltop. He'd been lucky Margo hadn't noticed that. Then he moved to the window and peered down the street, spotting Margo's petite figure bouncing away from him in the distance. He double-checked the appearance of the desk, fixed the sofa cushion, locked the back door and left through the bar. He was far from a seasoned criminal, he thought to himself, but he was getting better at this stuff.

CHAPTER 46

Boston 2013

Owen had always hated the smell of his father's home office. Once he left, he could never conjure the odor in his mind, so he wondered whether it was real or some sort of visceral reaction to the place. But when he was inside the windowless room, paneled in oak and furnished with leather chairs, a mutant funk of body odor, cologne, and cigars formed a fist and punched him square in the nose.

Nothing good ever happened to Owen in the room. For as long as he could remember, it was reserved for his father's diatribes of disappointment. Owen had been too weak as a boy, not interested enough in sports, not tough enough on the football field, not smart enough when it came to science, and not passionate enough about anything. He'd spent too much time reading—reading for pleasure, his father had disgustedly called it—and not enough time with his numbers. He'd been too lazy, too much of a mama's boy, too disorganized, and too cowardly to ever make something of himself.

Of course, turning down West Point had been the final straw. After all the strings his father had pulled, all the favors he'd called in to get the undeserving Owen the appointment; ungrateful Owen had opted for a liberal arts education. "You're a disgrace to the family," his father had said, his eyes filled with loathing. "You sicken me."

Now, as he stepped into the room, engulfed by the smell, he wondered what current aspect of his life his father had examined and found wanting. He was behind his giant desk, dressed, as he always was, in a three-piece suit. Behind him, on the wall, hung a painting of himself in full military dress. There were three others in the room. He recognized the short, stocky man with a shaved head who wore a black suit over a black turtleneck. His dad referred to him as his advisor and whenever he was around, tensions ran high. The other two had the sharp, useless look of attorneys.

Each time Owen returned to the office as an adult, he saw something he hadn't noticed as a child. He recalled a time in college when he'd first recognized the ridiculous portrait of his father for the egomaniacal symbol it was. Today, it was the gold nameplate on his father's desk. *What kind of asshole has a nameplate in their home office?*

Edgar Rockwell Prescott stood from his chair. "Sit down, Owen." It was an order, not an invitation, and all the men turned to face the desk, practically saluting. His dad looked at the advisor. "What do we know?"

"Our sources inside the District Attorney's Office have told us that Owen Prescott is a suspect in the murder of Professor Norvel Anendale. We know that there is no timeline for an arrest warrant and that they are awaiting certain laboratory tests. Presumably, these are DNA tests, but that has not been confirmed."

Owen heard the words spill from the advisor's mouth in slow motion at first before gaining speed to smack him in the forehead. Owen's first reaction, typically, focused on his father. *How typical of him not to address him personally, opting to have a lackey read the charges against him.* Then reality had struck.

"Wait, wait," he'd said, looking around the room at the men, all staring, clearly gauging his reaction. "Wait a minute. Don't they have to have evidence before they make me a suspect."

"Wallace?" His father turned to the older of the two attorneys, reflexively checking his pocket watch, billable hours on his mind.

"It is worth noting that young Mr. Prescott is—rather, was—being sued by the victim. So, he had motive to commit the crime." Owen squirmed in his seat and exhaled loudly but held his tongue. "However," the attorney continued, "motive alone would not be sufficient to designate him a suspect. If the information that Mr. Prescott is a suspect is correct," he continued, shooting a glance at Owen, "and I have no reason to doubt its veracity, then yes. It is safe to presume that the D.A.'s Office has, in its possession, some evidence that Owen is responsible for the murder."

Why are these fuckheads talking about me like I'm not here? Owen stood. "Listen," he said, "there is no evidence that I had anything to do with murder. This is absurd!"

"Look," the attorney said, both palms facing Owen, "no one here is saying they believe that you had anything to do with this. But the reality is that the legal system is based on perception. You wouldn't be a suspect if the D.A. didn't have some evidence besides motive. However misguided their perception of that evidence, that's the reality."

Owen had stopped listening sometime during his second or third sentence. *Typical attorney speak. No one was saying he had anything to do with this, but they weren't saying that he didn't either.*

His father sat with his arms crossed, disapproving look in place. "Next steps?" he grumbled, checking his pocket watch again. "We need some damage control." *We? Classic. To hell with my worthless son. This family has a reputation to protect.*

The junior attorney spoke up, his voice teaming with obsequium. "I'll prepare a statement. Condolences to the Anendale family, categorically deny allegations, yada, yada, yada."

"And I assume Owen is not to speak to the press or the police?" his father said, addressing the senior attorney, ignoring the junior. Owen seethed. Apparently, he was incapable of speaking directly to him.

"Guys, I'm sitting right here," Owen spoke up. "Also, listen carefully. I have nothing to hide. And I need for the people—the police, my readers, everybody—to know that I'm innocent." His father smiled condescendingly and again turned to his suited sycophant.

"His readers," he muttered under his breath. "Wallace," he said with disgust, "Owen needs to understand that playtime is over. Whatever's he's done or not done, it's time to face reality, is it not?"

"Again, dad, I'm sitting right here!" Owen complained, hating the whiny tone in his own voice. He was up out of his chair now and moving toward the desk when the squad advisor blocked his path.

"Owen," the attorney cut in with a hand on his shoulder, "obviously, tensions are high," he said with a smarmy smile. "I know you are eager to declare your innocence. That's very natural, of course. However, in the event you are contacted by the police, I must insist that you not agree to be interrogated. Simply inform them you are represented by an attorney who has counseled you to invoke your constitutional right to remain silent."

Owen's mind raced. "Are they going to arrest me?" he asked, addressing the attorney. The lawyer handed him a business card, then looked to the advisor for an answer.

The bald man addressed his boss. "They have no plans to do so at this point," he said blandly, as if reporting the empire's quarterly earnings. "Our sources will keep us apprised if anything changes."

Owen nodded to the attorney. At least he'd addressed him directly. Sort of. He walked out of the room and out the front door of his childhood home. He knew his mom would want to talk, but he couldn't face her now. *I need to get the fuck out of here before I actually kill someone.*

Hurrying to his car, he fired off a text to Joe.

—*They think I killed Anendale?!? Can you meet?*

CHAPTER 47

Boston 2013

Joe Turner was familiar with the look of someone who had just learned that they may be charged with a serious crime. Some handled it better than others, exhibiting varying levels of shock and confusion. But to all but the most hardened criminals, the overriding emotion was fear. Sitting across from him in his office, Owen was certainly no exception.

"I called my contact in the D.A.'s Office," Joe said, ruing his next sentence. "He confirmed you are a suspect in the murder."

Owen let out a groaning sigh, collapsing his head in his hands. "How can this be happening, Joe?" he asked, his voice weak.

"So, people are suspected all the time. That's how a criminal investigation works. Suspects are identified, investigation is conducted, and often suspects are eliminated. I also confirmed that the office is awaiting lab results."

Owen looked up at his friend. "What does that mean?" he asked, his face suddenly flushed.

"Are you okay?" Joe asked. "Take some deep breaths, O."

"It's just that…"

"Owen," Joe cut in. "Deep breaths. I need you to listen. I may not know how to be a literary agent, but this is my jam. You're in good hands, okay?"

Owen breathed deeply as Joe began to speak. "That they are waiting for lab results is good news for two reasons. First, if they had enough to charge, you'd be in jail already. My guess is they have motive and something else, probably circumstantial. Also, given the timing, the lab results are likely DNA tests. Presumably, once the test comes back, you'll be cleared."

Owen was nodding slowly. "Okay. So, my dad and his toadies say I shouldn't talk to the police. Do you agree?"

"Yes," Joe said firmly. "There is never any upside in speaking to the police."

"But won't it show that I'm willing to cooperate?" Owen asked.

Joe shook his head. "That won't matter. Cops don't interview suspects with an eye toward uncovering the truth. They do it to build a case against the suspect."

"But I don't have anything to hide, Joe," Owen countered.

"Owen, I know you believe you have nothing to hide. But without knowing what evidence the police have or think they have, I don't want to subject you to an interrogation."

Owen sat back in his chair, shaking his head. "Let me give you an example," Joe continued. "Say they asked if you ever told anyone you wished Anendale was dead. Your mind flashes to the time you joked with me about him being hit by a bus, so you hesitate. Then you decide to explain yourself to the cops, who have a field day. 'So you did want him dead, didn't you? I mean, you must have meant it on some level, right? Do you often joke about someone's death?' Get the picture?"

Owen shrugged, clearly unconvinced. "So what, I just do nothing?"

"No," Joe said calmly. "I'd like you to go home, get a shower, and relax. Then, when your mind is clear, write down what you did the day of Anendale's death. We don't know the time of death, so start from the moment you woke up. Every detail is critical. I'll make sure my contact with the D.A. keeps us informed. As soon as the test results come back and you're cleared, I'll schedule a press conference."

"Okay, Joe, thanks," Owen said standing to leave. "Sorry I'm a bit of an ass. This is all very surreal. As many times as I've joked about needing your services, I just never really thought I would."

Joe smiled. "I get that a lot."

CHAPTER 48

Needing a temporary distraction after a sleepless night worrying about Margot, Owen decided on his quarterly trip to Lundy's Grocery Shop. Sputtering through Tetbury in the Rover, he reminded himself for the one hundredth time he needed to have a mechanic look at the car. If nothing else, the sheer racket of the blasted thing called attention to him. Sure enough, a large, older woman strutting down the sidewalk in a hat fit for the Kentucky Derby seemed to stare as he parked at the curb.

Climbing out of the Rover, Owen stole a glance her way. She was definitely eyeballing him, and he cursed himself for not wearing his hoodie. The noise of her heels on the cement stopped, and Owen looked again to find that she had turned to look behind her, her heavily made-up eyes squinting toward him. "Fuck," Owen whispered to himself after his back was to her.

Something similar had happened to Owen a dozen or so times over the years, and he reminded himself that nothing had ever come of such incidents. Once, an Irish woman had stared at him while he sat in Bunson's, finally approaching to ask if he was a classmate she hadn't seen in twenty years. Another time, a man had eyed him from across a parking lot, only to inquire if he would consider selling the Rover.

The presence of his photo on a most-wanted poster in the next village had Owen more spooked than usual. Still, his was one of a dozen or so photos in the poster, and the odds that anyone would commit the faces to memory and be on the lookout for them seemed rather unlikely. He probably looked like this woman's long-lost relative or something similar.

On his way to the grocery store, Owen took a slight detour and ducked into Bunson's. "Hey, Tommy," he said, approaching the barista.

"Awright, Ancil, fancy a tea?"

"No, thanks. I was just wondering. Do you remember a quite buxom woman with long black hair stopping in to see you the other morning?"

"I do, yes," he said, smiling. "Fairly memorable woman, that one."

"Yes, well, just out of curiosity, Tommy, if you don't mind me asking, did she say what she was after?"

"Oh, yes," he said, wiping the counter in front of him. "It was crazy, really. She was asking about a video camera for security. Had I ever considered a video linked to some bloody government network. Sounded like a bit of a nutter if you ask me. I told her to piss off."

"Right." Owen stood silently for a few seconds, digesting the barista's news.

"Was there anything else, Ancil," Tommy asked, gesturing behind Owen, where a customer was ready to order.

"No. Sorry, Tommy." Walking out of Bunson's, Owen considered that the more he learned about the woman with black hair, the less Mrs. Pembroke's concerns seemed a product of her over-active imagination.

As he walked toward the grocery, Owen gradually became aware of a car in the street to his right. Feeling exposed without his hoodie, he resisted the urge to look toward the car. Surely, its driver was lost or perhaps looking for an address as it crept along. Owen was convinced he was imagining things and promised himself a nap when he got home.

But another twenty paces and the car was still there, moving parallel with him in the street. Well, now it would be strange if he didn't look its way. Perhaps it was a village acquaintance wanting to say hi, or someone who needed directions. But if either of these were the case, why weren't they speaking up?

As the car loomed, Owen's mind strayed down a dark path with each step. Was this thing going to track him all the way home, he thought, momentarily forgetting about his grocery shopping. Was it a cop, blocking his escape? Was he about to be arrested? But in his peripheral vision, the car looked large and black, not the blue and yellow checked cars favored by the English police. Perhaps it was an undercover cop. For God's sake, Owen, get a hold of yourself.

Another few paces and he would head into the grocery. That would tell the tale. He turned into Lundy's and spun to look behind him through the dark tinted glass of the market's front door. A shiny black sedan with sparkling chrome-spoked wheels idled in the middle of the street. The driver had removed her hat, but Owen immediately recognized the woman who gawked at him earlier. Her garishly painted face squinted to see him through the glass door, her eyes boring into him, sending a chill up his spine. Owen turned away, then heard the big car's engine rev as it rolled away.

This time there was no doubt, he thought, wandering aimlessly down an aisle. He'd been spotted.

CHAPTER 49

Boston 2013

"Damn it!" Detective Sevilla wadded up a piece of paper at his desk and tossed it through the hoop above the recycling bin against the wall of the precinct's bullpen. It had been ten days since Anendale's murder and Owen Prescott's status as a suspect had been leaked to the press. The chief was demanding daily updates and the detectives were feeling the pressure to make an arrest.

Detective Pete Jepson reclined, hands behind his head, and called to his partner across their facing desks. "So, Lew," he said grinning, "I'm done with my reports."

"Awesome. Very happy for you."

"Do you know why that is?" Sevilla was silent, as he fed a fresh piece of paper into his typewriter. "It's because I use a computer like literally every other cop in the civilized world."

"Look Pete, I'm loyal to Mabel. She makes me feel like…"

"Like a cop, I know. And so would smoking two packs a day, right?" he chided, but his partner had begun the loud operation of his antique. "Hey, Lew," he said after a time, "I've been thinking about our boy, Prescott."

"Yeah?" answered Sevilla, half listening while his index fingers pecked away.

"Something about this case stinks," Jepson said, channeling his favorite melodramatic tone of a clichéd detective. "It stinks like a dead skunk in a furnace. It stinks like Captain Bonilla's butt juice after a day of walking the harbor beat in July. It stinks…"

"I get it, Jepson," Sevilla cut in, chuckling. He stopped typing to crack his knuckles. "But don't overthink it. Prescott's got a truckload of motive. The old dude was trying to steal his baby, not to mention his fame and fortune. So, poetically, he killed him with a literary award, hoisting him on his own petard. That's from Hamlet, Pete. It means…"

"I know what it fucking means, but it doesn't fit." Jepson stood and walked to the coffeepot for a refill. "Look," he began, sipping from his paper cup, "you agree that the perp wouldn't have strangled him after impaling him, right?"

"Of course." answered Sevilla, slamming the return on his relic to the left, before resuming his typing. "That would have been like kicking a dead horse. Also Shakespeare, by the way," he said casually.

"I call bullshit, partner," said Jepson, laughing.

Sevilla smiled and kept typing. "Okay, you're right. I made that up. Could be Shakespeare, though."

"So," Jepson continued, "your theory is he tried to strangle him first, then when that didn't work, he impaled him?"

"Yes."

"So, Lew, you're telling me that Prescott, a young man, could sneak up behind him and loop the garrote around his neck but somehow wasn't able to strangle him?"

"It happens."

"So, Prescott already has a garrote around his neck. If the old guy was still breathing, wouldn't he just keep choking him?"

"He probably panicked."

"So, he panicked because he was in a hurry and he wanted to kill him and get the hell out of there, right?" asked Jepson.

"Sure."

"But he didn't kill him as quickly as possible. Instead, according to your theory, Prescott searched the house for a poetic way to kill him. We know the pyramid was taken off a shelf in another room. C'mon, Lew. It makes no sense." Met with his partner's silence, Jepson waved a hand at him in disgust and turned his attention to his computer.

Five minutes later, Sevilla stopped typing. "Pete, not only does Prescott have motive, the notes about his novel put him there. It makes perfect sense. Anendale had the papers, which was proof of their collaboration on the novel, and Prescott knew it."

Jepson thought for a minute. "So, if the papers were what Prescott was after, why in God's name would he leave them strewn all over the murder scene?"

"Again, he panicked. This is not a seasoned criminal, Pete. He probably freaked out. Did you catch the Prescott family press conference with that slimy attorney reading the statement? You know damn well if Prescott had an alibi, it would have been front and center. And, did you see the cell phone data? C'mon Pete, the guy turned off his phone less than an hour before the murder."

Jepson exhaled, exasperated. "Well, I guess the DNA evidence will tell the tale. Didn't Caruthers say we'd know this afternoon?"

The detectives had finally gotten a DNA sample from Owen. They'd followed him to a pub near his home and snatched his glass and the dregs of his gin and tonic. The traces of saliva had been more than enough for a DNA profile.

"Hey, Mr. Literary, do you know why Anendale didn't die right away?" Jepson asked, failing to suppress a grin.

"Lay it on me."

"He was in the living room."

Sevilla smiled. "Keep at it, partner. You'll get there."

Jepson's cell phone rattled on his desk.

"Jepson here….Okay, Ted…Really? That's interesting…Yeah, and thanks for the quick turnaround."

Jepson sat frowning, processing the information. "What's up?" asked Sevilla, moving toward the copier.

"DNA tests showed two donors."

Sevilla stopped in mid-stride and faced his partner. "Really?" There was genuine surprise in his voice. "So, including the victim, there were three people at the murder scene?"

"Yeah, but turns out you were right again, pards. At least I think so."

"Yeah?"

Jepson nodded. "One sample was a match for Owen Prescott."

CHAPTER 50

Back from his mid-day walk through the village holding a brown bag of fish and chips, Constable Whitworth walked into the humble police station looking forward to his lunch.

"Hello, Catherine," he said, removing his black felt bobby hat, greeting his secretary, the only other employee of the Nailsworth branch of the Cotswold Village Constabulary.

"Awright, Captain. You have a familiar visitor," she mumbled, without looking up from her newspaper. He sighed, a pained expression falling over his face as he peeked into the conference room through an interior window.

"Bloody hell," he muttered under his breath, ducking inside his office to toss his lunch on his desk.

"Would you two fancy a cup of tea?" his assistant asked, smiling into her paper.

"No, Catherine, we most definitely would not, and you know it," he said, pausing at the door of the conference room to compose himself.

"Hello, Mrs. Busby," he said, mustering a fake smile as he entered the room.

The middle-aged woman sat ramrod straight, her right hand resting atop the gold eagle's head handle of her cane. She wore a high-necked dress of purple and white lace, too much makeup, and a mink shawl across her shoulders. "Constable Whitworth," she said haughtily. "I trust you've made, at least, some inroads into the blatant disregard for our village council's very clear recommendations regarding residential specifications?"

"Mrs. Busby, as I have indicated in the past," until I was blue in the face, he wanted to add, "while the village council's recommendations for homeowners are well valued and appreciated by the public, they can hardly be enforced as the law."

She raised her chin to talk down her nose. "Constable, I'll remind you that thanks to our work on the council, Nailsworth is known for having some of the most picturesque villages...."

"Yes, but..." The constable's effort to cut in was in vain, as she merely increased her volume.

"...in all of England. And now, while law enforcement such as yourself sit idly by, Constable Whitworth, this reputation is in jeopardy as some residents of our village run roughshod over the most basic specifications. Just on my way here this afternoon, I passed three separate cottages with their vehicles parked outside their garages."

"Oh my, that is a travesty," he muttered, but his sarcasm was lost on his guest.

"And despite my newsletter, there remain throughout the village at least eleven cottages without post lanterns. Constable Whitworth, the black wrought-iron post lantern is the very iconic symbol of the Cotswolds. On this point I cannot bend," she said, eyes wide. "If law enforcement refuses to enforce the law, our community will soon dissolve into anarchy." She emphasized her last point with a forceful rap of her cane on the conference room's tile floor.

"Now," she said, shifting in her seat, "I have another matter to discuss. Yesterday, while shopping in Tetbury—now that's a village with beautiful cottages—I passed a man who bore an uncanny resemblance to the latest addition to the most-wanted poster in our post office."

"Really?" the constable asked, wearily. He had long since mentally checked out, thinking of his fish and chips going cold on his desk. "Imagine, a most wanted man right here in the Cotswolds."

"Yes, indeed. He was driving an old light green Rover with a terrible-sounding engine. Right here in Tetbury." Constable Whitworth's eyes flickered from his trance.

"An old green Rover, with a bad engine, you say?" he asked, now staring at his guest intently. "Mrs. Busby, that is quite interesting."

CHAPTER 51

The next morning, across the Atlantic, Alyssa Wagner pulled up Owen Prescott's shared digital file. After some initial correspondence with Mr. Norich, she hadn't opened it in a few weeks, having promised herself to give her colleague space to operate.

So far, Norich had proven to have been accurately described by his chief. Despite being a bit clumsy with their shared file, he had gained a thorough command of the case. He'd agreed that given the pattern of travel, the Cotswolds seemed a logical place for Prescott to land.

Norich had established an undercover presence and was "pursuing a few leads." Also, Alyssa was pleased to hear that with the help of Interpol, he was attempting to broaden the video network of Cyclops in the area, with particular attention to the coffee shops noted in her analysis.

Alyssa sat staring at the photos of her fugitive with various combinations of hair lengths and facial hair. The more she looked at them and read about Owen Prescott, the less any of them looked like a killer. She'd read the police reports in the case, but the autopsy, lab reports and crime scene photos had yet to arrive.

For starters, she wasn't sure Prescott could physically generate the force necessary to impale the victim. She'd done the rough calculations in her head. Assuming the sides and tip of the pyramid trophy weren't razor sharp, the amount of force necessary to run the thing through a human body was about eight hundred pounds of force. More, if bone. That was more force than is generated by the average professional boxer's punch, and Prescott had appeared fairly out of shape.

Even if capable of delivering the blow, it would take all his strength and a significant windup. But that meant delivering the strike from the front of the victim would be impossible, as the required coil and thrust would deprive him of the element of surprise. The detective's theory—that the victim was choked unconscious, then impaled seemed unlikely. If the initial plan was to strangle, why would the perpetrator abandon that plan?

Finally, the weapon of choice didn't fit. The motive of revenge for the lawsuit clearly suggested premeditation, which meant that Prescott arrived at the victim's residence with an intent to kill. However, the impaling was clearly a crime of passion, suggesting that the killer was overcome with emotion and grabbed the nearest weapon available.

Agent Wagner had just returned to her chair with coffee when an update from Scotland Yard flashed on her computer screen. "Agent Norich reports possible sighting of fugitive. Follow-up underway."

Alyssa's fingers were on her keyboard. "Well done, Agent Norich," she typed, smiling at her use of the English phrase.

Then she picked up her phone and dialed Boston P.D. to check on the expected arrival of the lab reports and photos. Her fugitive's capture was seeming inevitable. Now, Agent Wagner intended to find out what Prescott had or hadn't done.

CHAPTER 52

Spooked by the grocery trip, Owen holed up at home writing, then took a long hike in the sheep pastures west of the village. As he walked back home, he collected his thoughts about Margo. She was coming over later, and he hated confrontation. Since the previous day's daring mission, he'd evaluated the potential scenarios. They ranged from bad to a dumpster fire falling off a cliff.

The most hopeful was that their attendance at the lecture in Oxford had been a coincidence. Given their shared literary taste, it certainly wasn't out of the question. After calm reflection, he was no longer certain it had been her in the street. So, perhaps she had figured out his identity after meeting him. Were that the case, there seemed little chance that she had designs on turning him in.

Of course, Owen had been forced to consider the worst: that Margo was in law enforcement. If that were true, though, what was she waiting for? Had she fallen head over heels for him and now couldn't do her duty? That sounded farfetched, not to mention like the plot of a bad movie. After a bottle of wine last night, his mind had skidded off the rails, imagining other bizarre story lines. In one, Margo had been sent as a test by April, who secretly still pined for him. In another, she was Anendale's daughter, planning her vengeance.

Owen had contemplated not even mentioning it to Margo, given the sheer awkwardness of the situation. What would he say? "So, having broken into your apartment, I know that you know that I've been lying about my identity and am wanted for murder. Anyway, how about a hike tomorrow?"

Lost in thought, Owen hadn't noticed the portly man approaching him on the sidewalk until they were face to face.

"Hello, Ancil."

"Good afternoon, Mr. Boles. How are you?"

"I am well, thank you. I've just popped over to Mrs. Pembroke's and I'm on my way to get some grub and make some business calls."

"Okay. Your business was prosthetics, was it?" Owen asked.

"Yes, indeed."

"You know, my nephew has had a prosthesis for most of his life. He has one that's linked to the internet. Amazing what advances have been made."

"Ah, yes, it is truly a wonder." The big man smiled awkwardly. "Well, I won't keep you, then. Cheers."

"See you soon, Mr. Boles."

Owen walked home with his mind still on the Margo dilemma. He checked his letterbox, knowing it would be empty, then went inside and made pizza dough, wondering if the date would last until dinner.

Soon, Margo was walking into his cottage, kissing him hello, her hard body pressing into him. She wore tight jeans and a V-neck sweater with no bra. Owen immediately doubted his ability to broach the subject.

"What a cute cottage."

"Thanks. I realize I have done little in the way of decorating."

"Well, you're just settling in. It's only been ten years, right?"

"Very funny."

"I didn't know you had a cat."

"Yeah, this is Guildy. Guildenstern, actually. I didn't know she was a girl when I named her," Owen said, thinking that was one of the few things she didn't know about him.

"So," she said, leading him to the couch. "We should talk."

"Uh oh, this sounds serious," he said jokingly, while actually quite mortified.

Margo took a deep breath and exhaled, looking him in the eyes. "So, don't freak out, Owen," she said, emphasizing his name, "but I know who you are."

"Yeah, I know," he said, "or at least I suspected," he said, catching himself.

Her brown eyes widened in surprise, eyebrows arched in a question.

"I saw a copy of my book on your desk," he said. Technically, it was true, and Owen saw no need to tell her about his break-in.

"Ah," she said, quietly nodding. "I suppose I owe you an explanation."

"No, let's just have dinner," he deadpanned, desperate to inject humor.

"My name is Margo Stark. I'm a freelance journalist from the Boston area. I followed your story quite closely. I was at a lecture at Oxford when I recognized you."

Owen smiled to himself. This woman had quite a way about her. She had just dropped a bomb of information. Yet, her glassy eyes and placid air had calmed him with a reassurance that all would be well.

Still wary, Owen continued to study her. She still hadn't said what her plans were now. "How did you recognize me? It's been so long, and my appearance has changed quite a bit." It wasn't the most pressing issue, but he'd been curious about it.

"I wish I could tell you," Margo began. "I remember watching you on television. There was a clip of you walking into the police station. The news stations played it over and over. It was an image that stayed with me. I remembered wondering why you were alone and not flanked by attorneys. And you have this very distinctive walk. I saw you in the queue at the lecture and I just knew immediately it was you."

"So," Owen began, "I should apologize for my dishonesty. For me, it's sort of become a way of life." She waved it off. "So, now what?" he asked.

"My story was going to be about Owen Prescott's life as a fugitive. Obviously, I didn't expect us to connect ..." She breathed deeply and took his hand. Her eyes glistened with forming tears. "I mean, Ancil, sorry, Owen, I feel like I need to hear..." She paused again. "Um..."

He touched her face. "It's okay," he said quietly. "It would be weird if you didn't ask. And the answer is no." He looked into her eyes solemnly and shook his head. "I didn't kill him."

"I'm so sorry to ask," she said, audible relief in her voice. "I know you didn't. I have no idea why, but I know it for certain." Later, Owen would realize that it was the first time he'd heard anyone say those words. His mom and April's belief in his innocence had been understood and so never voiced.

"So, what about your Owen Prescott, the fugitive, feature?" he asked. "That would be quite a scoop."

"I've been thinking I might want to change the focus a bit."

"Yeah? More of a travel guide to hiking in the Cotswolds?"

She laughed. "So, were you ever told what the evidence was against you?"

"I never saw the police reports, no. The D.A. refused to release them until I was formally charged. But supposedly, my DNA was at the crime scene, which has always baffled me."

"Yes, I recall that being leaked to the press. So,..." She hesitated, as if unsure of his reaction. "I have a contact in the D.A.'s Office. What say we see what we're up against, solve the case and win your freedom?"

Owen sat back on the sofa, closed his eyes and exhaled, squeezing Margo's hand. Ten minutes ago, he'd wondered if she would be his ticket to prison. He sat up and held her face in his hands and kissed her through his smile. "That sounds like a wonderful idea."

CHAPTER 53

Boston 2013

"That sounds like a terrible idea." Shortly after his meeting with Joe, Owen had called Detective Sevilla at the number left on his voicemail, then driven straight to April's. She'd listened to him in disbelief as he shared the news of his suspect status and upcoming appointment with the police.

"Owen, I know you want to proclaim your innocence, but this is getting scary. As much as you despise your dad and his attorneys, you should probably follow their advice. At least, listen to Joe."

"The whole thing is just so ridiculous. I'm sure that if I could just talk to them. How can they think I'm a murderer? I'd never hurt a flea."

"But that's the thing, Owen. They don't want to just talk to you. They want to interrogate you. However slimy your dad's advisor is, he's probably got good sources. For whatever reason, the police think you committed a murder." She paused. "I can't even believe this is happening. Anyway, they're not going to just let you tell your side of the story. You've seen it on television. They're going to intimidate you and threaten you and twist your words. Please don't do it."

"April, I'm not an idiot. Give me a little credit. I know I can end the interview..."

"Interrogation..."

"...interrogation any time I want. I just don't understand what evidence they could have. They're awaiting some test results."

"What kind of test results?"

"He didn't know."

"Well, that's good. DNA or fingerprint or whatever they have will show it's not you. But in the meantime, I really don't think you should talk to them."

"Here's the thing, April," he said. "I'm being accused of killing someone." Now, he shook his head, dumbfounded by his own words. "You know it will be leaked to the press. Probably already has been. And what do you think people will think when they read, 'Prescott, through his attorney, Mr. Slimy Slickster, declined to be interviewed by the police?' You know what you'd think if you read that."

"I'd probably think the guy is following the advice of his attorney, Owen. It happens all the time."

"I know it does," he said, putting his hands over his face. "Just not to me." He looked up at her and smiled. "Sorry, Pril. I feel like I have to do this," he said, getting to his feet.

"I know you do," she said, nodding stoically. "At least let me give you a ride."

They rode in silence, holding hands. As the police station came into view, it became clear that Owen's suspect status had already been leaked. News vans were double parked in front, and a group of reporters and cameras guarded the entrance. "Babe, are you sure you want to do this?" April asked, squeezing his hand.

"Yeah, I'll be fine," he said, but she could hear fear in his voice. "I'll call you when it's over." Owen walked quickly to the front door as the reporters converged, yelling questions his way. "Are you taking the allegations seriously? Do you expect to be charged? Will your family have another statement?"

He was greeted by a uniformed officer who escorted him down a hallway into a room barely large enough for its table and three chairs. All that was missing, Owen thought, taking a seat, was the light bulb hanging from the ceiling. The cop told him someone would be with him shortly, then left.

Down the hall, Sevilla and Jepson gathered their notes for the interrogation.

"How do we play this?" asked Jepson. "We have PC for the arrest."

"Tough call," answered his partner. "If we Mirandize, he might clam up. I think just play it free and easy and let him go home. Besides, the Chief will probably want to orchestrate some high-profile arrest."

"Sounds good to me."

The detectives' dilemma was one common to criminal investigations. The motive and papers at the scene had given them probable cause to arrest Owen for murder. However, if they took him into custody, they would have to recite his Miranda warning, informing him he had a right to remain silent and a right to an attorney. If they didn't warn him, his statement could not be used against him in court. Also, as Sevilla had pointed out, the warning often resulted in the arrestees invoking their right to remain silent.

On the other hand, if Owen was not under arrest, but rather free to leave the police station at any time, then they could forego the Miranda warning and his statement would be fair game.

Sevilla stood. "Okay, pards, let's go get a confession."

"Yeah, this one's already in my win column," said Jepson, moving toward the door.

The detectives bumped knuckles.

"Yeah, and we didn't even have to resort to Plan B to solve it."

"What was Plan B?"

"Getting the word on the street."

"Dear God, Lew. Please stop."

CHAPTER 54

Boston 2013

"Hello, Owen, I'm Lew Sevilla. This is Pete Jepson."

Owen stood and offered a sweaty hand. "Hello."

Sevilla took the lead. "Have a seat here in our luxury accommodations, Owen. Listen, we really appreciate your taking the time to come in."

Owen sat facing the doorway, across from the two detectives. "Sure."

"And just so you know, you're free to leave at any time." The detective's words were for the benefit of the invisible recording device, mounted in the ceiling. The statement meant that even if they didn't read the Miranda warning, their conversation would be admissible in court.

"Coming in here to tell us your side of what happened is actually a very intelligent move," the detective continued. "But as you can see, that door is not locked," he said, gesturing behind him, "and if you ever feel you need a break or want to leave, that's totally fine."

"Okay, thanks."

The detectives offered Owen a soda—he declined—then proceeded to take down his contact information. They already had the information but used it to establish a rapport and help him relax. They'd both noticed his clammy hands.

"So, Owen, here's the thing," said Sevilla, staring earnestly at his suspect. "For starters, we don't believe that you killed Norvel Anendale." Owen's instinct was to exhale in relief, but it sounded like there was a 'but' coming. "However, we have some evidence—some incontrovertible evidence—that you were at the scene of the murder near the time that it happened."

Owen stared at the detective, confused. He shook his head. "I wasn't. I don't understand how…"

The detective put up his hand. "Now, hold on, Owen. Sorry to cut you off, but I just want to emphasize that we don't just suspect you were there, okay. There is absolute proof of that fact."

Owen looked at the detective, the hint of a smile forming on his lips. The cop was smooth. He had to admit it. The pleasant manner, the assurance that he didn't believe in his guilt. But now he knew he was being played.

"Look Detective Sevilla, I understand that you have a job to do. But I also know you're not being truthful with me. I know that because I wasn't anywhere near the murder scene and so you cannot possibly have that evidence. If I had been there, then your plan to trick me into admitting it might work."

The detective sighed and looked at his partner. Jepson took the cue. "Owen, you're a smart guy and you seem to know a little bit about how this works. You're right that on occasion, my partner and I lie to people like you. If we thought you committed this murder but couldn't prove you were at the scene, we might lie to you and say we had the proof, hoping you'd admit it."

"And that's what's going on here?" Owen said, staring hard at the detective.

Jepson stared back. "Sir, we just met and I realize you have no reason to trust me. But I can tell you, unequivocally, that is not what is happening here. We have proof that you were there."

Owen shook his head in frustration and started to stand. Jepson showed him both palms and remained seated. "Please, just hear me out." Owen sunk into his chair.

"Like my partner said, we don't believe you murdered anyone. Frankly, seeing you in person now, I'm sure you didn't. But if you saw something, or the old guy attacked you, or you got there after it went down. If any of those things happened, you've got to tell us. Otherwise, this is not going to go..."

But Owen was up out of his chair, shuffling around the table toward the open door.

"Where were you on the evening of September 22, Owen?" Sevilla asked, knowing that Owen wouldn't answer.

"You guys have any more questions, call my lawyer," Owen said, fishing the attorney's card from his wallet and tossing it on the table.

"No, that's fine," Sevilla said pleasantly. "Thanks again for coming in, Owen. We'll see you soon." The last sentence echoed in Owen's ears as he dialed April for a ride home.

CHAPTER 55

Owen had told Margo of being spied by the woman with the clownish makeup and his suspicions about the black-haired woman. As usual, she had taken the news in stride and had comforted him with her soothing tone.

Now she stood behind him, massaging his shoulders as he sat on the couch. She leaned down and whispered in his ear. "For this woman with the regrettably oversized chest who seems to have gotten your attention, I see only one solution," she said, biting his neck.

"Oh," he said, smiling, "I feel a very wicked Annabelle Steves-like solution percolating in that wonderfully wicked brain of yours."

"Not at all," she deadpanned. "I will simply bring her to you, tie her up and torture her until she reveals her business in Tetbury."

"Oh, good. I was afraid you'd overreact."

"Then," she said, giggling, "I'll hold her down and tattoo 'slut' on her forehead. That ought to take care of her strutting around town."

"Wow, I hope she isn't collecting money for a church charity," he said, and they dissolved in laughter.

"So, seriously, Owen," Margo said, after their laughing fit had ended. "If I understand you, this woman has been around town for a few weeks now. You've seen her a few times, and you'd agree that it is safe to assume that she has seen you as well?"

"Yes," he confirmed, as her fingers worked the tension from his neck.

"So, if she was in law enforcement, she would have already arrested you." Her conclusion seemed so obvious.

Although Margo didn't have an easy answer for the gawking motorist, she'd shrugged it off as nearly irrelevant, given her plans to solve his case and prove his innocence. More than her pragmatic approach, her calming vibe had again massaged his mind. "My darling," she'd told him, as if seeing into the future as she spoke, "all will be well in the end."

Later, snuggled together on the couch, sipping a French Pinot Noir, they talked about the murder charges. Margo had read every article written in the papers, which had generally described the evidence against Owen. "Obviously, the most baffling thing to me is the DNA," Owen said, after she'd summarized the evidence.

"Yes, but there's so much we don't know about that, right? Was it supposedly a strand of hair, blood, perspiration, saliva? And was it found on the victim's clothing, on his body, on the floor, or on the rim of a glass you may have drunk from? Not to mention we don't have any information about the DNA analysis itself. I realize that your dad's source in the D.A.'s Office was probably solid, but there are too many unknowns to waste time on it. The police reports should be here in a few days."

"I see your point. So, what then?" asked Owen, content to let her lead the discussion.

"How about these reports that something of yours was left at the scene? Any idea what it was?"

"My advisor said it was my handwritten notes from my novel, *Orchards of Grace*. Again, no idea how that's possible." Owen found himself suddenly extremely attracted to Margo. It was something about the combination of her analytical mind and tranquil presence. It reminded him of one of those sultry computer-generated voices that announced the next stop on trains in England.

"So, obviously, these notes would have been valuable to Anendale's lawsuit. Who would want him to succeed? An enemy of yours, right?"

"Makes sense," he said, trying to focus.

"So, did anyone at the college ask for your notes, for the library or anything?"

"No, not that I recall." Owen wished he'd thought of this ten years ago. He supposed he'd been too overwhelmed to think clearly. That and he hadn't wanted to believe it was happening.

Margo continued methodically. "How about recent thefts?" Owen searched his memory.

Owen thought of his former stalker for the first time since he'd fled. "Well, someone broke into my apartment a few weeks before the murder. My laptops were taken, but no hand-written notes." Now, Owen's mind leaped to his own break-in at Margo's and he immediately felt guilty.

"So, you don't think it was related to the lawsuit?"

"It was a weird situation," he said vaguely, wanting to change the subject. "I suppose the notes could have gone missing without me knowing it."

Margo looked at him with a sideways glance. "You wouldn't happen to know anything about break-ins, would you?"

Owen closed his eyes and winced. "Oh babe. I'm so sorry. I was going to tell you."

Margo smiled. "It's okay. You were probably freaked out after seeing your book."

"How did you know I was there?"

"It's hard to explain," she said. "I sort of sensed your presence when I came back to check the stove. So, back to your break-in. Your notes could have been stolen then." She stopped talking and was looking at the ceiling, clearly working something out in her mind.

"What is that wonderful mind of yours thinking?"

"Here's the thing that I can't quite figure out," she said, ignoring his compliment. "It looks like someone framed you, right?"

"Yes, I'd say so."

"But to murder just so you can frame someone. It's a bit extreme, isn't it? I mean, if they hated you that much and were willing to murder…"

"Why not just murder me?"

"Exactly." They shared a laugh, then sipped their wine, thinking. "So, were you seeing anyone romantically at the time?" Owen was taken aback by the question, and it showed. "Sorry, I'm just turning over stones here," she said. "Hell hath no fury, and all that."

"No, I get it," he said. "There was someone, but we parted on good terms. There was no one that felt jilted or anything like that." Owen's mind strayed to his stalker again. What was her name? Desiree Richards, no Richins. Technically, she had been very publicly rebuked. But she'd seemed barely capable of finding her way to court, let alone orchestrating a murder.

Owen and Margo talked more about the case. She asked about his life in Boston—friends, his writing, his daily routine—gently coaxing memories from him. After two hours, they took a break to pick vegetables from his garden and ate bread, cheese and a salad of broccoli, kale, and beets.

"Tell me about her—your romantic interest." Margo asked, opening a second bottle of wine.

Owen hesitated. "She was lovely," he said quietly. "But obviously, that was a long time ago."

"Was she at all like me?"

"A bit, I suppose," he answered, feeling uncomfortable thinking about April. "I don't know. It's been a long time since I've thought of her."

"Sorry if I've made you uncomfortable," she said, leaning in for a kiss. "You can ask me an uncomfortable question," she said with a coy smile.

"Okay, I will," Owen said, playing along. "What, in God's name, is up with your ridiculously ripped stomach?"

"That's the best you can do?" she asked, laughing.

"Yeah, I guess 'Why are you so hot?' is not exactly a ball buster."

"Well," she said, "I have a little ritual of pretty intense core exercises I do most nights. It's more for my mental health—just to lose myself in the battle of the workout."

"Interesting," he said. "Maybe that's what allows you to exude such a soothing vibe."

"Flattery will get you everywhere, Owen Prescott," she said, wrapping her arms around his neck. "And I'm sorry again about the questions about your ex. I suppose I'm just wanting to know what makes you happy."

Owen smiled into Margo's brown eyes. "Especially given recent events," he said, "I can't imagine being in a better frame of mind. I owe that to you." He paused. "And I'm sorry about not telling you about my break-in." She pulled away from him and walked toward his bedroom.

"C'mon and make it up to me, cowboy," she said, peaking over her shoulder. "I'm skipping my core workout tonight, so I need some exercise."

CHAPTER 56

Boston 2013

As Owen entered his father's office for his second visit with him and his band of sycophants, the nauseating smell enveloping him, a collage of memories like the wooden car race and the goose incident flooded his mind. He heard the closet door slam tight, sealing him in complete darkness, his dad's angry barks echoing throughout the house, his mother's soft, mournful weeping.

The men were discussing the logistics and timing of his flight as if it was a foregone conclusion. "My sources predict charges by the end of the week," baldy was saying, addressing his boss. "Likely Thursday morning to optimize the news cycle. They'll expect a surrender by evening, so he should be on a plane by Wednesday, just to be safe.

"I've prepared some choices of locations, optimizing security. I'm partial to South America but we can make any of the options work. Passports, visas, and credit cards and a secured bank account are all in the works. I'll review the travel and communication protocols before he leaves."

"What the fuck is happening?" Owen asked, scarcely believing his ears.

"Look, Owen, South America is just a suggestion. We can make somewhere else work."

"No, I mean, why are we talking about me leaving?"

But the men talked over him, continuing about specifics of a trip that had already been planned. Finally, the older attorney, sensing that Owen was about to lose it, addressed him. "Owen, we've received some new information from our source inside the D.A.'s Office. Apparently, the victim was impaled on a literary award, which obviously plays into your motive. Also, there are several witnesses who saw your rather violent outburst in a bar last week when asked about the lawsuit. Finally, and most damming, there is evidence that the fatal struggle was over pages filled with your handwriting—apparently, notes about your book."

The attorney's words buckled Owen's knees. He grasped the back of a chair, steadying himself, and tried to make sense of them. The men began talking logistics again, their comments muffled by the questions pounding against his skull. Anendale was impaled on his Cupcarthe Pyramid? An image of the old man with a wedge driven in his chest flashed through his mind, turning his stomach. It was the first time Owen had pictured the death. And they think I did that? And what was this about pages of his writing?

"How do they know the pages were mine?" he asked lamely.

The attorney turned toward him while in mid-sentence, frowning at the interruption. "Handwriting analysis," he replied curtly, before turning back to address Owen's father.

Owen's mind went to his interview with the police. Apparently, they hadn't been bluffing. "But I'm innocent," Owen mumbled.

"Owen," the attorney said, irritably. "The evidence is not overwhelming, but it is very strong. Upon arrest, you'd be jailed. There is no bail available for murder charges. You'd sit in a cell for a year awaiting trial. Then, in my estimation, and that of our trial team, you'd likely be convicted and sentenced to life in prison without the possibility of parole. You would die in a cell."

Over the years to come, Owen would think about this meeting, remembering it like it was yesterday. But it would be months before he recognized it had been orchestrated by his father to play on all of his insecurities. Later in the meeting, when Owen had voiced opposition to the plan, the advisor had repeated the reference to a lifetime in a cell. Not just in prison, but in a cell. Owen was sure the words had been chosen by his father, selected to play on his claustrophobia.

"You couldn't possibly do that to your mother," his dad had told him, addressing him personally for once. "You know how she could never bear to see you suffer." He'd used everything at his disposal. Anything to avoid a drawn-out trial that would sully his reputation and, no doubt, somehow hurt his precious bottom line.

Owen also questioned whether his relationship with April, in a bizarre way, may have contributed to his decision to leave. Given his history, he'd been wondering how he would manage to sabotage the relationship. Perhaps his flight was simply a different, albeit more spectacular battle in his mind's reckless war against his own happiness.

He'd ruined everything with April. Although she'd said she understood, he knew it wasn't true. No sane person would have. In fact, April had said exactly that when he first mentioned leaving. "This is insane, Owen. You're innocent. You need to stay and fight."

At least for that night, Owen held firm against the men. He would stay, he'd told them emphatically, before storming out. In the end, though, his dad had known that he hated confrontation. Compared to his encounter with his friend at the stupid wooden car race, the thought of a trial—the ultimate confrontation—made him sick to his stomach. He had barely handled the court date with the stalker.

Deep down, just as his father had planned, Owen knew that thoughts of a lifetime in a cramped cell and the whimpers of his grieving mother would be too much to overcome.

CHAPTER 57

Owen awoke with Margo's head on his chest, feeling the rejuvenation of a long, deep sleep. He gently slid from beneath her body and stood, looking down at her lean form and tousled hair. Their sex had been as intense and physical as the first time, and he stretched his back on the way to the bathroom. Dousing his face in the sink, he rose and smiled into the mirror at the sight of a rather savage looking bruise on the left side of his neck.

This woman was a wonderful enigma, he thought, as he showered. On one hand, her placid demeanor had an almost hypnotizing effect on him. But somewhere below the surface, whether she was forcing her body to its physical limit or ravaging him in bed, a firestorm of energy and emotion raged. She seemed so composed and upbeat, and yet he'd seen scars on her wrists and she'd referenced a difficult childhood.

After he dressed and made coffee, he kneeled and whispered in her ear. "Back soon. Going for breakfast." She murmured something and burrowed under the covers. Then, as he was walking out the front door, she called out, "Wear a hoodie, babe."

"Thanks," he called back, taking the sweatshirt off its peg. "Case in point," Owen said to himself, pulling on the hoodie as he walked down the path to the street. "Her brain never really stops."

On his walk, he assessed his whirlwind ride with his new lover. While he couldn't say he was yet head over heels for Margo, it was trending that way. Apart from the thrilling sex, he thought, smiling as he touched his hickey, she gave him someone with whom he could be completely honest. Amidst his life of lies in Tetbury, it was an immense relief to have someone he wasn't constantly deceiving.

Margo's actions also showed that she cared about him in a way few others had. She had never questioned his innocence and had obviously put a lot of time into thinking about his murder charges. Also, as her call from slumber had shown this morning, she seemed determined to keep him safe.

More than anything, though, Margo had given Owen hope that someday he could reclaim his life. This was the reason for the bounce in his step as he strode down the sidewalk in downtown Tetbury. He thought of her hard body, sharp mind, and mesmerizing vibe. Okay, he said to himself, maybe he was head over heels for her.

He walked into Balfrey's and ordered croissants to go. If he hadn't looked up on the chalkboard behind the counter to read the soup of the day, he would have missed it. There, mounted in the corner at the ceiling was a slender, pistol shaped camera, its lens angled down to the counter. Owen quickly looked down. Thank goodness for Margo and her last-second reminder about his hoodie.

On the way back, the ample form of Mr. Boles crossed the street in front of him, no doubt on his way to visit Mrs. Pembroke. They greeted each other and shared small talk on the way.

"Mr. Boles, I mentioned before that my nephew has a prosthesis. I've heard they are developing ones with the sense of touch. Have you heard of such a thing?"

"Oh, yes. Yes, indeed," he said. "Quite amazing stuff."

"Do you know? Are those on the market yet?"

"As an actual matter of fact, Ancil, I'm more on the distribution side. I haven't come across a model with that feature."

"I see. Well, Mr. Boles, have a nice day."

"And you do the same."

Margo had showered and was wearing one of his shirts, sipping coffee on his couch, when he arrived. "Hi, lover," she said, standing to greet him with a kiss. "Thanks for the coffee. I'll pour you a cup." Owen had to admit, her presence in his house seemed very natural.

He told her about the camera at Balfrey's. "Thanks so much for the hoodie reminder," he said, helping himself to a croissant.

"Stick with me, kid," she said, winking. "I'll take care of you."

"I'm getting that distinct impression," he said, failing to hide a goofy smile.

"Listen," she said, sounding serious, "I hate to say it, but it seems like with your photos up in the post office, it's only a matter of time before someone recognizes you."

"Seems that way, yes," he conceded. "So," he paused, his eyebrows raised in a question.

"So, either you confine yourself to your home to be my sex slave or we'd better solve this murder mystery."

"I choose all the above," he said, leaning in to kiss her.

"Good. Now, back to work, tiger," she said, gently pushing him away.

"Okay," he said, moving to the other side of the couch. "Where were we?"

"I was about to ask you about the night Anendale was murdered. According to the newspaper account, the time of death on the evening of September 22 was around 9:30 p.m."

"Yes. I had plans to have dinner with Joe. Unbelievably, he ended up having a date for the first time in a decade. I met him for a beer at about 5:00 p.m., then walked home to write."

"I assume you've thought about all this, but did you make any calls around the time of the murder? Order a pizza, anything?"

"No. Got home around 6:45p.m. and then turned off my phone to write."

Margo closed her eyes, concentrating. "Well," she said finally, "I suppose Joe could testify that you originally had plans for dinner. That would mean that you would have planned to murder

Anendale on the spur of the moment." She stood, walked to the kitchen and poured a cup of coffee.

"That's actually good. What, did I supposedly say, 'Oh well, Joe canceled; guess I'll go commit a murder?' You're good at this, Margo."

"Okay, so what did you see when you got home?" She handed him the coffee.

"I don't know. It's been so long."

"You know," she said, "as an undergraduate, I studied how memory works," she said, pulling Owen's shirt over her head and tossing it on the floor.

"Really?" Owen whispered, his wide eyes devouring her rippling stomach and perky breasts.

"Yes," she said. "It turns out that our brain stores memories in a labyrinth of pathways. And when we try hard to remember something, we often search down the same path over and over. Follow me?" she asked, moving a step closer to him.

"Yes," he nodded, maintaining his gaze.

"But," she continued, "it turns out that when our minds are distracted—when we stop trying so hard to remember—it frees us to travel down different paths. That's why when you stop trying to remember something, it suddenly pops into your head."

"Interesting. Well, consider me distracted," he said, smiling, as Margo walked behind him.

"So relax and take me through what you saw that night," she said, rubbing his shoulders.

"Let's see," Owen said, breathing deeply. "I walked home from the bar. I remember being anxious. This woman had been stalking me and there'd been a few break-ins at our apartment."

"That's creepy. Okay, you're walking home, anxious. What did you see when you got home?" she asked.

"Will had ordered a pizza. I had a piece and put the rest on our porch for a homeless guy in the neighborhood."

"Is your desk in your room visible from the street?"

"Yes."

"Well, if the homeless guy picked up the pizza, he may have seen you."

"I never thought of that," he said. "Of course, good luck finding him now."

"Was Will home?"

"Yes. I saw a light on in his room."

"What else, Owen?"

"I think his girlfriend was there," he said, pausing. "Yes, I smelled cookies. Then I went in my room, turned off my phone, and wrote."

Margo sat next to him on the couch. Owen could see her wheels were turning. "Did you see the cookies," she asked after a time.

"What?"

"The cookies. Did you see them or were they still in the oven when you got home?"

Owen searched his memory. "I don't remember seeing them."

"And the door to your bedroom was closed?" she asked.

"Maybe ajar, but I would have likely closed it."

"And if, for example, Will's girlfriend came out of his room to get the cookies out of the oven…"

"Jesus," Owen said, as recognition spread across his face, "she would have passed by my room. Would have seen my light on, maybe even heard me typing." He collapsed back on the couch, shaking his head. He'd asked Will if he knew he was home but hadn't thought to have him ask his girlfriend. Now, if she had noticed him, Owen wondered if there was any chance she would remember. Margo read his mind.

"I know," she said, holding his hand. "If only you'd thought of these things back then. But you were freaked out and scared."

"Or if I would have just stuck around, eventually, the cops would have interviewed Will and his girlfriend."

"I know, Owen, but the past is the past. We can piece this together now. I know we can." They embraced and kissed.

"Hey, by the way, nice hickey, Dracula," he teased, pulling down his shirt to show her handiwork.

Margo smiled. "Good. I figured I'd send a message to all these buxom women strutting around town."

"All these buxom women?" he asked, chuckling. "Here, in Tetbury?"

"Yes. I heard they're coming out with a calendar soon."

"Well," he said, taking her face in his hands for another kiss, "I'm partial to the petite, fit type, anyway."

"Good answer, Prescott. I'm going for a run."

"Okay. By the way, Margo, would you think a prosthetics company in the Cotwolds needs a distributor?"

CHAPTER 58

Boston 2013

Even as Owen dialed Joe's number, he knew it was a mistake. It was never the crime, but always the coverup, after all. But the meeting with his dad and his lackeys had him rattled to the core.

He couldn't imagine saying goodbye to his life, to April. After all, he was innocent, wasn't he? He'd even begun to doubt that, his mind wandering down blind alleys, searching to make sense of everything. Was it possible something horrible had happened and he'd blocked it out? He'd been known to sleepwalk from time to time but surely he'd recall something like this. "Jesus, Owen," he'd said aloud to himself, driving away from the meeting. "Get a fucking grip."

Of course, rationally, he knew he was innocent. He also knew that he should stay and sort everything out. Running, especially in the age of digital footprints, seemed absurd. Maybe there were DNA samples that would prove his innocence. Still, the prospect of prison sent a surge of panic through his body. He could barely withstand a two-minute elevator ride, let alone a lifetime in a cell.

"Hi, Joe. Thanks for meeting me," he said, taking a seat in a coffee shop near his apartment. "Look, I know you probably think I don't trust your judgment, but…"

Joe cut in, dismissing the words with a wave. "Hey, Owen. Forget it. How are you holding up?" his friend asked, compassion in his voice.

"Not well, actually."

Joe scooted his chair closer and lowered his voice. "So, for what it's worth, I hear from the D.A.'s Office that you'll be charged."

"That's what I hear. Typically, my dad is freaking out."

"What's he have in mind?"

Owen hesitated. If he really was going to go through with this, the fewer people he told the better, if only for their sakes. "Just the usual bullshit. Trying to bully me."

"Well, your dad probably arranged for some high-priced attorney, but just know that I'm here if you need me?" Joe wanted to tell him he'd be making a mistake going with some white-collar defense attorney who rarely went to trial. He wanted to tell him that in front of a jury, he was the best and if anyone was going to argue for his freedom, he wanted it to be him.

But he didn't. Joe didn't want to appear boastful, but that wasn't the reason. He owed Owen the truth, after all. In the end, he held his tongue because he could see the familiar, beaten look in his friend's eyes. Once again, Owen was going to obey his father, whatever his advice. Like when he'd gone out for the high school football team despite having no interest in the sport, or when he'd taken an internship with an investment banker in college. "Any progress on your alibi?" Joe asked.

Owen shook his head. "According to what the D.A. said in their press conference, the murder occurred around 9:30 p.m. After our beer, I just went home and there's literally no way to prove it. Didn't order food or make an online purchase. Will was home, but he was in his room with his girlfriend. Had no idea I was home."

"Phone calls?"

"No, I turned my phone off."

Joe nodded. "Which you always do when you write, but now it looks like you were trying to hide your location."

"Exactly."

"What's your attorney advise?" Joe asked. "Not that you'll follow his advice," he chided.

"I don't know. All the attorney ever does is recite the damning evidence against me and tell me how bleak prison is, which I'm well aware of."

Joe paused, as a patron walked by their table. "So," he said quietly, leaning in. "How can I help?"

Owen was staring off into space, thinking of a tiny prison cell. "Huh?"

"You said it was urgent. How can I help?"

On the drive to meet his agent, Owen had imagined a conversation that now seemed absurd. "So, what time did you leave the pub that night?" Owen would ask, feigning actual confusion. Then he'd add casually, "Because apparently, the murder happened sometime after 9:30 p.m."

"Oh, I'm not sure," Joe would respond, also attempting to sound sincere, "but I'm pretty sure we were together until 9:20 p.m., maybe later."

Now, sitting across the table from his friend, Owen was ashamed he'd even considered dragging Joe into his mess. "Sorry to drag you down here. I think I just needed to vent to someone."

"No problem. I can't imagine the stress you must be under," Joe said, getting up to leave. "If you think of anything—anything at all—call me. Also, so if you want to ditch your dad's attorney, like I said, I'm a better attorney than an agent."

Owen looked him in the eye. "Thanks, Joe. For everything." Then he reached into his pocket and presented a plain white envelope. "Hopefully, we can go together. If not, have fun."

"Thanks, Owen. Wow, game six. If they win tonight, that might be the clincher. We have to go together, right?"

"Take care, Joe."

Joe hesitated, a thought running through his mind as he turned to leave. He wondered whether he'd ever see Owen again.

CHAPTER 59

Boston 2013

Owen drove to April's apartment and, to her horror, recounted the meeting with his father. As usual, she settled his frenzied mind. Owen could tell she thought that leaving wasn't the answer, no matter the state of the evidence. "You're innocent, Owen. I have to believe that the truth will come out. Have you asked Joe? This is his profession, after all."

"Yeah," he said absently.

But April had seen his father's effect on Owen before. No matter how much Owen said he despised him, she sensed that years of Owen's mental torture still hung from his neck like a shock collar. She'd seen him flinch at the mere mention of his father and had witnessed his panic attacks when faced with the slightest confinement.

Owen sat on a kitchen stool and opened a bottle of Cabernet while April boiled pasta. "Last time, the advisor told you the D.A. was awaiting some sort of scientific test results. Did he have an update on those?"

Owen shrugged and shook his head. "This time he mentioned a handwriting analysis, but I don't know if there are other tests outstanding."

"So, there's still a chance that a DNA test will clear you, right?" Owen nodded. "Promise me you won't do anything rash until we find out about the tests?"

Owen took a deep breath and managed a smile as he poured wine into two glasses. "Yes, of course," he said, "and thanks for talking me off the ledge. Sorry I'm such a wreck."

She came over for a kiss, then stepped back to gaze at him, her warm brown eyes caressing his soul. They smiled at each other, sharing an unspoken message.

Owen's phone rattled loudly on the countertop, abruptly ending the moment. He read Private on the screen and guessed the caller.

"Hello." His serious tone caught April's attention. "Yes, the DNA test. Well?" he asked anxiously. April watched his face turn from concern to bewilderment and finally to horror as he looked into her eyes. She knew the news before he spoke.

"How the fuck is it your DNA, Owen?" she asked after he'd hung up, desperation in her voice.

It didn't occur to Owen that April, just for a moment, may have doubted his innocence. Over the years, though, as he replayed the worst moment of his life, he wondered.

CHAPTER 60

Owen tried to control his breathing as the trail snaked up the hill on steep switchbacks. Ahead of him, Margo seemed weightless under her backpack, her tight shorts in his field of vision, the perfect motivation to keep up. They had left at dawn and driven north, arriving in England's Peak District on a warm spring day. Margo had scouted out a trail that was not for the faint of heart.

"How are you doing back there?" she called back without stopping.

"Couldn't be better," Owen replied between breaths.

"Yeah?" she asked, hearing his labored breathing. "How about a break?" she asked at the end of a long switchback, turning to offer a water bottle.

"Oh, I mean, I feel awesome," he said between breaths.

"Oh, I can see that. No question," she said, beaming, as he drank from her bottle. "Okay," she said, and turned uphill again.

"Of course," Owen said, gasping after his drink, "if you'd like a quick break, that would be just fine." She laughed and turned back to him, moving close.

"Well," she said, pausing for a kiss, "I think I want a break."

"Bless you, Margo," he said, collapsing back against the hillside.

"Seriously," she said. I hope this has been okay. I thought it would be good to get away. Forget about things for a day."

"It's great, really. Thank you." They took in the view of emerald hills, checkered with short, stone fences and valleys of pine and poplar. "The scenery is beautiful," Owen said, pulling her close, "especially the view from behind my guide."

"Okay, Prescott, keep your pants on. Another half mile, then it's downhill to a surprise," she said, and kissed him again.

"I love surprises."

"Really?" she asked, starting up the trail.

"Yes," he said, catching up, "tell me something I don't know about you."

"Okay, remember when that woman fell on her face in front of you in the street in Oxford?" she asked.

"Oh! You little scamp!" he said, swatting her butt. "It actually crossed my mind that it was you for a second. What in God's name were you doing?" he asked, laughing.

"Well," she giggled, "I wasn't entirely sure it was you, so my plan was to walk past you for a closer look. I didn't plan on falling at your feet."

"Yes," he said, "I suppose not."

"Then I followed you to your car," she said.

"Really?"

Margo paused, remembering the evening. "It was thrilling, actually," she said. "I recall you kept looking behind you and I'd have to duck behind a car."

"Wow, a true sleuth."

"Then, as you drove away, I was able to make out a 'Try Tetbury' bumper sticker."

"Of course," Owen sighed, picturing the peeling sticker on the Rover's back bumper. He thought for a moment as the trail turned downhill. "And did you happen to follow me in your car that night?"

"I may have," she said coyly, then laughed. "All the way to Tetbury, until you pulled some slick maneuver and lost me."

"The old Rover was put to its limits that night. Anyway, I'm very happy you tracked me down."

"Me too," she said, and turned to face him for a kiss.

Owen held her hands in front of his face. He'd seen the scars on her wrists before but figured she'd talk about them when she was ready. He kissed each wrist and looked deep into her eyes, smiling an unspoken message. She smiled and nodded. "Thanks," she whispered, and kissed his cheek.

Soon they emerged through a shaded grove of silver birch to a shimmering lake. "What do you think?" she asked, throwing down her pack at the base of a tree.

"I think you are full of surprises, Margo Cummings," Owen said, his eyes finally leaving her ass. "It's gorgeous."

"Derwent Lake. Or maybe Reservoir. Doesn't it look perfect?" she asked, kicking off her boots.

"You're going in?" he asked.

Margo peeled off her shirt. "After that hike, are you kidding?"

Owen steeled himself with a deep breath, "Okay, so, we're doing this."

She smiled, raised her eyebrows, and nodded, flinging her panties on her backpack. She tiptoed across a narrow beach of crushed stone and was in with a shallow dive.

Owen followed, the cold taking his breath as he swam to her. All at once, as he smiled into Margo's face, he felt an exhilarating relief. There, naked in nature and spirit, he felt freedom from the heavy cloak of his secret life. "I'm falling for you," he said, the words slipping past his lips just as she bobbed underwater to clear the hair from her face. He didn't think she'd heard him, but kissed her before she could respond, just in case.

And even though he'd skinny-dipped once before on a memorable first date, on this night his beloved April never crossed his mind.

CHAPTER 61

Boston 2013

Owen and April both knew it would be their last night together. Given the news of the DNA evidence, April realized that convincing Owen to stay was out of reach. Still, she needed to sort out the murder for her own peace of mind. She sipped wine on the couch, leaning against him. "So, before we found out about the DNA," she said, "I thought the evidence against you was just a series of unfortunate coincidences."

"And now?" he asked.

"I mean, not to sound alarmist, but…" She paused.

"Babe, I'm being charged with murder. By all means, sound the alarm."

She smiled, admiring Owen's ability to find humor in his plight. "Well, it certainly seems like you're being framed. And not by some half-crazed stalker. Getting your DNA to the murder scene, stealing your notes. This is a well-orchestrated plan by someone with means."

"Yeah, seems that way," Owen said, drinking his wine, then staring at the ceiling. "And funny you mention the stalker," he added. "I wish you could have seen her in court. It's hard to explain, but she seemed straight out of central casting—almost like she was putting on an act."

"Interesting. Maybe someone somehow used her as a ruse to get your DNA and steal your notes." April shook her head at the absurdity of it all. "I can't even believe any of this."

They talked about his potential enemies—jealous former classmates, jilted exes, someone he'd unwittingly offended in his book. None of them seemed remotely motivated enough to launch such an extreme attack, and they went to bed as confused as ever.

They both agreed that it didn't seem right to make love, nor even to speak about their feelings for each other. They knew how each other felt and neither wanted the other to suffer more than was necessary.

Both Owen and April had experienced emotional break-ups, but this was much different. They weren't breaking up, after all. Cruelly, amidst their zenith of happiness, their relationship was about to end. And there would be no reconciliations or second chances. As a couple, they were simply about to vanish, with the finality of and emptiness of death. There weren't the pangs of guilt, nor the sting of rejection. As they lay in bed, holding each other for one last night, waiting for their relationship to die, there was only profound sadness.

They spoke briefly of staying in touch, laying out the depressing ground rules. There would be no calls, texts or online communication. Owen would write when it was safe, mailing to a private mailbox under the name Prill Nesnom—Monsen spelled backwards.

Owen was up early in the morning, quietly packing as April slept. His departure was surreal. He didn't know what to take with him—a photo of his mom, a few changes of clothes and toiletries. He looked back at April one last time, his vision blurred by tears. Then he headed to his family's home.

There, he found his mother, who was strong, telling him it would all be sorted out and he'd be home in no time. She told him she'd chosen the Cotswolds for him as his home, recalling his love of the area. She'd chosen his name as well. He would be Ancil Bradford—after two of their favorite modern artists. She'd baked him cookies for the trip, of course, and Owen promised to return some day, intending to keep his promise.

Then it was one last trip inside his father's office. Owen was surprised to find only the advisor there. He'd assumed that his father would be there to gloat. The bald man distributed his various identifications and credit cards, then walked Owen through a thirty-page protocol for his life as a fugitive. He would travel under a second alias in a circuitous route to Berlin, then make his way to his home in the Cotswolds on trains, buses, and a ferry across the North Sea. "Ancil Bradford," he said to himself, as he rode to the airport, still not quite believing what was happening.

As he arrived at Logan Airport, April was stirring for the first time in his bed. She smelled a box of donuts on the bed next to her and smiled through tears as she read a hand-written note taped to the box.

April,

I'm sorry I wasn't stronger. The donuts are a reminder of our first night together. The following is a far cry from your brother's poetry, but at least it rhymes.

For witty quips and brown eyes warm
Lips on fire and luscious form
For showing me my soul's true mate
And riding through our waves of fate
For baring hearts, so many laughs
Forgiving all my many gaffes
For golf and sex and sleeping late
Then morning sex, more sleeping late
For sharing minds and stopping time
While linking hands or drinking wine
From skinny-dip to our last night
From our first glance until my flight
Please know I will always love you.

CHAPTER 62

Owen was shocked at the police report's clinical description of the macabre scene.

...The victim, later identified as Norvel Anendale, was prone on his back, with a pyramid-shaped instrument protruding from his abdomen. Closer inspection revealed the weapon to be a trophy. Blood was still oozing from the wound and had pooled on the floor. Advanced rigor mortis was apparent. A garrote was cinched tight around his neck. No petechia was visible.

The reports had arrived from Margo's contact in the D.A.'s Office the afternoon after their hiking excursion, and they sat on his couch, poring over them.

Owen searched his memory to recall Anendale's face, then pictured him savagely attacked and dying alone. His mind flashed on the goose from his childhood, frightened and suffering. "It's just so awful," he said.

"I just can't believe they think I am responsible for this," Owen said, his thoughts returning to the present.

Margo turned to kiss his cheek. "I know, babe. But we have to focus."

"You're right," he said, exhaling. "What are your impressions?"

"Well, honestly, I can certainly see why you were charged," Margo said, thumbing through the reports.

Owen nodded. "Yeah, the motive, the symbolic use of the Cupcarthe, the papers scattered around the body, not to mention the DNA. I hate to say it, but my dad was right. I can't imagine a jury not convicting me with this evidence."

"I wonder if the killer stuck around to watch him suffer," Margo wondered out loud.

Owen turned his head slowly toward her and broke into laughter. "Babe, that is one sick and twisted thought."

"Well, just wondering," she said, returning the laugh. "Maybe one too many Annabelle Steves novels for me. I was hoping to get the DNA reports. My guy in the D.A.'s Office said he'd send them soon, along with copies of the crime scene photos."

"Those will be pleasant to see," Owen said sarcastically.

"It would be nice to know what it was—blood, hair, saliva, sweat…"

"Semen," added Owen.

"Ugh, Owen," Margo said, elbowing him in the shoulder. "Who's twisted now?"

"Sorry, but absolutely nothing would surprise me now. And you're right, it seems like knowing what it was will give us a clue who put it there."

Owen looked at the address of the victim. "3768 College Drive," he said, searching his memory. "For some reason, that sounds familiar."

"Well, if you'd been there before, that would obviously be important. Is there any chance that Anendale hosted a mixer for the English Department?" Margo asked.

"I don't think so. Maybe the address is familiar because I saw it on some of Anendale's lawsuit paperwork."

Margo got up to stretch. "By the way," she said, kicking off her boots, "I saw your black-haired friend chatting up Brodie as I was leaving."

"Yeah? What'd you think?"

"Well, buxom, as advertised," she said, shooting an exaggerated frown his way. "I'm going to pretend you didn't notice, though. I only saw them chatting from a distance, but it didn't appear that he was at all interested in what she was selling."

"That's not surprising. I can't imagine Brodie thinking that a video camera was a good idea. He strikes me as not exactly a fan of the government."

"Yeah, he probably cursed her in Gaelic."

They were quiet for a time, both thinking about the police reports.

"You know," Owen said finally, "when I'd heard about my hand-written notes being at the scene, I'd assumed they'd been found stacked somewhere, hidden away. The description in the police report makes clear they were scattered around the body—as if there had been a struggle over them."

Margo bent over and touched her palms to the floor. "Why did you assume that?"

"I'm not sure," said Owen, trying to piece things together in his mind. "Well, presumably," he began, "Anendale's possession of the papers would be potentially bad news for my lawsuit. So, if I went to the trouble of killing him…"

"Yes," she said, standing, her eyes brightening in recognition, "you would absolutely make sure you took the papers with you."

They talked about the odd combination of strangulation and bludgeoning. "It's very weird," said Margo. "You mentioned the stalker seemed fake, somehow. The whole murder scene seems staged."

"And yet, Anendale was killed. That part was real," Owen said solemnly.

"It will be helpful when we know where the DNA was found. If it was on a glass that you drank from, it would be easy for someone to just leave it at the scene. Join me for a run?" she asked, lacing up her running shoes.

"Pass," said Owen. "I'd slow you down. Dinner later?"

"Sure."

After she'd gone, Owen sat at his desk to write, blinking away images of Anendale's corpse, conjured in his mind from the police reports. Soon, he heard the familiar sound of Mrs. Pembroke's heels on his stone path.

He opened the door and she breezed in. "Hello, Owen," she said cheerfully. "Isn't it a splendid spring day?" She wore a pink and purple dress, its neck and sleeves lined with ruffles, and matching pink heels.

"Yes, it is, Mrs. Pembroke, and don't you look nice."

"Oh," she said, waving off the compliment, "it is a fun dress, I must say, but I'm afraid I look a bit like an over-decorated Easter egg."

"Don't be silly," Owen said, putting the kettle on the stove. "You look great. May I offer you some tea and biscuits?"

"Oh no, I'm on my way out."

"I don't suppose you have a date later with a certain purveyor of artificial limbs?"

"Goodness, what a morbid sounding description. But as a matter of fact, I do."

"Mrs. Pembroke, you're seeing quite a lot of this fellow."

"Oh, you're one to talk," she said, shooting him a scolding look over her glasses, "or will you be wearing a skirt with those?" she asked, gesturing toward Margo's boots.

"Very well played," replied Owen, chuckling.

"Tell me though, how many people in the Cotswolds do you suppose have prosthetics?"

"Well, I surely would have no idea. I don't like to bother him with talk about his work."

"Does he have an office nearby?"

"Yes, in Swindon, apparently. He's very high up in the company," she said proudly.

"Is that right? Do you know what his duties are, exactly?"

"My, you're full of questions, Ancil. Why so curious?"

"I don't mean to be impertinent," Owen replied. "I suppose I'm just feeling a bit protective of you."

"Well, that's nice, I suppose, but Mr. Boles has proven quite a gentleman." Mrs. Pembroke flashed a mischievous smile. "In fact, in some ways," she said, blushing, "I quite wish he were less of one, if you get my meaning?"

"Mrs. Pembroke, you surprise me," he said with a chuckle. "Well, I'm glad I have nothing to worry about."

"No indeed," she said. "In fact, it seems that Mr. Boles has taken an interest in you."

"How so?" Owen asked, suddenly serious.

"He just asks about you. Says he wouldn't mind having a pint with you sometime," she said, making her way to the door.

Owen sighed audibly as he opened the door for her. "Mrs. Pembroke, given my, um, situation, I have to say that makes me a little nervous."

"Oh, not to worry a bit, Ancil. I can say for sure that Mr. Boles is not exactly the literary type. Wouldn't know you from Shakespeare himself. Your secret is safe," she said, pausing in the doorway to inhale the spring air. "And what a wonderful day it is."

CHAPTER 63

Joe sat in his office, holding the ticket stubs, remembering the game. Over the last decade, he'd thought of Owen from time to time, wondering in what corner of the world he'd landed. There'd been a feature story about his disappearance on the five-year anniversary in the *Post*, and a few reported sightings of the fugitive on social media.

Joe recalled his disbelief when he found out that Owen had fled the country. He'd been angry that Owen had ignored his advice— that he hadn't trusted him to defend him. He was also mad at himself for not making his case more forcefully. Not once, though, had Joe ever doubted his friend's innocence.

From time to time, Joe had considered trying to help. Usually, though, he'd brushed aside the thought as a waste of time. After ten years, dredging up the case to prove Owen's innocence would surely be an exercise in futility. But Joe wondered if that was the reason. Or was he just being petty because Owen hadn't thought him up to the task?

Now, staring at the ticket stubs, Joe recalled seeing his friend for the last time. He took his phone from his pocket. "Why not?" he heard himself say aloud as he dialed an old friend in the Suffolk County D.A.'s Office.

CHAPTER 64

After her run and core workout, Margo checked her email and found one from her husband. Expecting documents regarding their divorce, she instead read a heartfelt message of concern for her safety. Apparently, he'd run into her editor, who had mentioned the story she was investigating. She'd lied to Ken about it, knowing his reaction.

But there was none of the vitriol she'd expected in the email— no name-calling, jealous rants, or railing about her frivolous excursions. "My dearest," he'd written, "I find myself worried sick about your safety. Owen Prescott is an extremely dangerous man. Please stay away from him and leave his capture to the authorities. Please respond and let me know you're safe."

Margo found herself touched by his concern. They had suffered through some ugly break-ups, and she acknowledged that she'd been far from blameless. She didn't love him now, but she once had. She certainly cared about his wellbeing, and it was nice to know that the feeling was mutual.

A quarter mile away, Owen pulled a ball cap down tight for the walk to the Piper's Arms and his dinner date. At the end of his stone path, he saw the postman, no doubt ready to fill his letterbox with bills and junk mail. He'd not spoken to him before, so was surprised when the portly man waited for him.

"And you must be Mr. Bradford," he said, extending a chubby hand for a firm handshake.

"Yes, hello. And you are?"

"Ainsworth Muggins, Postal Clerk III, at your service," he said grandly. "I'm new to this route. Filling in for old Tom Flynn, who's retiring."

"I see. Pleasure to meet you. And thank you for all your, er, deliveries," Owen said, awkwardly.

"You know, Mr. Bradford, I've been wanting to speak with you, I have."

"Really?"

"Yes," he began cryptically, "it just so happens that I'm a man who notices things. Even the smallest things that most people don't give a second look to. For me, these little irregularities seem to sort of leap to my attention."

"I see," Owen said, wondering what was coming. "So you're very perceptive."

"Exactly," the postman said, slapping Owen's shoulder, as if he had chosen the perfect word. "Yes, indeed, I would say I am extremely perceptive."

Owen waited in silence as Mr. Muggins stared at him, grinning. "Well," Owen finally said, "what is it you've seen that I should know about."

The postman frowned. "Seen?" he asked, confused. "I haven't necessarily seen anything yet. This is my first day on the job, mind you. But I just wanted you to know that I don't miss much. Nothing much gets past me, no siree," he said.

"Brilliant, then. That's great," said Owen, somewhat relieved. He started to say his farewell when Ainsworth spoke again. "Also," he said, moving a bit too close for Owen's comfort, "you'll notice another thing about me."

"And what's that?" Owen asked, taking a step back.

"You should know that I'm never one to flap my gums. I treat the mail as serious business and you'll find I'm the model of discretion. Your address, your mail, where you send to and from whom you receive is in what I like to call the old Muggins vault."

"That's very comforting," Owen said, walking away, thinking that he'd never worried about mail security before now. Between Mr. Boles, Mrs. Pembroke, the black-haired lady and now Ainsworth Muggins, Postal Clerk III, he was beginning to think that the entire village of Tetbury belonged in an old-fashioned whodunnit.

He walked briskly to the Piper's Arms and found his date waiting outside. "You clean up, nice," he said, greeting Margo with a kiss. They walked in holding hands, to the delight of Brodie Dundas.

"Guid eenin!" he said, smiling like a proud parent. "Look at you two. Pure dead brilliant, it is."

"Hello, Brodie. You're a long time dead, right?" Owen said, attempting a Scottish brogue as the proprietor led them to a table.

"Aye!" the big man said.

"Talking in code now, are we?" Margo asked, after Brodie had gone.

Owen smiled. "It just so happens that Brodie Dundas was instrumental in our Prescott-Cummings…" Owen paused, interlocked his fingers, looking for a lifeline from Margo.

"Collaboration?" she asked.

"Collaboration," Owen repeated, nodding. "Thank you. Anyway, Brodie thought he saw me staring at you before we met—I was actually admiring your chicken dinner—and encouraged me to go for it. He said I'd better have fun in life, because you're a long time dead."

"Who wouldn't admire the boiled chicken here? It's divine," she said, laughing. "And Brodie is a wise man. I knew I liked him."

They ordered a Sauvignon Blanc with ice and fish and chips, then Owen shared his strange encounter with the postman. "Sometimes I swear this village is full of amateur sleuths," he said scanning the pub. In the corner, a young couple sat on the same side of a booth, sipping pints between kisses.

Margo followed his gaze. "International spies plotting an assassination?" she asked.

"No, they're clearly local," he said. "Probably just a modern-day Bonnie and Clyde, planning a heist at the Royal Bank of England."

"Ah, of course. And here comes your favorite couple." She gestured out the front window, where Mrs. Pembroke and Mr. Boles were making their way toward the pub's entrance.

Brodie brought over a carafe of wine over ice. "Brodie, I saw you having a chat with a woman earlier today," said Margo. "Jet black hair?" she asked, prompting his memory.

"Aye, full of bum and parsley, that one was," he said. "Going on about a video camera that's linked to the government." He leaned down to the table. "I told her to bugger off," he said with a wink.

"Thank goodness for that," said Owen, after Brodie had left.

Margo nodded. "Yes, if you couldn't come here, it would be a huge problem," she said, raising her eyebrows provocatively.

"In that case, you'd just have to come live with me," Owen said, and watched Margo's eyes light up across the table. Then, as she looked past him, he saw her eyes narrow and her smile disappear.

"You look like you've seen a ghost," he said, turning to follow her stare.

Then Owen saw too. Across the pub, as Mr. Boles reached over the table to pour water into Mrs. Pembroke's glass, his jacket lifted to reveal a leather shoulder holster and the butt of a pistol.

CHAPTER 65

"The Prescott file, Turner? Are you kidding me? What's next? You going to have a go at the Lizzie Borden caper?" Joe and Dan Moriarty had met in law school and kept in touch. Now, Moriarty was second in command at the Suffolk County District Attorney's Office.

"I know it sounds ridiculous, Dan. But the file is in storage, right?"

"Actually, the feds have been poking around. They're making a push to solve some fugitive cold cases, and Prescott made their list. Did the family hire you?" the prosecutor asked.

"God no. I grew up with Owen. I just need to see it for myself."

"Okay, Joe. Technically, the case is ongoing, but I can forward you the police reports. Obviously, the file is confidential, so be careful with it. I'll send an encrypted email."

"Thanks, Dan."

"Sure," Moriarty answered. "And if he ever surfaces and you represent him, I'll make sure I try the case against you."

"You're on. Thanks again."

CHAPTER 66

Even after finishing off two bottles of wine with Owen, Margo hadn't been able to sleep. Back from an early morning run, it was still dark outside when she opened her mailbox to find a thick manila envelope, sent from her contact in the Suffolk County District Attorney's Office in Boston.

It would have been easier to have her friend in the D.A.'s Office email her the file, but her divorce experience had left her leery of hacking. If her husband's private eye had been capable of hacking her email, she was certain law enforcement could use it to track her to Tetbury. She would never forgive herself if it led to Owen's arrest.

Seeing the package, a surprising surge of relief passed through Margo. She hated to admit it, but her husband's cautions about Owen had caused her, ever so slightly, to wonder about him. Seeing Mr. Boles armed hadn't helped. Even if Boles's presence in Tetbury was a coincidence, she knew that law enforcement considered Owen dangerous. Sure, people could be wrongly accused, but she knew it was rare. And if Owen was innocent, would he really have left behind a wonderful life as a writer and a woman he cared about? Also, how in the world had his DNA made its way to the murder scene?

Still, Margo couldn't imagine him perpetrating violence. She just didn't think he was capable. Also, while she understood his motive in theory, would he actually kill someone for trying to steal his book? Wouldn't he just let the courts resolve it with the lawsuit? She supposed it was possible Owen had stolen the idea from Anendale, but even if that were the case, killing wouldn't settle that issue. Wouldn't the professor's heirs just take up the lawsuit on his behalf?

Now, with the package in her possession, Margo felt certain the DNA evidence would put an end to the internal debate that waged in her mind. Tiptoeing into her apartment, seeing Owen sleeping peacefully in her bed, she felt a wave of affection for him. He had trusted her with his life and she knew he cared about her. She'd pretended not to hear him in the lake, when he'd said he was falling for her. She'd been taken aback and wanted to be sure before responding. Now, though, hearing his gentle snores, she was sure, and planned to tell him so soon.

Margo looked at the package and felt guilty for doubting him. She made coffee and lay next to him in bed. Staring at the ceiling, she allowed herself to think of a future with Owen. Deep down, she knew that solving the murder mystery from an ocean away would be a stretch. Barring that, there was life as a fugitive couple. While there was definitely an excitement factor, she wondered whether it was sustainable.

Next to her, Owen continued to sleep peacefully. Her eyes wandered to the envelope on her desk. Surely, he wouldn't fault her eagerness. It was addressed to her, after all. She rose quietly and brought the letter back to bed. She picked up a dagger-shaped letter opener she'd found in the nightstand and slit open the envelope. A note from her D.A. friend told her that the contents of the envelope included the photos and all lab results. The only thing missing was the autopsy protocol, which would be mailed in a day or two.

Margo thought she was prepared for the photos. She'd braced herself for the gore, and it certainly was there. Anendale had literally died in a large puddle of his own blood. The base of the

Cupcarthe Pyramid, protruding grotesquely from his stomach, was wider than she'd pictured it. Only three or four inches of the trophy was visible above his stomach, its green felt bottom facing the ceiling.

Another photo of the pyramid next to a ruler, clearly taken after the autopsy, revealed the trophy to be a shade under one foot in height. Margo shuddered at the thought of how much force would be necessary to drive it through nine inches of human flesh.

Looking past the gruesome carnage, Margo found the photos overwhelmingly sad. The look frozen on Anendale's face, no doubt capturing his last coherent thought, was one of surprise, mixed with the terror of approaching death. A pair of reading glasses lay near his body. Perhaps they'd been in the breast pocket of his shirt at the time of the attack.

Wide angle photographs that captured more of the old man's house told a depressing story. A half empty bourbon bottle on the kitchen counter meant he'd likely been drinking alone. Margo saw a photograph of a much younger woman on a side table near the body, perhaps his daughter or his lover from years ago. She wondered whether it had been in his field of vision when he lay dying.

Another close-up photo of the Cupcarthe revealed its inscription. *Cake Batter Blues: Norvel Anendale, Cupcarthe Award for Literary Excellence, 1977.* Margo flipped back to the shots of the victim's body. It looked as if Anendale could have read the inscription upside down in his last moments on earth. Perhaps he had fumbled with his reading glasses for that very reason.

Margo was so caught up with the story told by the photos, she almost forgot about the DNA results. Hurriedly, she flipped through the loose pages until arriving at the DNA Lab Report. Ten different samples of blood had been tested. The "donor" of all ten samples was the victim, Norvel Anendale.

A single strand of hair was found on the victim's clothing. The donor was determined to have been someone other than the victim. This DNA sample was compared to the sample obtained from Owen Prescott and determined not to have matched. Margo reread the paragraph again. This was very good news. It meant that someone other than Owen had almost assuredly been present at the murder scene, perhaps to deposit his DNA there.

Margo read the final paragraph. *The garrote around the victim's neck was a narrow strip of cloth. It was analyzed and found to contain DNA material, most likely from perspiration. This DNA was compared to the known sample from Owen Prescott and determined to be a match.*

Margo's eyes stopped cold. The DNA she assumed was planted wasn't saliva obtained from a glass he'd used at a bar or taken from his toothbrush during a burglary. It had come from his perspiration on what the killer used to choke his victim. Margo thought back to her first introduction to Owen, just downstairs in the Piper's Arms. She recalled his warm smile and very sweaty palms. An image flashed in her mind. It was Owen, kneeling beside the victim, the pyramid raised high above his head with both hands.

"Morning babe," came a sleepy voice at Margo's side. "What's up?"

CHAPTER 67

Joe was walking out of the Alameda County Courthouse in Oakland when his phone buzzed, showing an unknown number. Usually, this meant law enforcement, so he answered.

"Joe Turner, this is Special Agent Alyssa Wagner, FBI. I understand you've inquired about the Owen Prescott case."

"Uh, no. I mean, yes," Joe stammered. He'd only called about the file yesterday, and he was sure Dan wouldn't have told anyone. "I'm just an old friend of Prescott, and I've always been curious about his case. How did you…" Joe's voice trailed off.

Alyssa smiled into the phone. "We tend to know most things. Don't be alarmed, though. I have no problem with you reviewing the file. I'm curious about one thing, though. I have Prescott listed at 6'2", 190 lbs. back in 2013. Does that sound right?"

"Yeah, Joe answered," still reeling from the surprise call.

"This is going to seem like a strange question," Wagner began, "but was your friend unusually strong for his size?"

Joe chuckled. "No," he said, recalling Owen's rather rounded frame, "not at all. He used to joke that he had a writer's body. Why do you ask?"

"If you wouldn't mind, Joe, I'd like to pick your brain about the case once you've reviewed the file. You may provide some insight. I'll text you my number."

Joe hesitated. "You mean so I can help you catch him?"

"Frankly, no." the Special Agent answered. "So I can determine whether he should be a fugitive at all." The line went dead, leaving Joe thoroughly confused.

CHAPTER 68

On Margo's birthday, Joe sat across from her at Bunson's, each with a cup of their favorite tea. Outside, the dreary weather matched their moods. They had spent the night together at her place, trying to make sense of the police reports. The news that his DNA had been found on a garrote around Anendale's neck was devastating, all but proving that Owen had once held the strip of cloth used to choke Anendale. DNA research done on Margo's computer had made every other plausible explanation inconceivable.

Now, it was common knowledge that touching an object could leave behind minute skin cells containing DNA. But this "touch DNA" evidence hadn't been around ten years ago. Owen's positive DNA test wasn't the result of "touch DNA," which foreclosed the possibility that Owen could have somehow been tricked into handling the garrote before it was used.

Owen's DNA on the strip of cloth used to strangle Anendale had to have been either saliva, perspiration, or blood. Fluids like these could not possibly have been obtained on one item, like a drinking glass, and then transferred to the garrote.

The unknown third party's strand of hair at least provided a sliver of hope, but not much more. The police had no doubt logged the DNA sample into CODIS, the FBI's Combined DNA Index System. But a future "cold hit" relied on the killer either voluntarily undergoing DNA testing or being arrested again. Even if that happened, a stray hair on the victim's body seemed much more easily explainable than DNA on the garrote. Exhausted, Owen and Margo had fallen asleep, their outlook bleak.

Sometime during his restless sleep, it had occurred to Owen that doubt might creep into Margo's mind about his innocence. She'd shown no signs of it, but even he had to admit that the evidence was overwhelming.

Today, though, sitting in Bunson's, Owen was determined that they both forget about the mess for a while.

"Happy birthday," he said cheerfully. "Anything special planned for the big day?"

"Spending it with you, I hope. Maybe a hike later if the weather holds?"

"Sounds good. And how about a fancy dinner?"

"Are you cooking?" she asked, chuckling. "I wasn't aware that fancy was in your repertoire."

"Well, Ms. Smartass, it just so happens that I've made reservations at the Charlatan House in Oxford."

Margo's face lit up. "Are you kidding, Owen? You know, I was just reading about that place in the *Times*. It is over-the-top fancy. That's awesome!"

"Well, happy birthday."

"Thank you. And are you sure it's okay? It doesn't exactly fit with our recent vow to keep you cloistered."

"Oh well," Owen said, with a wave. "If I'm about to get arrested," he whispered, leaning across the table, "then I might as well have a good meal in me."

"Don't say that," she said. "But I am excited. You may not know this about me, but I love to get dressed up and go out to a fancy dinner once in a while."

"I think I sensed that about you."

"So, it's a set menu, right? Whatever it is, I know it will be super chichi."

"Well, I'm happy to report that I avoided Thursday night's roasted hare."

"Oh, thank goodness."

"Yes, I recall you had pet bunnies as a child."

"Oh, they were just feed for my pet anaconda," she deadpanned.

"And there it is," Owen said laughing, "Stark's wicked sense of humor comes when you least expect it. Anyway, I believe tonight's offering is duck à l'orange. But yes, undoubtedly tons of utensils, a pretentious menu, tiny portions, the whole thing. Endive-infused foam over roasted chanterelles with harvested figs. That sort of thing."

"Yes, probably some locally sourced microgreens with the essence of lavender."

"Perhaps a deconstructed bone marrow mousse with a balsamic reduction?" he asked.

Margo laughed. "Now you're just making shit up. Wow, I need to get a dress. And do you have a coat and tie?"

"I do. My mom made me bring one. Ten years later, it makes its debut tonight."

"Well, even though your birthday isn't until tomorrow, I have a little gift for you," she said, producing a small box from her purse.

"Really? A gift for me on your birthday? How unconventional."

"It's more of a practical gift," she said, as he opened the box. "I got one for both of us." Owen paused briefly, realizing it was the first gift he had received in more than ten years.

"Wow," he said, taking the phone out of the box.

"It's a burner phone," she said, taking a matching phone out of her purse. "No risk whatsoever. I paid cash for them on the street the other day in Oxford. I just thought given recent events, it would be good to be able to communicate."

"Yes, it's a great idea. And thank you."

"Well," Margo said, glancing at her watch, "forget the hike, Prescott. I have so much to plan. What time tonight?"

"I believe 7:00 p.m., but I'll call to confirm on my new phone."

"Awesome. Are we getting a ride or are you driving?"

Owen raised his chin and attempted his best British accent of the upper crust. "My lady, I will squire you to dinner in my carriage, also known as the Rover."

"Excellent. I shall await the carriage then, Sir Owen," she said, matching the accent before they kissed goodbye.

CHAPTER 69

Joe sat in his mustard-colored recliner, cracked open a beer and considered the formidable case against his friend. He wouldn't have advised Owen to flee the country back in 2013, but the evidence against him was strong. Even so, the motive, opportunity, his flight, and lack of alibi could all be explained away. Even the papers at the scene.

But not his DNA on the garrote.

Still, something about the evidence seemed a little off. For starters, it had been immediately clear why the FBI agent had asked about Owen's strength. Joe seriously doubted him physically capable of the crime. Every gym teacher they'd had growing up would testify to that. Then there was the strange combined strangulation and bludgeoning.

His cell phone buzzed. It was Chuck, his intrepid investigator. "Just remember," Joe said preemptively, "we're starting from the premise that he's innocent." He'd emailed the reports to the investigator earlier in the day.

Joe used Chuck Argenal on almost all his cases. He had an amazing knack for getting people to open up to him. An aging hippie, Chuck spoke in a mix of southern idioms and movie lines. Joe followed only about half of it, but found him wildly entertaining.

Chuck exhaled into the phone. "Okay," he said, clearly rethinking his remarks, "then that means someone framed him. And good luck finding out who did it ten years after the fact."

"We don't have to figure out who did it, Chuck, just that Owen didn't do it."

"Well then, he has to have an alibi," the investigator answered. "No other way."

"Okay," Joe answered, leafing through the autopsy report, "Anendale's time of death is listed between 9:15 p.m. and 9:45 p.m. I was with Owen until 6:30ish, when he went home and spent the night working alone in his room with his phone off. Still, I'll bet the alibi is there somewhere. If only he were around to answer some questions."

"If all the ifs and buts were candy and nuts, every day would be Christmas," Chuck answered, accentuating his southern drawl.

Joe laughed. "I'll send you Owen's old address and the name of his former roommate. I have no idea where he is now."

"Counselor, I will conduct a hard target search of every gas station, residence, supermarket, movie theater, video arcade, studio, school, skyscraper, amusement park, warehouse, farmhouse, pool house, henhouse, outhouse, doghouse and waffle house."

"I assume that's a movie line?"

"Tommy Lee Jones in *The Fugitive*. Movie about a wrongfully accused man on the lam. As usual, my genius is lost on you, Turner."

CHAPTER 70

Walking back to his apartment, snuggling himself against a bracing wind, Owen once again crossed paths with Mr. Boles. The big man stopped in front of him to block his path on the sidewalk. "Top of the morning, Ancil. What are you up to on this dreadful spring morning?"

"Hello, Mr. Boles. Just had some tea at Bunson's," Owen replied, wondering whether Boles was armed.

"Ah, Bunson's. That's one of your spots, is it?"

"Yes, I suppose so."

"Listen, Ancil. I've been meaning to ask you. Do you suppose you could spare a few minutes sometime? I need to bend your ear about something that's nagging me. It's a conversation that should be had privately, if you get my meaning."

"Oh, um, I mean, sure, Mr. Boles," Owen stammered, his heart suddenly racing. "I suppose that would be fine. Well, I'm actually in a bit of a hurry now, though."

"Oh, course," Boles said, as Owen walked away, nervously. "I'll see you another time, then," he called after him.

Owen walked home, thoroughly confused. Boles was clearly law enforcement and on to him. But what was giving him pause? Was he still unsure?

As Owen was arriving at his cottage, Margo assumed he was the one knocking on her back door. No one else had ever visited, and she wondered if he had come up for a surprise late-morning romp. "C'mon in, silly," she called, walking to the door. She opened it and stood staring, mouth agape, at Ken, her soon-to-be ex-husband.

"Ken," she said. "I can't believe it. Come in."

"I know I should have called, Margo, but I felt I needed to address you in person." The sixty-year-old's tone was characteristically formal.

"No, it's fine," she smiled, still getting her bearings. "I'm just so shocked to see someone here from home. I just never expected it. How, um, did you even find me?" she asked nervously.

"Well, as I said in my email, I'm quite concerned about your safety. Worried sick, actually. I got the name of the village from your editor, who, by the way, is quite eager for you to send him some copy.

"Anyway," Ken continued, "it's a small village. I got in this morning and within an hour, with some gentle prodding, a very talkative postman was telling me more than I wanted to know about a certain famous writer who'd settled in town and where he liked to have tea. I'm afraid to say that I spied you there this morning and saw you walk here afterwards. Terribly sorry for the snooping."

"No, it's okay, Ken. I appreciate your concern. I really do. But I can take care of myself."

"Margo," he said gravely. "Owen Prescott has killed. Everyone knows that. I don't understand why you would risk your life just to write a silly feature," he said, raising his voice. Margo let his comment hang in the air and smirked.

"And there it is," she said, venom in her voice. "Just when I was wondering who this thoughtful man was standing here, you reminded me of exactly who you are."

"Honestly, Margo," he said, showing her both palms. "Please, I don't want to fight."

"I don't either," she said, breathing deeply.

"Listen, I'm not here to win you back. I know that ship has sailed and you're better off without an old codger like me. But that doesn't mean that I don't care about you. So, please know that I'm very concerned for your safety. I wouldn't have flown across the Atlantic if I wasn't. What if this guy finds out you've found him? If he'll kill over a lawsuit, he'll certainly do so to avoid capture. Promise me you'll at least think about what I'm saying," he pleaded. Margo heard uncharacteristic desperation in his voice.

"I will," she said quietly, as he turned to leave. "And Ken? Your traveling all this way means a lot to me."

"Sorry again for ambushing you," he said, smiling. "I panicked. Lunch tomorrow, perhaps?"

"Okay, sure."

Margo sat on her sofa after Ken had gone, thoughts racing through her head. His visit had touched her. She knew he wasn't right for her, but that didn't mean that Owen was a rational choice either. Soon, though, she thought of her night ahead—a legitimate night out on the town on the arm of Owen Prescott. She decided big decisions could wait.

CHAPTER 71

Joe was catching up on some billing in his office when Chuck walked in unannounced and took a seat across his desk. "Hey Chuck, how goes the Prescott caper?"

"We're as lost as last year's Easter egg, I'm afraid. I found the roommate, Will. He was home that night but can't vouch for Prescott. Never left his room. His girlfriend was there, too, but has no recollection of the evening."

"Shit, Chuck. Any other ideas?"

"I got a virtual tour of his apartment online. Prescott's room was visible from the street, and his roommate said his desk faced the window. Ten years ago, we could have canvassed the neighborhood for witnesses. Now, though..." Chuck shrugged.

"Okay, thanks," Joe said with a sigh.

"You know, Joe," Chuck said after a time, "what if our dog is on the skunk scent?" Chuck asked.

"English please?"

"Sorry," Chuck said, rolling his eyes. "What if we're laboring under a misapprehension? What if the time of death is wrong? The county lab isn't exactly Scotland Yard."

"Now you're talking, Chuck!" Joe said with enthusiasm. "Should we run it by Dr. Death?" Joe asked. "I'll set it up."

"I'll handle it," Chuck replied, getting up to leave. "Look at me!" he said dramatically. "I am the captain now."

"Oh, I know that one," Joe said, searching his memory. "Captain Phillips!"

"There's hope for you yet."

CHAPTER 72

Desiree Richins stood in front of a mirror in her apartment in Tetbury and put on her jet-black wig just for fun, letting the smooth synthetic locks fall over her shoulders. She hadn't worn the disguise in more than a week. The fake boobs were cumbersome, but she liked the way she looked with long hair.

It had taken her years, but she had finally found Owen Prescott and soon he would be hers. The restraining order was a distant memory.

CHAPTER 73

"Sam, killers are crazy, right?" Alyssa called over the wall of her cubicle.

After a pause, Sam's bespectacled face appeared atop the wall. "Prescott, I assume?"

"Why would you assume that?" she asked, smiling?

"Because it's Friday night, and the young star of the agency, who could be out painting the town red—I've never understood that, painting the town red." He paused. "Anyway, the darling of the agency, who could cruise on prior accomplishments for the next decade, instead is grinding away in her cubicle at 7:00 p.m. It has to be Prescott."

"Actually, painting the town red originated in the early eighteen hundreds when the Marquis de Waterford, a notorious scoundrel, actually painted a town red. Ironically, it got him kicked out of Oxford, near where Prescott is currently living his last days of freedom."

"Shocking that you know that," Sam deadpanned.

"Well, since you know so much about my psyche, to what do you attribute my, admittedly, unusual interest in the case?"

"Oh, that's easy. You're in love with him." Alyssa laughed.

"No, I'm serious. First, you get to know the author, learn everything there is to know about him, then track him down, then feel guilty about it. It's some sort of reverse Stockholm Syndrome, where the captors identify with their hostages."

"That's called Lima Syndrome, Sam, but I haven't captured anyone."

"I don't know, Al," he said with exaggerated skepticism. "You were just about to tell me that you don't think he's capable of killing, right? Because killers are crazy and he's not."

"Something like that," she said, smiling, "but authors aren't my type. I tend to go for the guys who have trouble expressing themselves," she said, shooting him a look.

"Well, to answer your original question, while not every murderer is nuts," he said, "it is true that a very high percentage of killers suffer from some level of personality disorder."

"And," Alyssa continued, "personality disorders are characterized by an inability to empathize and a lack of compassion."

"True."

"And that's just not Prescott," Alyssa said, shaking her head. "He writes with a lot of compassion. He volunteered at a food bank in college, for God's sake."

Sam walked around the cubicle and pulled up a chair next to Alyssa. "But not every killer has a mental affliction," he said. "He could have flown into a rage. The victim was trying to steal something he'd put his soul into. Not to mention his livelihood. And maybe he did steal the old guy's novel and knew the lawsuit had merit."

Alyssa shook her head. "I don't buy it. Nothing about this guy says violent rage."

"How do you explain the DNA on the garrote?" he asked.

"I don't know, but there were two DNA donors and it sure wouldn't have taken two to do the job. Anendale was feeble. And I still don't have the autopsy protocol. I don't trust the metro lab."

"So, Prescott was framed? C'mon, Al," he said, standing. "Anyway, I'm heading out. So, um, I think, er, I was …"

Alyssa shook her head, ending the painful stammering. "I'm going to press on for a bit. See you Monday, Sam."

Alyssa had spent the last two days dissecting the Prescott file—the reports, autopsy, lab results and photos. She knew she was close to piecing it together. She pulled up the digitized images. A photo from directly above the body showed Anendale's form framed in red, the blood pooled in two uneven puddles that stretched three feet from the body. Just as Alyssa clicked to the next photo, her brain registered an irregularity.

She clicked back to the photo and zoomed in on the edge of the puddle to Anendale's left. There was an imperfection—a slight smear at the edge of the pool. Something had caused it—more than likely a shoe. The cops wouldn't have been that sloppy. By the time they arrived, there was no chance to save a life, so they'd had time to be meticulous. The blood would have taken several minutes to pool that far from the body, and still longer for it to dry enough to smear. Even a single drop took an hour to completely dry.

Someone had been there, stepping around the body, long after Anendale was impaled.

CHAPTER 74

Owen arrived home to find Mrs. Pembroke in his kitchen. "Hello, Ancil," she said, wiping his counter with a dishcloth. "I've just come by to drop off some chocolate chip cookies. They're still warm if you'd like one."

"Don't mind if I do, Mrs. Pembroke," he said, taking one off the plate. "Thank you, but it appears you're also cleaning my kitchen, which, as I've told you, makes me feel quite domestically inadequate."

"Nonsense," she said, ignoring his comment. "Biscuits are a doddle."

"Oh my." Owen sighed, chewing warm chocolaty goodness. "You continue to make it very difficult for me to stay in any semblance of shape."

"Don't be silly, Owen. You're skin and bones. Both you and your new friend. What's her name, Marge or Margo?"

"Yes, Mrs. Pembroke, Margo. I'd like you to know her name."

"Anyway, I made a batch for Mr. Boles and these are the extras. Lord knows he could stand to skip a few trips to the dessert table."

"Mrs. Pembroke," Owen said, searching for the right words, "speaking of your friend Mr. Boles, how much would you say you know about him?"

"Quite a bit by now, I'd say. Why do you ask?" she said, wiping Owen's stove top.

"I don't know, Mrs. Pembroke. He just seems mysterious to me?"

She stopped wiping and laughed. "George Boles, mysterious? I'd hardly say that. What are you getting at? Speak plainly, Ancil."

"Well, he carries a gun, for example."

"Oh, he explained that," she said dismissively. "He was shot years ago and ever since has carried one for protection. Perhaps it's a bit extreme, but we all have our eccentricities, wouldn't you say?" she asked, her eyebrows raised.

"I suppose you're right. But he did mention that he wants to meet with me. Do you know what about?"

"I have no idea. I should think he just would enjoy some male companionship. He's out here in the country and doesn't know a soul. Most likely, he'd just like to have a pint, watch a football match, throw darts. Isn't that what you gents do?"

"I suppose so."

"Since you're asking about Mr. Boles," Mrs. Pembroke said casually, "I may ask similar questions about how well you know Margo. I don't mind telling you, Ancil, I don't like the cut of her jib."

Just then, Owen glanced out his kitchen window to see a uniformed officer walking up the path toward his front door. He knew the face, but from where? A wave of heat flushed through Owen and his stomach turned. Fuck! It was the bobby from outside the post office in Nailsworth.

"Um, Mrs. Pembroke," he said, moving from the window, "I hate to ask, but would you mind answering my door?" She looked out the window, then turned to see the panic etched in Owen's face. Without a reply, she walked to the front door and paused as Owen retreated into his bedroom.

"Hello, may I help you?" she asked, opening the door.

"Good afternoon. Might you be Mrs. Abigail Pembroke?"

"I am. How can I help you, Constable?"

"Captain, actually. Captain Alec Whitworth, at your service. I was over at your home when the gardener said I might find you here."

"Well, what's this about, Constable?" Mrs. Pembroke asked, intentionally ignoring his title.

"Mrs. Pembroke, are you the owner of a green Leyland Rover?"

"I am. And why do you ask?"

"Are you the only driver of the vehicle?"

Mrs. Pembroke frowned. "Constable Whitley..."

"Whitworth."

"Again," she continued, "I must insist that you do me the courtesy of telling me what this is about."

"Mrs. Pembroke, as I'm sure you will understand, during the course of an investigation, there are certain police precautions that must be taken, and I must insist..."

"Constable Wiggins, I'll have you know that my father was a constable before your mum was out of nappies, as was his father before him. I daresay, I don't need any lectures about the duties of a proper constable," she said, raising her voice. "But to answer your question, I am widowed and live alone. I am the sole driver of the Rover."

"And have you had occasion to allow anyone to borrow the vehicle lately?"

"No, of course not."

"Are you sure of that?"

"Am I sure about whether or not someone has borrowed my car, Constable? Do I look daft?"

"Of course, not, Mrs. Pembroke." He fished a photograph out of his pocket. "Tell me, have you ever seen this man?"

"Just a minute," she said, putting on the spectacles that hung from her neck. Watching her closely, the Captain thought he may have noticed the briefest of flashes of recognition in her face. "No," she said, slowly shaking her head, "can't say as I have."

The constable stared at her for several seconds with a poker face. "Mrs. Pembroke, would you mind having a second look?"

"As an actual matter of fact, Constable Wiggins…"

"Whitworth."

"…I do quite mind. You've come to my home, unannounced, had a gander around my grounds, interrogated my gardener, and now, sir, you may kindly leave."

"Mrs. Pembroke," the captain said calmly, beginning to suspect something was afoot, "would you mind if I stepped inside?" he asked and stepped forward. Ms. Pembroke sidestepped to block his path.

"Constable, does your impertinence know no bounds?" she asked, as if appalled by his behavior. "And I've just noticed that your badge says Nailsworth. Does our Constable Dreyer know your business here?"

"Mrs. Pembroke, as I'm sure you know, both Constable Dreyer and I serve the Cotswold Village Constabulary, and it is well within my jurisdiction to…"

"I'll take that as a no, Constable, and I'll have you know I am past secretary of this district's Counsel, not to mention, as proprietor of this estate, I pay your salary."

"Mrs. Pembroke, I don't mean to trouble you further," he said, maintaining a quiet, polite tone. "Could I at least trouble you for a look at the Rover."

"No, you may not, Constable. Consider your business here concluded," she said sternly. "And I suggest, before you come back nosing about in Tetbury, you might look after your own regrettable village, where, in case you haven't noticed, your residents are making a mockery of the Cotswold District's Residential Guidelines."

"Very well Mrs. Pembroke. Good day." Good God, he thought, walking away from the cottage. I managed to find the Mrs. Busby of Tetbury.

By the time Owen emerged from the bedroom, looking stunned, Mrs. Pembroke had gone back to wiping his stove. Finished, she placed the dishcloth in the sink and dried her hands on a towel.

"Mrs. Pembroke, thank you. I suppose…"

"Don't mention it, Ancil," she said, picking up her purse to leave. "However, if I didn't have what you Americans call a hot date tonight, I should think we would have a lot to discuss."

"Yes, Mrs. Pembroke, and another thing," he said, haltingly, "those comments that I made about Mr. Boles. I suppose it would be awkward if he was privy to them. I hope you will exercise discretion."

Mrs. Pembroke turned to face Owen at the door. "Ancil, I should hope that today I have more than demonstrated my capacity for discretion. Also," she added with a smirk, "my Rolls is at your service. You might want to keep the Rover locked away for a while."

CHAPTER 75

Desiree took off her wig and stowed it in a box under her bed. It was time for her core workout. She stretched, then reached for the bar and hung from it, feeling her shoulders loosen. Next, she curled her knees to her chest and thrust her feet into the air, looping her legs over the bar. Hanging upside down, she began the first of her daily routine of three hundred inverted sit-ups. With each rhythmic breath, she recited the same quiet mantra she'd repeated for more than a decade. "Owen will be mine. Owen will be mine."

Within minutes, she had entered a trance-like state, her body on autopilot as she blew out the words in forceful breaths, her stomach rippling under her t-shirt. Eight minutes later, her workout complete, Desiree dismounted and leaned against the wall, recovering. She pulled off her dampened shirt and walked to the kitchen for water. Her phone rattled on her table.

"Hi there," she said, still catching her breath and beaming.

"My lady, your carriage will arrive promptly at 7:00 p.m.," came the faux British accent from her phone.

"Excellent, Sir Owen. I await your arrival."

CHAPTER 76

Dr. Death, also known as retired Alameda County Coroner Curtis Berrian, waved Joe and Chuck into his cramped office. The room was filled with test tubes, beakers and microscopes of various vintages and smelled of formaldehyde.

The doctor didn't know that Joe and Chuck had dubbed him Dr. Death because of his appearance rather than his occupation. Tall and thin, in his early seventies, ashen skin sagged from his boney features. Long wisps of unruly white grew from his balding pate. A wrinkled, pale blue sport coat hung from his spindly frame. His shoulders were powdered with dandruff.

Forced into an early retirement at the Coroner's Office, undoubtedly for a lack of people skills, there was no disputing Berrian's brilliance. Respected as one of the foremost experts in his field, he always delighted in pointing out mistakes made by his former employer and others in the field.

In typical fashion, the doctor began speaking about the case without a greeting. "Turns out the Suffolk County Coroner is no more competent than our locals. They didn't bother going to the crime scene, which I believe is essential. One must spend time with the corpse, feel it, get to know it," he said, as if the comment was completely normal.

"Dr. D, we were curious about the time of death," Joe mentioned.

"I read your email," the doctor answered brusquely. "That's precisely what I'm addressing. The county hacks determined the time of death by plugging in the standard algor mortis rate. When the body was found at 4:30 a.m., its temperature was 88 degrees, having fallen from 98.6. The standard body cooling rate is 1.5 degrees per hour, yielding a time of death of approximately 9:30 p.m.

"This simplistic approach failed to account for several factors that should have been obvious. First, the victim's body-fat ratio was high, which slows the cooling of the body. He was also wearing multiple layers of clothing, which served the same purpose.

"The paramedic's report noted that the home was unusually warm. Crime scene photos show a heating vent on the floor within a few feet of the body. The corpse was found by a jogger who noticed the front door open. This probably had the heat running nonstop."

Joe was getting excited but didn't dare interrupt. "All these factors severely slowed the body's cooling process, probably by several hours. The autopsy photos reveal advanced rigor mortis, more consistent with an earlier death. It is difficult to be precise, but I believe the time of death was more like 5:00 p.m., certainly no later than 5:30 p.m."

As was his custom, the doctor stood and walked out of his office without a farewell, leaving Joe and Chuck sitting in stunned silence. "You met with Prescott at 6:00 p.m.," Chuck said. "Do you know where he was before that?"

CHAPTER 77

George Boles sat on a bench in the village garden, hunching against the damp chill as he thought about his predicament. Out of habit, he scanned his surroundings for potential threats, feeling the comfort of his pistol against his side.

He took out a cigar and struck a match, puffing it to life. He knew very well what had to be done. Momentum was gathering quickly and if he didn't take action soon, he knew someone else would. It had been a while since an opportunity like this presented itself and he knew he wasn't getting any younger.

Mrs. Pembroke was certainly a pleasant distraction from his job, and one he hadn't expected. Boles hated lying to her about his employment, but perhaps she would understand. He even made room for the possibility that she'd already worked it out. She was a sharp one, after all, and had seemed skeptical about his explanation for carrying a gun. He'd told her he'd been shot once years ago, which was technically true. As a young officer, he'd taken a bullet in the line of duty during a drug raid in the Tower Hamlets in London.

Perhaps he was losing his edge, he mused, and laughed at the thought. He'd taken on some of the country's most hardened criminals in his career, and here he was going soft over a woman.

Boles wasn't sure, but it seemed like Owen was avoiding him, perhaps sensing what was coming. He certainly seemed nervous around him. The big man rose, straightened his flat cap and flicked ash from his cigar to the wet grass. It was time. He would pay the writer a visit this afternoon.

CHAPTER 78

Joe sat at his office desk, thumbing through the Prescott police report with renewed enthusiasm. Dr. Death's revelation about the time of death wasn't exactly Owen's get-out-of-jail-free card. As Chuck had pointed out, it would mean nothing unless Owen could prove where he'd been at 5:00 p.m.

Owen had told him about being at a book club somewhere on the coast, but had given no specifics. He'd booked the event himself, so Joe wouldn't know where to begin.

Still, though, the doctor's news had brought Joe a strange sense of relief and calm. It was almost as if the alibi had already been proven. He sensed it was here, somewhere, just waiting to be found.

After two hours of poring over the file, he got up to stretch, and wandered to the box of Red Sox memorabilia, spying the envelope that had launched his quest. He brought it to his desk and emptied its contents—the two ticket stubs, the photo of his mom at the game, and the crinkled up credit card receipt, studying them one at a time.

Joe began to smile even before he smoothed out the yellowed receipt on his desk. He'd seen it before and had noted the hefty fee for the tickets. He just hadn't noticed the fine print: *September 22, 2013, 4:37 p.m., Padanaram, Mass.*

He collapsed back in his chair, pumped his fist, and reached for his phone. When Anendale was murdered, Joe had been more than an hour away, and now he had proof.

CHAPTER 79

Margo had first seen Owen at Breastwing, back when her name was Desiree Richins. She'd been two years ahead of him and had served as a teacher's assistant in his Intro to Composition class. She would never forget the first time she saw him on the first day of class. He was quiet, but self-assured for a first-year student. He had smiled at her that day—not a polite smile that never reached his eyes and not a sly, flirty one either. Owen Prescott's smile had been warm and genuine. Their relationship would continue to grow, of course, but it was that first moment when Desiree knew that he would belong to her someday.

Not surprisingly, he had resisted at first. Something as exciting and transcendent as their perfection together was always going to be scary, but she knew he would eventually come around.

Margo would recall her first exchange with Owen for the rest of her life. He had just turned in an essay assignment. As a teacher's assistant, it hadn't been assigned to her to grade, but he must have known she'd read it. In his own way, in that essay, he'd professed his love for her. The day after she'd read it, she'd caught his eye before class and they'd exchanged passionate looks of longing. No words were exchanged because none were necessary.

She and Owen had only spoken once. She'd waited for him to arrive at the campus coffee shop and had approached him while he was in line. "Hi Owen," she'd said nervously as she walked past.

Owen hadn't just nodded his head or uttered a flippant greeting. He'd smiled and said, "Hello," with passion in his eyes, letting his true feelings flow between them. She could still hear his greeting floating to her and wrapping her in a warm blanket of love.

Now, though, even as Margo showered after her workout, her mind wandered to her husband's recent attempt to rescue her. She knew it meant that he cared about her, especially given what she had put him through over the years.

Margo began dating Ken while still studying at Breastwing, at first, for a distraction from Owen on the advice of her therapist. But Ken's wealth had made her life as a freelance writer so easy and, she was embarrassed to admit, gave her more free time to spend tracking Owen around Boston. Even upon their engagement, she'd never stopped her pursuit of Owen—her obsession, as her therapist insisted on calling it.

One big mistake she'd made was telling Ken the truth. One day, shortly after their engagement, he found her sitting at her desk surrounded with Owen's books, early writings, copies of his press interviews, and photos she'd taken when he wasn't looking. On some level, she thought that once Ken saw how perfect she and Owen were for each other, he would understand. In hindsight, of course, that had been stupid. Only she and Owen could comprehend their connection as spirit mates.

After her admission, she promised Ken to forget about Owen. Logically, it made sense for their upcoming marriage. But even as she said the words, Margo knew that she would never give up her dream. It would mean giving up her life's destiny. Her first separation from Ken had come six months later when he caught her pleasuring herself to Owen's photo on the back cover of *Orchards of Grace*. She'd read the book countless times and had memorized most of it.

Owen's Cupcarthe Pyramid was well deserved, but he'd clearly been robbed of a Nobel Prize in Literature. Margo suspected a conspiracy of some sort. Reading between the beautiful lines of prose, she could hear his voice in the pages, calling for her. The subtext of their love was so obvious. She'd wondered why it hadn't been mentioned in the book's reviews.

The restraining order had been a setback for their relationship, for sure. Margo knew the corporate suits were behind it. It certainly hadn't been Owen's idea. She could tell the way he'd looked at her in court that his heart wasn't in the proceedings. Still, the judge's order had been difficult to take.

She'd started cutting herself after that day in court. Of course, Ken had freaked out and made her start the bullshit therapy sessions, but the cutting wasn't a big deal. It wasn't as if she wanted to kill herself, just a little self-motivation to make her life with Owen a reality.

Besides, her blood on the knife blade had given a little flare to her present on April's door.

CHAPTER 80

"Interesting," Special Agent Wagner said pensively, digesting Joe's summary. News of an alibi from a criminal defense attorney had to be taken with a grain of salt, but it was worth checking out.

"Let me guess," she said after Joe mentioned the new time of death, "the idiots at county forgot to account for the warmth of the place?"

"How'd you know?" asked Joe, impressed.

"It wouldn't be the first time they plugged in the algor mortis rate and rubber-stamped the time of death. Besides," she asked, "have you been in your parents' home recently?"

"True," Joe agreed, chuckling. "It's usually a tad warm."

Alyssa promised to verify Dr. Berrian's conclusions with her lab and get back to Joe. Now, she stretched in her chair, and pulled up the Prescott file with renewed resolve.

She had never bought the idea that Prescott had been framed. Who would go to the trouble of committing a murder just to frame someone for it? It seemed like ordering lobster bisque for the crackers. But now, she wondered.

She clicked through more photos, stopping on a close-up of one of the handwritten notes that was scattered on the floor around the body. She had noticed before that a few of the notes appeared to have been water damaged, their blue ink blurred in places. Now, she scrolled through the rest of them rapidly, letting the photos tell a story.

"What is missing?" she whispered to herself. Anendale had obviously been drinking. His high blood-alcohol level and the half-empty bourbon bottle proved that. A light went on. She clicked through the photos again, searching intently. There were more than 200 images in all, covering nearly every square inch of Anendale's study, living room and kitchen. None of them showed a glass or a cup. It would have been in plain sight, either on a side table or broken on the floor. But why would someone remove it?

Alyssa breathed deeply, concentrating. She pictured someone crouching at the edge of the pool of blood, leaning over to tie the garrote around the neck of the dead body. She saw them picking up pieces of the broken glass, and placing papers over splashes of spilled bourbon, their pages soggy from the liquid. She opened her eyes and quickly scrolled to another photo. Zooming in, she began to nod in recognition and smiled.

CHAPTER 81

Margo collapsed into her office chair and scrolled through emails to find one sent from her friend in the District Attorney's Office in Boston. She sighed with mild irritation, having specifically asked for him to avoid email. She opened an attachment labeled "Supplemental Lab Report" and printed it while she turned on the shower.

She was beyond excited about the evening's birthday date with Owen. It meant a lot to her that he'd remembered, and it was a milestone in their relationship—the first of many birthdays spent together. She took a long shower, luxuriating in the hot water, dreaming of her life with Owen. While part of her never doubted they would eventually find each other, the relationship was also surreal.

Over the years, at times, it had seemed like the world was conspiring against them. There'd been his natural shyness to contend with, his meaningless fling with April, then the restraining order, all blocking their path to perfect love.

Admittedly, she'd gone overboard a few times, but drugging him had been for his own good. She'd noticed him getting behind on his sleep, and someone needed to take care of him. And she hadn't taken advantage of him sexually that night. God knows she'd wanted him.

The graphic message she'd stabbed to that slut's door had also been for Owen's own good. She'd been watching April's reaction from a building across the street and had delighted in her quivering in fear—aroused by it, even.

But she knew the break-ins had probably crossed the line. Sometimes, though, the need to possess Owen had been overwhelming. The next best thing was to be close to him, but even that wasn't always possible. The burglaries had been a last resort to share in some part of his life—to sit at his dinner table or bury her face in his pillow. She'd only done it once in Tetbury and thank goodness for that cat. But it was all out of love. She knew Owen's life would be better with her in it, and sometimes she'd been carried away with the need to make him happy.

After Owen fled the country, Ken convinced her to move to Connecticut and she'd vowed to start fresh. She stopped smoking pot—at least not three times a day, anyway. She stopped cutting herself, died her hair, and got in shape. That's when she changed her name to Margo, Owen's mother's name. She'd heard him say in an interview how close they were.

Her marriage had been a series of explosive fights, counseling, and reconciliations. Ken never struck her but countered her loyalty to Owen with a barrage of verbal abuse, affairs, and invasions of her privacy, including hidden video cameras and hacked email accounts. For her part, Margo had promised to forget about Owen at least a half dozen times, always knowing it was impossible. Their last separation in Boston was triggered by Ken finding a stash of her memorabilia of Owen, stuffed in a box at the back of her closet.

Once in Connecticut, Margo embarked on a quest to find Owen, and after this recent final break-up, it had become her full-time occupation. Most of what she knew about him came from shadowing him around in Boston, where she'd learned his routine, interests, likes, and dislikes. She began scouring his family's history for ties to foreign countries and re-reading his books and essays for clues.

Finally, after years of frustration, Margo had figured out his pen name, Ancil Bradford, through a painstaking search of the International Directory of Authors. At Breastwing, she'd taken an art and literature class because Owen was enrolled and recalled two of his favorites were Ancil Dupre and Allen Bradford. Of course, she'd devoured the books written under Owen's pen name and was relieved to find subtle references to her sprinkled throughout the pages. She knew he still loved her.

Ancil Bradford's publisher was based in England, which was her first clue. Then she'd seen the interview where Owen had mentioned his dream of a quiet life as a writer in the Cotswolds. Margo had convinced her editor she could uncover Owen's whereabouts and she was off to England. She'd spent a month wandering around the different Cotswold villages, checking tea shops and pubs and scrolling through residence records. She'd taken a brief break from the search for a writer's conference in London when she'd heard about the lecture at Oxford. Sir Alex Wixom had so influenced Owen's writing, she'd thought he might attend.

After her face plant in the street, Margo had followed Owen to Tetbury. Meeting him was the easy part. From her days of shadowing him in Boston, it seemed as if they'd already spent a lifetime together.

So many hours, Margo had watched him typing away, picturing herself with him in their apartment. She'd noticed that he rubbed his neck after a few hours of writing and dreamed of being there to relieve his stress. She would make him tea and rub his shoulders as he wrote. She smiled, thinking of tonight's slightly different plan to relieve her lover's stress.

Sometimes she thought she knew more about him than she did herself—his favorite author, preferred tea, and interest in international soccer. There was much more, of course, but she didn't want to overdo it. Their birthdays being only a day apart had been real, and she'd celebrated them together for years.

Margo wasn't concerned about him recognizing her as her appearance had changed quite a bit from her days at Breastwing. The wild blonde hair was now brown and styled, she'd gotten very fit, and brown contacts veiled her shocking blue eyes.

Once they were together, she knew Owen would stop his silly infatuation with that April woman from Boston. She was obviously wrong for him and Margo had always suspected that she'd somehow blackmailed him into the relationship. It didn't matter now.

From their first electrifying kiss, she knew thoughts of April would soon be washed away. He'd even gone skinny dipping with her, too. Margo often replayed in her mind Owen's fateful jump into the lake. That's when she knew April was history. Take that, bitch, she'd thought to herself.

CHAPTER 82

Boston, September 22, 2013

The loose tile on the step from Professor Anendale's study to his living room was something Lydia would have made sure was repaired. It was exactly the type of thing she would have gotten done while her husband was in his own world, typing away in his study. Money hadn't been a second thought back then, with revenues streaming in from *Cake Batter Blues*, speaking engagements, and a new book deal. Now, the repair seemed an extravagance.

On his way to prominently display his Cupcarthe Pyramid on the mantel in his living room, Anendale wobbled past Lydia's photo, her face so full of life. He wished she could be here now. He should have been driving that night. After all, he knew how to handle his liquor. But she had insisted. She loved driving the roadster. He stopped to tip his glass toward her photo and continued on his way to the mantel.

He'd heard a noise on the porch and expected a doorbell, but none came. The professor raised his glass to his lips again, feeling for the step up to his living room. The toe of his loafer caught the front edge of the step. The tile shifted under his foot, upsetting his balance and propelling him forward.

His addled mind's first thought was his drink, holding it upright in his right hand as he fell. His instinct to brace himself with his left hand was too late, still clutching the pyramid as the floor rushed toward him. He released his grip on the trophy only an instant before its pointed tip punctured his soft belly, his full weight driving the pyramid through his liver. Glancing off his vertebrae, the sharp granite popped through the pale skin on the right side of his back.

Stunned at first, his dulled senses felt only the pain in his face, where his wire spectacles had been driven into the bridge of his nose. Slowly, reality took hold. There was a dull throb in his stomach that would soon turn to a searing pain. He turned his head to the side, his face feeling the cool tile of the hearth. Without his spectacles, his pooling blood was too blurry to make out. Soon, though, he would feel its warmth seeping under his splayed arms.

CHAPTER 83

George Boles knew it was time for himself to make a move. He was seeing Mrs. Pembroke tonight and he needed to take action. After lunch, he had stopped by the Piper's Arms for a spot of liquid courage. Now, making his way down the cobblestones of Tetbury, he steeled himself for what was to come. It wouldn't be pleasant by any means, but he had to get on with it. Approaching the door, he made a fist and knocked loudly.

CHAPTER 84

After her shower, Margo caught a glimpse of herself walking naked past the full-length mirror attached to the inside of the door of her modest closet. For thirty-seven, she looked damn hot—so much sexier than her old Desiree body. And she and Owen were going out on the town.

Lately, she allowed her mind to stray down the dark road of Owen's eventual capture. Surely, fate would not be so cruel. Now that they both had overcome so much, an abrupt ending to their bliss would be too much for her to bear. Some wrist cuts wouldn't be enough to dull that pain.

But now, on her birthday, Margo was determined just to enjoy the precious present. After her shower, she took out her backless, sequined dress she'd brought from home with exactly such an occasion in mind. She dressed, pulled on high heels, then admired herself in a full-length mirror on her closet door. Owen wouldn't be here for a few hours, but she wanted to get used to wearing heels again.

She looked in the mirror again, this time imagining Owen next to her, where he belonged. The dress was a showstopper, and she couldn't wait for him to see her. She blow-dried and brushed her hair and put in her brown contacts.

She poured a glass of Sancerre, then walked to the printer and picked up the DNA report. Strolling toward her front window, she scanned the pages, which documented in narrative form, every step in the DNA testing protocol. Suddenly, she stopped in mid-stride, her eyes falling on the last paragraph on the second page. "The DNA of suspect Prescott was found on the garrote. Specifically, testing revealed that suspect Prescott's perspiration was present on the narrow strip of blue paisley fabric cinched around the victim's neck."

Margo's mind leaped back to one of her more memorable splits with Ken. It had been about a week before Anendale's murder. She'd come home to find that he'd moved out. He'd found her stash of memorabilia from her "chance" encounters with Owen—a name card lifted from a dais, programs from his lectures, even napkins left behind at coffee shops. They'd been her prized possessions. Sometimes, she would sift through the box just to be close to Owen.

Hidden in a duffle bag at the back of her closet, her treasures had gone missing the night her husband left. There'd been Owen's name tag from a writer's conference, his hand-written notes about his novel, taken from his satchel one night in a bar, and one sweat-stained blue paisley shirt, lifted from a deck chair at a hotel in Hanover, New Hampshire.

Margo's wine glass slipped from her fingers, shattering on the floor as her mind traced the evidence to its horrifying conclusion. Ken had the shirt, so he was a murderer? How was that possible? Her knees buckled and she sat heavily on her bed. Shaking, she tried to collect her thoughts. Her eyes darted to her computer. The email! What if he'd hacked her account, again? What if he knew that she knew? She breathed deeply, desperate to stay calm. "Think, Margo," she heard herself whisper. Surely, she was just being paranoid.

Then a forceful knock on her front door shook her out of her skin. She sat trembling in place, paralyzed with fear, as the knocks grew louder.

CHAPTER 85

An instant after the last forceful knock, the front door swung open. "Mr. Boles," said Owen, startled by the imposing presence of the big man in his doorway. "How can I help you?"

"Sorry to pop in unannounced," he said, shouldering past Owen. "Nice little cottage you have." For a split second, Owen thought of running, but realized that he had already made his decision. Come what may, it was time for his life on the run to end.

"Thank you, Mr. Boles. May I offer you some tea?"

"For starters," Boles said, with a smile, "you can call me George. You make me feel old enough as it is."

"Right," Owen said, laughing nervously. "George, it is."

"And, if you don't mind, a pint of bitter would do the trick."

"Sure," Owen said, more than a little confused. Perhaps this was the solo good cop routine interrogation. He poured two cans of ale into frosty glasses. "Would you like to sit on the back patio, George," he asked, embracing the faux niceties of his imminent capture. *What the hell, I might as well have a few pints on my last night of freedom.*

"That would be lovely," Boles replied, turning his back to Owen to walk through his patio door. Owen brought out a salami and some crackers. "Ah," said his guest, eyeing the offering, "I recently learned from Mrs. Pembroke that what you've presented is something called charcuterie. Had avoided it in restaurants for years out of sheer ignorance, much to my detriment," he said, raising his glass.

"Cheers," Owen said, wondering when the conversation would, inevitably, turn deadly serious. The answer was immediate.

"You know, Ancil," Boles said seriously, his tone suddenly grave, "You may have gathered this already, but the truth is I'm not actually in prosthetics."

"Well, yes, Mr., er George, I did gather that."

"Actually," Boles continued before a healthy drink of ale, "I'm in Tetbury on official police business."

"Again, sir, I had a feeling that was the case." Owen sighed. Boles continued to speak, but Owen didn't hear him. His mind was all at once flooded with thoughts of his life in Tetbury. To his surprise, more than fear of prison or the stress and pain of the days ahead, his singular concern was leaving behind his life in the village. Until then, Owen hadn't realized how much he'd grown to love his simple life. The prospect of losing it all at once was devastating. Slowly, the man moving his lips in front of Owen came back into focus, and his words were again audible.

"In actual matter of fact, I'm in town investigating a fairly extensive counterfeit ring," he said, washing down a slice of salami with another gulp of beer.

The big man's words were slow to register with Owen. He blinked away lingering thoughts of Tetbury. "Come again," he asked, sure that he'd misheard his guest.

"Yes, believe it or not. They're actually based in Didmarton, just south of here. I've been on this undercover detail now for three years. It's grown on me, actually," he continued, but Owen wasn't listening.

"Mr. Boles, what is it, exactly, that you needed to speak to me about?"

"Well, here's the thing, Ancil. It's just not easy to talk about," the big man said, fidgeting, "but I suppose I'll just jump in." He sighed. "As you know, Mrs. Pembroke and I are seeing quite a lot of each other."

"Yes, I've noticed," answered Owen, still confused.

"The truth is," Boles continued, haltingly, "it's been a while since I've been with a woman, you know, sexually. It's been..."

"Mr. Boles," said Owen, holding up his hand to interrupt, "You're telling me that the reason..." He stopped in mid-sentence, allowing a smile to spread over his face, and let out an audible sigh of relief. "Sorry," he said, starting again. "The reason you wanted to speak to me is to ask for sexual advice?" he asked.

Boles looked unsettled. "Ancil, as I said, this isn't an easy topic for me, and I'd appreciate if you wouldn't make light of it."

Owen covered his smile with his hand and shook his head. "Oh, so sorry, George. Believe me, I would never do that. It's just that I'm actually very relieved to hear you say that."

"What's that? Thought I'd come after you for a speeding violation?" joked Boles.

"Something like that," Owen said, then took a long drink of beer. "So, how can I help?"

"For starters, it's been a while since I took a trip down petticoat lane, if you get my meaning. I was never one for experimenting. Is the old missionary still acceptable?"

"By all means." said Owen, still giddy with relief. "And I would remind you that in the recent experience department, it's unlikely that Mrs. Pembroke has much of a head start on you."

"Okay," Boles said, seeming satisfied. "And what's this business about me having to shave my undercarriage? Is that now required?"

Owen frowned to keep from laughing. "Well, George, that has become quite popular among both men and women, but it's hardly required. I think you're safe playing by the rules as you remember them."

"Well, that's a relief. I wouldn't be very comfortable wielding a razor down near my dangly bits," Boles said with a chuckle.

Owen returned the laugh. "No one is, George." He got up and retrieved two more beers, on the way realizing that he was actually enjoying himself.

"Cheers," said his guest, taking his glass. "So, just one more question on this topic. Mrs. Pembroke is such a proper lady. And frankly, I'm no day at the beach, I realize. My question is, Ancil, do you think she would be up for a shag with the likes of me?"

"George, my friend," Owen said, recalling Mrs. Pembroke's risqué comment that morning, "I have total confidence that she would be. So, are you employed by local police?" Owen asked, eager to change the subject.

"No, Scotland Yard. I'm what they call a roving investigator. They send me out on individual cases. Usually multiple-person scams. Auto theft rings, embezzlement schemes, that sort of thing. And how's your writing coming along, Ancil?"

"Quite well, thank you. The quiet of village life is perfect for it. I love it here in Tetbury. Do you enjoy your work as a roving investigator?" asked Owen, now thoroughly relaxed.

"Oh, yes. I spent years on the London Police Force, walking a beat, but I prefer my current assignment. I'm tasked with catching specific criminals, so I don't have to be bothered if I stumble across other crimes." Owen wasn't sure, but he thought Boles shot him a look.

The men talked about the various characters in Tetbury and English football. After a time, Boles rose to leave and thanked Owen for the advice.

"Good luck, tonight," Owen said, with a pat on his shoulder. "You'll be fine."

Boles paused on his way to the door. "You know, Ancil, I've actually read your latest book, *Commiski Flats.*"

"Have you? I'm flattered. What'd you think?"

"I liked it. Of course," the roving inspector said with a wink, "it's not quite *Orchards of Grace* now, is it?"

CHAPTER 86

When Ken Stark read the DNA report, hacked from Margo's email account, he'd felt a distant yet familiar emotion bubbling up within him. He'd last felt it in 2013.

Stark had gone to Anendale's home that night to offer assistance in the lawsuit against Owen Prescott, the object of his wife's obsession. He loved Margo back then and had witnessed his marriage crumble for a reason that made no sense. Prescott wanted nothing to do with his wife. Her delusional infatuation—it was a mental illness, really—would never succeed. The restraining order had made that clear to everyone but her.

And it wasn't as if their marriage was rife with problems. Sure, she spent a bit more of his money than he liked, and the sex was prone to dry spells, but mostly, except for this one glaring issue, their marriage was on solid ground.

In the years to come, Stark had figured that his desperate actions that fateful night had been born of helplessness. He was a captain of industry. If there was a problem, money and time would usually solve it. Not so with Margo's obsession. Years of therapy, romantic vacations, and even hypnosis had failed. And it wasn't as if he'd thought that helping Anendale was the answer to his prayers. For all he knew, the lawsuit would be dismissed the following day. But at least it had been something to try.

So, on September 22, 2013, he'd traveled to Anendale's home to deliver notes about Prescott's famous novel that his deranged wife had somehow gotten her hands on. She'd forced him to read the damn thing, so when he found the hand-written pages stuffed in a duffel bag with other sordid memorabilia, he'd recognized them right away.

Holding the duffel bag of notes and other items, Stark knocked on Anendale's front door. After a minute or two, he heard footsteps inside, followed by a distant thud. After more knocks and three minutes of waiting, he tried the door. It was unlocked, so he cautiously pushed it open, calling Anendale's name as he entered the foyer. The house was warm and musty, and the smell of liquor hung in the heavy air.

Approaching the living room, he heard a low moaning sound and rounded the corner to find a site that would be singed into his memory forever. Anendale—he assumed it was him—was on his stomach. The tip of some sort of metal spike protruded from the middle of his back and blood was pooling on both sides of his motionless body.

Not knowing if the responsible party was still around, Stark had ducked behind a sofa, fumbling with his phone. In the years since, he'd often considered how things might have been different if his cell phone had been charged. In his panic, looking for a landline had never occurred to him.

He squatted there, behind the sofa, thinking. After five minutes, assured that he was alone in the home with Anendale, he crept closer to the body, grimacing as the bloody scene came into view. Anendale was alive, each breath now producing a labored gurgle. It was clear there was no saving him now. The spike, which Stark now saw to be a three-sided pyramid, had surely ripped through vital organs, and the pools of blood were now a small pond.

Stark surveyed the scene. A broken glass lay shattered across the tile floor up near Anendale's head, its liquid contents sprayed out ahead of him. A cracked tile was askew on what had clearly been the man's last step. Now, the gurgling sounds had stopped, and the body lay motionless.

In the years to come, Stark would try to piece together his disjointed thought process. Standing there, still clutching his crazy wife's duffel bag, without a cell phone to call an ambulance, he recalled not knowing what to do. His first coherent thought was that he may as well deliver the pages he'd promised Anendale. He stacked them on a side table, in plain view.

Then, all at once, it dawned on him that what lay before him could be mistaken for a murder scene, and that his fingerprints were on the pages and even the front door. Panic set in. *What was he doing here?* Answering his own question, his panic turned to rage. The only reason he was here was Margo and her maniacal, selfish obsession.

Stark had never harbored ill will toward Owen Prescott. He'd been a victim, in fact. Certainly, he had nothing against poor Norvel Anendale. But at that moment, finding himself in jeopardy, he hated his wife very much. She had tortured him for years, lusting after another and repeatedly lying about it. And now, he'd allowed himself to be lured into her sordid, imaginary world.

Unhinged with rage, Ken Stark channeled his hatred in a series of frenzied but calculated moves. *You love Owen Prescott, you conniving bitch? You can love him when he's in prison.* He was so quick to retrieve Owen's sweat-stained shirt from the duffel, he would later wonder if the scheme was already there, percolating in the back of his mind as soon as he saw the body.

He tore a long strip from the shirt and walked to the head of the body, stepping over the pools of blood. Grabbing the man by the shoulders, he rolled him to his back, recoiling at the sight of the old man's distorted face. Determined, he looped the strip around Anendale's neck and cinched it tight. Looking down at Anendale, he pictured Margo's taunting face looking up at him. With rage coursing through his veins, he pulled the garrote tight until his arms gave out. Breathing heavily, Stark recovered and pulled again, the victim's eyes bulging through the image of his wife.

Finally, Stark stood on wobbly legs, looking down at his handiwork, his vision clearing. The strip of cloth was lined with blood and his wife's face was replaced by that of a frightened old man. Mortified by his actions, he turned to the side and nearly retched. But now, he was all in. He picked up the broken glass, then retrieved the papers from the table and placed them over the spilled alcohol. Finally, he replaced the loose tile and wiped his prints from every surface he recalled touching.

One last look at the scene and he was off into the cool fall evening.

All these years later, as Ken pounded on Margo's door, he felt the familiar rage welling up inside him.

CHAPTER 87

Hunched and trembling on her bed, Margo wished she had a gun. She'd thought about getting one in Boston, when her fights with Ken had been the most volatile. Even though he'd never struck her, she'd seen him shake with rage and had known violence wasn't far behind.

As the knocking on the door became more forceful, she stood, just as Ken burst into the room, crashing the door off its hinges. Margo took two strides in her high heels before he was on her, dragging her by her hair and tackling her to the bed. She clawed at him like an animal, but he was too strong, outweighing her by over one hundred pounds.

Margo got off a scream, but it was quickly muted by his hand, squeezing her face as he straddled her on the bed. She gnashed her teeth, chomping down on a finger. He yanked it free, then moved his hands to her neck as she squirmed desperately under him. She looked up to see his face distorted in a demonic smile and panicked.

Arms flailing, desperate for air, her hands felt for the letter opener on her nightstand. She grabbed it and drove it deep into his forearm. Ken yelped in pain and straightened atop her, one hand clutching the weapon stuck in his arm. Gasping for air, Margo scooted toward the head of the bed, wiggling up from between his knees. She brought her right knee to her chin, her taught body coiling before driving a stiletto heel into his groin, the spike knifing through his pants and ripping into his scrotum.

Ken fell to the bed beside her, moaning in agony. Still catching her breath, Margo sprang off the bed and stood over him, fierce hatred in her eyes. Her first thought was murder. Not for vengeance, but for trying to derail her dream with Owen. She took off her other heel and held it in her hand like a hammer, crawling atop him on the bed as he continued to writhe on his back in pain, his hands now on his bloody groin. She grabbed his hair with her free hand, pressing the spike of the heel into his throat with the other.

His face flushed beneath her as he choked, the spike threatening to pierce his neck. She kept the pressure steady, glaring down at him as his arms and legs began to spasm. Finally, as his eyes appeared set to burst from his face, she released the pressure, and climbed off him, sending him into violent gasps for air.

Calmly, Margo scooted a chair to the edge of the bed and sat, watching him suffer. He was bleeding from two different wounds and appeared dazed from oxygen deprivation. Wheezing, his trembling hands unzipped his bloody trousers. He tugged down pants and underwear to mid-thigh and held his ruptured groin with both hands.

"No one will take him from me, Ken. Is that understood?" she asked, speaking plainly.

"Fuck you," he said, his words dissolving into a guttural moan of pain.

Margo smiled, as if she'd been hoping for that answer. She stood again and stepped out of her dress. "I have a date with Owen, later. Can't have blood on my dress, can I?" she asked with a wicked smile.

Then she climbed on the bed again, wearing only her panties, clutching the heel, its spike moist with blood. On her knees, she leaned over him, moving the heel again toward his neck. She saw panic in his eyes.

"No, Margo," he pleaded, rolling away from her to the fetal position, exposing his white buttocks as his hands moved to protect his neck.

She leaned down to whisper in his ear. "At your advanced age, Ken, have you been keeping up with your rectal exams?" She watched as a look of horror slowly spread over his face. Then, a roundhouse swing with her wiry arm and the stiletto found its mark. She kept it there, grinding it into him with all her strength, feeling it tearing through his rectum as he wailed like a wounded animal. After a full thirty seconds, she finally released her grip on the shoe and covered his face with a pillow to muffle his groans. She chuckled when the heel remained stuck in place.

Margo stepped back to admire her handiwork. Ken was whimpering quietly now, groping pathetically behind him to dislodge the heel. She resumed her seat, still topless in her underwear, her nipples hard with arousal. "No one, Ken," she smiled pleasantly, a glazed look in her eyes. "No one will take him from me. You understand that now, don't you, honey?"

Ken was nodding before she'd finished the question.

She clasped her hands in front of her, smiling. "That's more like it," she said pleasantly.

All at once, her expression changed yet again. "Now listen," she sneered, her tone now venomous, "you are going to stagger out through the back door, walk down the stairs and collapse in the alley outside. It's a busy time of day, so you'll get someone's attention. Understood?"

"Yes," he whispered through sobs, nodding his head furiously.

"Good," she said matter-of-factly. "You'll be mended in no time. You will fly home, and the name Owen Prescott will never pass your lips again. You will not tell a soul where we are. If you do, you will surely go to prison." She paused with raised eyebrows and he nodded again.

"We will finalize our divorce in short order, with significantly more generous terms than we have discussed." Another pause, and he closed his eyes, nodding a final time. "Now, Ken," she said, "thanks to you, I need to clean up. So, get the fuck out of my flat."

CHAPTER 88

"So, Boles knows who you are?" Margo asked, staring across the table at The Charlatan House. "How fascinating. Does that mean Mrs. Pembroke knows as well?"

"Not yet, I don't think, but I'm sure she will soon," Owen said, refilling her wineglass.

The couple had ordered their second bottle of Pinot Noir, both having reason to drink. Owen had decided against Mrs. Pembroke's Rolls, leery of navigating the narrow roads of the Cotswolds in the giant car. Instead, he'd surprised Margo with a limo, and the sight of her in the dress had taken his breath away. The restaurant had been as posh as advertised, and they'd poked fun at the stuffiness of the scene.

"So, Boles just showed up unannounced?" she asked. "You must have been frightened to death."

"Yes, I was all but prepared to be led away in handcuffs when he started asking me about shaving his undercarriage," he said, laughing at the memory. "I actually enjoyed myself. And how was the rest of your afternoon?"

"Oh, rather uneventful," she said, then broke into a sly giggle at the image of Ken with her heel stuck up his ass.

"What's so funny?"

"Oh, nothing," she lied. "I suppose it's poor Mr. Boles worrying about his undercarriage."

Their tall waiter with perfect posture seemed to materialize at their table, silently presenting the wine as if cradling an infant. Owen nodded, and the waiter straightened, brushing imaginary lint from his black jacket before uncorking the bottle. He placed the cork on the table in front of Owen. Again, he nodded, rolling his eyes at Margo across the table.

"Sir, do you wish your wine decanted? Our sommelier recommends against for this vintage, but I am at your service, of course."

"No, thank you," Owen said.

"Very good, sir," he said, and was gone.

"He needs a blowjob," whispered Owen.

"Yes," Margo said, laughing. "Too bad he won't be in our car on the way home."

"Well then, check please," he joked. "And speaking of such things, I'd guess the Boles and Pembroke couple are busy making the double-backed monster as we speak."

"Well, that's an image I can't unsee," she said. "Thanks. How's your duck?"

"Excuse me," Owen laughed, feeling the effects of the wine. "Did you just ask me how my dick was?"

Margo burst out laughing, covering her mouth. "Owen Bradley Prescott, this is a reputable restaurant. I said, 'duck,'" she said, giggling. She pried off a heel under the table and delicately placed her foot between Owen's legs. "I wonder where your mind is?" she asked coyly, wiggling her toes against him.

"Well, I'm liking this restaurant more and more," he said, inhaling as he held her ankle under the table.

"Yeah?" she asked innocently. "Must be the wine."

They were gazing at each other when the waiter appeared again. "And how are you finding your duck?" he asked. Owen and Margo locked eyes, both feeling laughter surge within them.

"It's hard," Owen said, fighting to keep a straight face. Across the table, Margo closed her eyes and silently convulsed with laughter. "It's hard to understand how duck can be this tender."

"Very good, sir," the waiter said, without expression, and left them to dissolve into hysteria.

They were still wiping tears from their eyes when the dessert menus arrived. "Thank you for tonight, Owen," Margo said, looking at the ceiling, staring into space. "It's been magical." He looked across the table, sensing the familiar celestial aura about her. When he'd first met Margo, her unique vibe had seemed familiar somehow, and now an even stronger feeling of déjà vu swept over him.

"Well, thank you," he replied, staring into her eyes. "For everything. When I'm with you, I truly feel that everything will work out in the end. It's as if you know it somehow and I believe you."

"Of course, it will," she said with absolute conviction. "We are meant to be, Owen. "

After sharing a treacle tart with port, they stumbled to their limo for the ride home.

"How did you know my middle name?" he asked, as they climbed in the back seat.

"What?"

"How did you know my middle name is Bradley. I hate that name and never tell anybody."

She kissed him deeply. "I guess I'm not just anybody, am I?"

"No, you're not," he answered, forgetting his question.

Margo pushed a button, closing the partition to the driver and kneeled before him, unbuckling his belt. "How's your duck, Owen," she asked, and they shared a laugh. "Tell me," she asked, feeling tipsy and daring, "can you ever remember skinny dipping before last week?"

She pulled down his underwear, springing him free. "No," he said, not wanting to think of April. "What a strange thing to ask."

"Good," she said, quite happy with his answer.

"Ever had a blowjob in a limo?"

CHAPTER 89

Margo lay in Owen's bed, relaxed and content. They had fallen asleep in each other's arms last night, too tipsy for sex. This morning, though, she had nuzzled him awake to share an especially slow and sensual intimacy. Now, as he lay beside her, sated and sleeping, she thought about her next move.

After she found Owen in Tetbury, her priority had been keeping him safe from arrest. She couldn't very well build their relationship with him in prison. She'd seen a special on how the web of law enforcement cameras were being used to track fugitives and knew it was Owen's biggest threat. Then she'd been in Balfrey's when a camera had been installed and had overheard the owners discussing the system.

So, under the guise of peddling the cameras, Margo had set about discouraging their installation in other local businesses. Leaving her flat through the back alley door in the early morning hours, dressed in her disguise, she'd given "informational" talks to local proprietors, overemphasizing the intrusive nature of the system. Once it was up and running, she'd said, it couldn't be turned off. Every square inch of the property would be under surveillance, even after hours. Thankfully, after her anti-pitch, most businesses had wanted nothing to do with the cameras.

It had been Margo's plan from the beginning, after finally possessing Owen, to help him win his freedom. She'd known he was innocent all along. Only his DNA on the garrote had given her the slightest pause, and now that had been explained.

Before Ken's revelation, she considered giving an anonymous tip to the Boston Police. She knew his roommate's girlfriend knew he was home that night. She would have noticed his light on and heard him typing when she checked on the cookies.

Quietly, she got out of bed and walked to the bathroom. The more nights she stayed with Owen, the more her colored contact lenses were becoming a problem. Wearing them to bed was uncomfortable and she'd resolved to reveal her blue eyes to him soon. Her appearance had changed so dramatically, she knew for Owen, Desiree Richins was a distant memory. For now, though, she took the brown contacts out, rinsed and replaced them.

Next, she retrieved her laptop from her overnight bag and sat on the couch in the front room to catch up on her journal. For the past ten years, she chronicled every encounter with Owen, documenting every sighting, no matter how brief. In the early years, of course, she'd had less to write about, but now she could barely keep up. She really had never lied to Owen. She was there in England to write about him. After an entry about her birthday date, she climbed back into bed next to him and resumed plotting their course.

Ken had made proving Owen's innocence much easier. She knew he had garroted the victim. She could prove the source of the strip of cloth. That slut, April, would no doubt remember the paisley shirt disappearing from the pool deck. And Margo, herself, could swear to its disappearance from her home the night Ken moved out. The DNA extracted from the hair found on Anendale's body would be Ken's and that would seal his fate. She smiled at the thought of celebrating with Owen, toasting his freedom.

Then Margo had another thought as she looked around the room—their room. Owen belonged to her now, as she always knew he would. So long as he remained a fugitive, he would remain in seclusion with her—if not here in the Cotswolds, then somewhere. It would be a wonderfully simple life with nothing but each other.

And not that Owen ever would, but he certainly couldn't leave her. He had entrusted her with his secret, after all. If he was free, though, there were bound to be complications in his life that would distract him from her. She'd let agents and attorneys pollute his mind once, but never again. Now that she had him, she would never allow him to leave. Margo breathed deeply, smiling at Owen, sleeping next to her. So long as my secret is safe, she thought to herself, he remained trapped in their perfect life.

His freedom could wait a while. She kissed his cheek and got up for a morning run.

By the time Owen awoke, Mrs. Pembroke was in his kitchen, having made her customary Saturday morning run for croissants. "Hello, birthday boy," she said cheerfully.

Owen headed for the coffeepot. "Thank you, Mrs. Pembroke," he said, yawning. "You're in a good mood this morning."

"And you apparently had a late evening?"

"Yes, late and fun-filled. How was your date with Mr. Boles?"

"Oh, fine," she said, blandly, "we always enjoy each other's company."

"Isn't it interesting how the coffee's made," she said, feigning confusion. "So odd of you to get up and make a pot, then go back to bed."

"Very funny. You're certainly full of piss and vinegar this morning."

"I don't know why you'd say that," she said defensively.

Owen sipped his coffee and looked at her, frowning. "No, no," he said pensively, holding his stare, "there's something about you this morning. Sort of a youthful glow. You seem quite contented," he teased.

Blushing, she turned away from him. "Watch your step, Mr. Bradford. I may have some secrets up my sleeve. Where are you two lovebirds off to today?" she asked.

"A quiet day here, hopefully," he said. "Margo is on a run. What about you?" he asked as she made for the front door.

She turned to him with a gleam in her eye. "You might say I have something in the hopper."

CHAPTER 90

Owen spent a contented birthday writing while Margo pored over police reports on the couch. He got up to stretch and moved behind her.

"I know I've said it before," Owen said, leaning down to kiss her neck, "but thank you for all your work on my case. You've spent so much time on it. I only hope it's not for a lost cause."

She looked at him with her patented other-worldly stare. "Don't be silly, Owen," she said, as if she was gazing into the future. "Everything will be absolutely perfect." This time he didn't find her words quite so comforting. After recent events, they seemed almost divorced from reality.

After they shared an evening glass of wine on the patio, she pulled him from his chair. "I have a surprise for you," she said, guiding him to the kitchen, where two place settings were arranged across from each other, each with a slice of white birthday cake and a wineglass.

"Cheers," she said, "Here's to us. Spirit mates," Owen heard her say, as he focused on the eerily familiar place setting. A chill went up Owen's spine. "Are you okay?" Margo asked. "You look like you've seen a ghost."

"Sorry, I just had a very unpleasant flashback," he said, shaking away the distant memory. "Anyway," he said, regaining his composure, "thank you very much for the cake. I love it. Let's have a piece."

"Excuse me a minute," she said, rubbing her eyes and heading toward the bathroom. It was time to be rid of her contacts, she thought.

Owen heard a knock on his front door, and opened it to find Mrs. Pembroke, carrying a paper bag.

"Oh, hello," he said, wondering why she had bothered to knock. "Please come in."

"Is Margo here?" she asked, walking in cautiously.

"Yes, just in the bathroom. Why?"

"I was going to wait," she said in a low voice, "but I thought you should know straight away. I've been to Margo's," she said, glancing toward the bathroom door.

"You've what? I'm confused, Mrs. Pembroke."

With another glance toward the door, she reached into her bag and pulled out a long black wig resting atop a stack of papers. She put the items on the kitchen table as Owen stared in wonder.

Within seconds, the bathroom door opened. "Hello, Mrs. Pem..." Margo stopped in mid-stride, seeing the items on the table. Then she forced a smile, "Oh," she said, "you've come across my wig. It's sort of embarrassing," she said, moving next to Owen, "I picked that up the other day. I thought it might be fun in the bedroom," she whispered, smiling up at him.

"Margo, your eyes," he said, stepping back, his mind sifting through facts and memories, trying to make sense of it all.

"Oh, do you like them?" she asked. "They're my natural color, but I just always wanted dark eyes." Owen held his stare at Margo's shocking blue eyes, and it all clicked—her ethereal presence, their chance meeting, all of it. Owen's mind traveled to the court hearing. "Of course, I won't obey the restraining order," her mystical tone had seemed to say, her glassy eyes staring somewhere far away. And to think he'd been attracted to her celestial vibe, comforted by her aura.

Owen turned to Mrs. Pembroke. "Perhaps we need some time alone," he said quietly.

"Of course," she said, and was gone.

Margo sat at the table and touched his arm. "Babe," she said, still smiling her creepy smile into his eyes, "I was waiting for the right moment to tell you."

"Tell me what, Margo," he said, pulling his arm from her, "that you're a fucking stalker?"

"No, silly, that I've solved your case. That you'll be free because of me," she said. "Let's celebrate," she said, pouring wine in a glass. As she poured, Owen's eyes traveled across the table. He moved the wig to reveal a stack of notepaper filled with a handwriting he recognized immediately. He thought about April's trembling face the night she'd found the bloody knife in her door. Then he thought of his intimacy with this monster and nearly vomited, collapsing on a kitchen chair.

Until that moment, Owen had never considered murdering anyone. He hadn't thought himself capable. But now it would be so easy. As Margo poured the wine, he rose from the table. As he imagined crashing the bottle against her skull, a random thought passed through his addled mind. Mrs. Pembroke would be scrubbing the blood from his kitchen for days.

He held Margot's face in both hands—this crazed face of evil. He thought of April, sitting at home wondering why he'd stopped writing. He slid his hands down to her fragile neck.

CHAPTER 91

"So, let me get this straight," Sam said, calling over his cubicle to Alyssa. "You took an assigned fugitive case, which wasn't even supposed to be a priority, and became so obsessed with catching the target, you invented a new technology."

Alyssa shrugged. "Pretty much," she replied, typing away at her computer.

"You then used the technology to find the fugitive minding his own business, walking the streets of Amsterdam…"

"Rotterdam."

"Then," Sam continued, walking around the partition between them, "without authorization, you utilized an asset who was probably busy tracking a dangerous terrorist—I would have been fired over it—and choreographed a foot pursuit on a different continent. Next, you tracked him to Nowheresville, England, enlisting the help of Scotland fucking Yard.

"But," he said, raising an index finger in the air, "just as you were about to capture him, completing one of the greatest manhunts in history, you decide—based on some pseudo psych training we got in the academy—that he just didn't seem like a murderer," Sam said, using air quotes.

"Best class I took in the academy," Alyssa put in, "but go on."

"So naturally, you re-investigate the crime—which in no way resembles your assigned task of catching the fugitive—prove his innocence, and convince the Suffolk County D.A. to drop the charges?"

Alyssa stopped typing and turned to face him. "It's not a done deal yet, but it looks that way, yeah. Luckily, both cops who worked the case were retired, so I didn't have them to contend with. The D.A. wasn't thrilled, but again, he wasn't the prosecutor who filed charges in the first place, so I'm sure he'll spin it as his predecessor's botch."

"Of course," Sam said, sitting on her side desk. "And being the honest D.A. who would never prosecute an innocent man, he's dismissing the case."

"Exactly."

"What have I missed? Last I heard, your theory that the victim tripped and fell was short on evidence."

"So," she said, allowing herself a smile, "I enhanced the photo of the broken tile, showing it was clearly loose. Then I had the lab guys run some tests to nail down exactly how many pounds of pressure it would take to drive the pyramid through a human body, given its dimensions. It turns out only a very strong person could have done it."

"So, someone like me," Sam deadpanned.

"Yes, like you or an Olympic power lifter. Also, Prescott's scattered notes were tested and parts of them were found to have been soaked in alcohol. All of them just happened to avoid the giant pool of blood, indicating they'd been placed there to hide the accident. Also, one item of evidence didn't make the reports. A tiny shard of glass was found stuck in the victim's shirt sleeve. Had to have been part of the broken glass.

"Finally, I spied what looked like one of those old-school daily planners in one of the wide-angle photos of the living room. The cops didn't collect it but I contacted Anendale's brother, who eventually sold his house. Turns out he kept the planner because it had a bunch of photos stuffed inside."

"Nice, old-school police work, Wagner."

"Thanks, I thought so. Anyway, at 6:30 p.m. on the night he was murdered, Anendale had an appointment labeled 'Prescott lawsuit meeting.' Who makes an appointment to commit a murder? I still don't know how Prescott's DNA was on the garrote, but that wasn't the cause of death. Whoever left the hair behind on the body—obviously, an enemy of Prescott—likely went there to deliver his notes, found the body and decided to frame him."

"So, is that it?" Sam asked. "The Prescott saga finally ends?"

"It will take a few days for it to be approved, but the case will be dismissed, and the arrest warrant recalled." A smile played at the corners of Alyssa's mouth.

Sam read her mind. "You're kidding?" he said, exasperated. "How do you expect to find the guy who framed him?"

"Sam," she said, "let's go get drinks." Not waiting for his stammering reply, Alyssa stood and headed for the exit. Sam hurried to catch up, punching the air in victory on his way.

CHAPTER 92

Owen closed his eyes, caressing Margo's soft neck. Feeling the chords within, his mind drifted to a childhood memory—his hands on the neck of the goose, its limp body dead weight on his shoulder. But this would be nothing like murdering that poor, innocent creature.

He imagined staring into her cold blue eyes before beginning to gently squeeze. Her eyes would narrow as his grip tightened. Her haunting smile would disappear as she realized what was happening. He imagined his thumbs gouging into her windpipe, as her taut body began to spasm, desperate for air.

In the weeks to come, Owen wasn't sure why he hadn't done it. Part of it had been sheer curiosity. Bits of information floated in his brain without context. Apart from assuming she'd had something to do with Anendale's death, he was lost. Then he'd thought of April. He knew it was likely too late, but if Margo really could prove his innocence, it was his only chance.

He sat back down and managed a smile, gesturing for Margo to sit. "I'm sorry, babe. This is all so overwhelming," he said, grinning through the venom on his lips. "Why don't you start at the beginning and tell me what you know."

And she did.

Without a hint of contrition, she told him about her pilfering his notes from the satchel and his shirt from the pool deck. Ken's theft of the items, of course, had been a crime against humanity. "Can you imagine that monster taking my prized possessions?" she asked Owen, with a look of dismay.

She told him how Ken must have torn the shirt and used it as a garrote to kill Anendale and scattered his notes at the scene. Not once was there the slightest recognition that it had been her obsession that had driven Ken to frame him.

Margo told him about breaking into the apartment and spiking his drink that night in the bar. "I suppose I was out of line. I shouldn't have taken your laptops," she said, smiling. "But there was so much I needed to know about you. It was all born of love, Owen. I knew you'd forgive me. Besides, the night I drugged you, I got my first kiss. You were so adorable in your boxers."

When she was done, Owen sat, trying to digest it all. Presumably, assuming this was all true, the missing DNA donor was Ken. Still, there were gaps in the story. "Margo," he said after a time, "how did you know I was innocent? Or did you?" he asked, doing his best to appear calm.

"Well, of course you're innocent, my love," she said, as if stating the obvious. "Remember, we figured out that your roommate's girlfriend would have seen the light in your room when she got up and checked on the cookies. Then, again when she took them out of the oven."

"Margo," he began, then stopped. "Wait, what did you say?" Owen turned his head from her face, thinking. "When she took them out of the oven, Margo? How did you know…"

"Of course," she said, interrupting him, "you were at home that evening, babe. Typing away at your desk, sipping tea from your Red Sox mug."

"Oh my God," whispered Owen, as the realization washed over him. "You were there."

"The homeless guy could vouch for you, too. He took the pizza box off your porch and waved at you through the window, but you wouldn't have seen him. I even tracked him down and got his name after you left the country," she said with pride.

"You were there, watching me," Owen repeated, stunned.

"Of course I was there, babe, until about 8:30 p.m.," she said, as if stating the obvious. "I was there every night. Sitting in that giant, beautiful tree across the street. Sometimes, I'd bring a carafe of wine or a joint and just relax and read or listen to music. It was so comforting knowing we were together."

Margo gazed up at the ceiling, smiling at a memory. "That night, I remember you rubbed your neck after a few hours of writing. You'd been doing that a lot. I so wished I could have massaged it for you." She looked at Owen. "Babe, you knew I was there, right?" she asked, rolling her eyes. "I mean, I was always there, close to you. How else do you think I knew so much about you?" she asked with a giggle.

"No, I didn't," Owen said, still trying to comprehend.

"Oh, you knew, Owen," she chided, and leaned over to kiss his cheek. "Of course you did. You were just playing along so we could have our own private world together here in Tetbury."

Owen shuddered. "So, you knew I was at home at the time of the murder," he said, slowly, his voice quaking with rage.

"Of course, babe. I followed you home from the bar. I thought about telling the police, but they wouldn't have believed me, us being lovers and all. In fact," she said, searching her memory, "I think I probably took a photo of you at your desk that evening. I did most nights." Owen breathed deeply, suppressing his anger.

"Anyway," she continued with a playful push to his shoulder, "I thought you were being quite naughty, carrying on with that April woman. I hope you aren't upset about those silly letters. It was just so obvious she wasn't right for you. And now we know I was right," she said, creepy smile in place.

Owen tried to process the events in his mind, but there were too many facts, too much emotion. He knew no matter how much he despised her, he likely needed this monster. She was an eyewitness, after all. "Margo," he said quietly, touching her arm, "this has been a crazy birthday for me. I think I need some time to process it, if you don't mind."

"Of course," she said, rising to leave. "I'll come back in the morning and we can celebrate."

Owen pulled her close. "Let's get together tomorrow evening, babe. I have some errands to run in the afternoon." They kissed.

"Happy birthday, my love. I've given you your freedom, Owen." Owen heard the slightest hint of a threat in her syrupy voice.

CHAPTER 93

Owen had stayed up late, sorting it all out. He'd made notes on Margo's revelations and lists of the evidence, trying to determine how much he needed her cooperation. Presumably, the hair would be Ken's. Of course, Margo had the photograph, if there was one, and she hadn't told him the name of the homeless guy. Will's girlfriend, the cookie baker, was still a possibility as an alibi witness.

Sometime that evening, Owen decided he was going home, come what may. His reaction to Margo's bombshells had told him all he needed to know. He was enraged about facing prison for her actions, to be sure. But the agony of losing April had dominated his thoughts. You'd better start enjoying your life, he told himself, for you're a long time dead.

In the morning, he went for a run, trying to fathom his unthinkable romance with Margo and her incomprehensible obsession. He was embarrassed to admit to himself that he'd been completely taken in by her deception. Of course, the solitude of his life had probably made him vulnerable, but there had been signs he ignored.

Owen thought of her wicked sense of humor and shuddered at the prospect that she hadn't been joking at all. He'd stupidly chalked it up to Annabelle Steves novels, which, by the way, she'd probably never read. Not to mention, he thought to himself, shaking his head, the novels were fictional. There'd been nothing fake about her sinister side. It had been her true depraved self all along.

He recalled her random question about whether the killer stuck around to watch Anendale suffer. She probably wished she'd been there to see it. She'd promised to torture and tattoo "slut" on the black-haired woman. Of course, she had been the black-haired woman, but best not crawl inside her head too far, thought Owen, lest he never get out. Hell, she probably had fed her childhood bunnies to an anaconda.

Finally, he thought about the bloody dagger stuck in April's front door, with the note calling her a slut. It must have been one of her favorite words. Had the blood on the knife been her own? She had proven capable of anything.

Maybe he hadn't missed signs so much as failed to comprehend how another human being could be so depraved. Arriving back at his cottage, he vowed, for his own mental health, to think of Margo Stark as little as possible.

After his run, he charged his burner phone while he showered, then dialed one of the few numbers he'd memorized. In California, fresh off receiving the news from Agent Wagner of the official dismissal, Joe sat staring at his buzzing phone, showing a strange set of numbers. Something told him he should pick up. "Hello."

"Hey Turner," Owen said, smiling at the sound of his friend's name on his lips. Joe paused, getting his bearings. "Joe?"

"Holy shit, Owen. I can't even believe this."

"Yeah, me neither. Listen, first off, I want to tell you I'm sorry. I know you…"

"Forget about that, Owen," Joe interrupted, his voice teeming with excitement.

"No, seriously, I need to…"

"Owen, you're free," he cut in again.

"What? I don't understand?"

"It was just confirmed. It's a long story, but the case against you has been dismissed. You're fucking free, Owen."

Joe went on for a while, talking excitedly about the arrest warrant being recalled and the logistics of a return to the states, but Owen wasn't listening. He let the phone slip through his fingers and collapsed on the couch as waves of relief washed over him. He sat there for several minutes, imagining his new life free of secrets and deceit.

After breakfast, he walked to Bunson's. Strolling outside without his hoodie, he smelled the sweet country air of spring. He gazed at the village as if for the first time, the morning sun shining on its gabled roofs and honey-colored stone.

"Hello, Ancil, your usual?" asked Tommy from behind the counter at the coffee shop.

"Actually, Tommy, the name's Owen. Owen Prescott," he said, extending his hand.

Later, he would do the same with Brodie Dundas inside the Piper's Arms. "Well done, then," the Scotsman said, without batting an eye. "We're all Jock Tamson's bairns." As usual, Owen got the gist of the remark. He told the pub owner that he'd be gone for a few months but would surely be back. "Then lang may yer lum reek. That means, 'good luck to you.'"

"To you as well, Brodie," Owen said, and the two grasped hands.

Back at his cottage, Owen poured himself a cold beer and brought April's letters to his sunny patio. He leafed through them, smiling through tears. Then he picked up his phone, breathed deeply, and dialed. Soon, he heard the sweetness of her husky voice on the line.

"Hi, April," he said. "It's Owen."

ABOUT THE AUTHOR

T.L. Bequette is a criminal defense attorney turned writer from Lafayette, California. His debut novel, *Good Lookin'*, won the 2022 Independent Press Award for Crime Fiction, a Chanticleer International Book Award, and was a Finalist for a National Indie Excellence Award. *Blood Perfect*, second in the *Joe Turner* mystery series, was named a 5-Star Best Book by Chanticleer Book Reviews. The book was hailed by Kirkus Reviews as "a tale that solidifies Turner as a charmingly-reliable champion of the innocent." Much of Bequette's law practice involves defending young men from Oakland accused of murder. He holds degrees from The University of the Pacific and Georgetown Law School and serves annually on the faculty of the Stanford Law School Trial Advocacy Clinic.

OTHER TITLES BY T.L. BEQUETTE

"After his rousing debut, *Good Lookin'* (2021)...Bequette returns with a tale ...that solidifies Turner as a charmingly reliable champion of the innocent."
–Kirkus Reviews

BLOOD PERFECT

A Joe Turner Mystery

5 Stars!
★★★★★
BEST BOOK
Chanticleer
Book Reviews

T.L. BEQUETTE

NOTE FROM T.L. BEQUETTE

Word-of-mouth is crucial for any author to succeed. If you enjoyed *A LONG TIME DEAD*, please leave a review online—anywhere you are able. Even if it's just a sentence or two. It would make all the difference and would be very much appreciated.

Thanks!
T.L. Bequette

We hope you enjoyed reading this title from:

www.blackrosewriting.com

Subscribe to our mailing list – *The Rosevine* – and receive **FREE** books, daily deals, and stay current with news about upcoming releases and our hottest authors.
Scan the QR code below to sign up.

Already a subscriber? Please accept a sincere thank you for being a fan of Black Rose Writing authors.

View other Black Rose Writing titles at www.blackrosewriting.com/books and use promo code **PRINT** to receive a **20% discount** when purchasing.